FOREVER

Forever

Red Team Ink (DBA) of Zealot Solutions Idaho

Red Team Ink

DBA of Zealot Solutions, Idaho LLC

9480 W. River Beach Lane

Garden City, ID 83714

Copyright © 2021 by Red Team Ink

This is a work of fiction. Names, characters, businesses, places, events and incidents are either the products of the author's imagination or used in a fictitious manner. Any resemblance to actual persons, living or dead, or actual events is purely coincidental.

For permission requests or information about discounts for special bulk purchases please contact: redteamink@gmail.com. Substantial discounts on bulk orders are available to corporations, professional associations, and small businesses.

Printed in The United States of America

Library of Congress Control Number: 2017930051

ISBN: 978-0-9982349-7-7

Title: Forever

Description: Second Edition

Glossary of terms used in this book

Bad – A prefix used in front of German town names to denote that the town is a spa town. (*ex. Bad Tölz, Germany*)

Bitte – This German word can mean: *Please, You're welcome, Here you go* (when handing something over), *May I help you?*, or *Pardon?*, depending on the context of how it's used.

Da – The Russian word for *yes*.

Danke – The German word for *thank you*.

Das ist gut – A German expression meaning *That is good*.

Der Führer – German for *The Führer*, referring to Adolf Hitler.

EMP – EMP (electromagnetic pulse) interference is generally disruptive or damaging to electronic equipment. Weapons have been developed to create the damaging effects of high-energy EMP. These are typically divided into nuclear and non-nuclear devices.

Führerwohnung – German for *Führer apartment*. This was where Hitler resided at the Old Chancellery.

Gestapo – The Gestapo was the official secret police of Nazi Germany and German-occupied Europe.

Glashütte – A German watch brand. As of this writing, the company is still in business and making watches with a modern design.

Guten Tag – A German greeting that translates to *Good day*.

Hematite – The mineral form of iron oxide. Ores containing very high quantities of hematite or magnetite (greater than ~60% iron) are known as "natural ore" or "direct shipping ore," meaning they can be fed directly into iron-making blast furnaces.

Hitlergrub – The famous Nazi salute where the arm is extended out in front at an upward angle, with the hand open and extended.

Ja – German for *yes*.

Jahwol – A German word indicating a strong affirmative.

Jerry – A slang term for a British chamber pot. German soldiers were referred to as Jerries because their helmets resembled chamber pots.

Junker – The SS rank of Junker was a paramilitary rank used by the SS from the years 1933 to 1945. It was a special position held by those aspiring for officer commissions in the armed wing of the SS.

Junkerschüle – Junkerschüle Bad Tölz was an officers' training school for the Waffen-SS. The school was established in 1937 and constructed by Alois Degano, in the town of Bad Tölz, which is about 30 miles south of Munich.

Kapo – A prisoner in a Nazi concentration camp that was assigned by the SS guards to supervise forced labor, or to carry out administrative tasks.

Lebkuchen Cookies – A German traditional baked Christmas treat that somewhat resembles gingerbread.

Liebchen – A German term of endearment that translates to *dear* or *sweetheart.*

Mein Gott – A German expression meaning *Oh my God.*

Mein Herr – The word *herr* used by itself is the German equivalent of the English prefix for mister. Herr Schultz, for example, would translate to Mr. Schultz. Mein Herr on the other hand translates to my lord and was used as a term of respect for those higher in rank or station.

Metzgerbräu Keller – A Metzgerbräu is a German brewery, and Keller is the German word for cellar, so in this case, Metzgerbräu Keller translated into English would be *Cellar Brewery.*

Nationalsozialismus – The German National Socialist party. The Nazis.

Nein – The German word for *no.*

OBI – A major do it yourself store chain in Germany, similar to Home Depot or Lowes.

Panzerkampfwagen – A German super heavy tank that was developed toward the end of World War II.

Polizei – German police/police officers.

Radschlepper Ost – This was a German heavy four-wheel drive military tractor used during World War II. Its name translates to *Wheeled Tractor East.*

Reichsführer – This was a special title and rank that existed between the years of 1925 and 1945 for the commander of the Schutzstaffel (SS).

Reichskanzlei – Translates to Reich Chancellery. This was the traditional name of the office of the Chancellor of Germany.

Reichsmark – Monetary currency that was used in Germany from 1924 to 1948.

Rottenführer – A Nazi Party paramilitary rank that was first created in the year 1932. The rank of Rottenführer was used by several Nazi paramilitary groups and is the equivalent of a lance-corporal. This was the first SS and SA position to have command over other paramilitary groups.

Schütze – In German, it means *rifleman* or *shooter*.

SchützenPanzerwagen – There were numerous variants of this German vehicle used during World War II for a variety of purposes. Each of the variants had a designation after the name. In this book, the vehicle referred to is the standard troop carrier variant, Sd.Kfz. 250.

Sieg heil – A German expression used by the Nazis that translates to *Hail victory!*

Signalbuch – German for *signal codes.*

Standartenführer – This was a Nazi Party paramilitary rank that was the equivalent of a full colonel. The rank became one of the first commissioned Nazi ranks, and was bestowed upon those SA and SS officers who commanded units known as Standarten, which were regiment-sized formations of between three hundred and five hundred men.

Sturmbannführer – A Nazi Party paramilitary rank equivalent to major that was used in several Nazi organizations, such as the SA, the SS, and the NSFK.

Totenkopfverbände – Known in English as Death's Head Units, these SS units were made up of concentration camp guards. The SS-TV also provided troops for the first combat unit of the Waffen-SS, the Totenkopf Division, which eventually evolved into one of Nazi Germany's most formidable combat formations.

Übermensch – The ideal superior man of the future who could rise above conventional Christian morality to create and impose his own values, originally described by Friedrich Nietzsche in *Thus Spake Zarathustra* (1883–85).

Üntermenschen – A term that became infamous when the Nazis used it to describe inferior people, often referred to as the masses from the East.

Untersturmführer – The first commissioned SS officer rank, equivalent to a second lieutenant in other military organizations.

Vater – The German word for *father*.

Volksgrenadier – This was the name given to a type of German Army division formed in the autumn of 1944. There were 78 of these divisions formed during the war.

Volkssturm – A German national militia established during the last months of World War II. It was set up by the Nazi Party on the orders of Adolf Hitler and was staffed by conscripting males between the ages of 16 and 60 years who were not already serving in the military to be a part of a German Home Guard.

Vyrus 987 Motorcycle – One of the world's most powerful production motorcycles, and extremely expensive.

Waffen-SS – The armed wing of the Nazi Party. Hitler resisted incorporating the Waffen-SS troops into the army, because they were intended to be used as an elite police force after the war was won.

Wunderbar – The German word for wonderful.

PROLOGUE:

GATHERING WINDS

Prologue

December 2014

Outside of Stuttgart, Germany

Baldwin pulled the *Polizei* cap down over his brow, his dark eyes reflecting a trio of headlamps in the distance. The freight train was fast approaching, and he was parked on the tracks facing it.

He switched on his car's blue flashing lights. In response, a screeching sound pierced the night, accompanied by what felt like a small earthquake as the rails shook from the sudden braking of the locomotive. Its horn blared, long and baritone in a warning for him to move.

He clenched the steering wheel tighter as a bead of sweat slid down from his temple and dripped off his cheek.

"What are you doing?" a distressed German accent called through his earbud. "Move you fool, or you'll be killed!"

"This isn't a mission for the weak," Baldwin said calmly in his Romani accent.

"You're crazy …" came the response, and perhaps he was, but *The King* needed true believers, and he'd do whatever it took to succeed.

The ground continued to tremble as the headlamps' fiery glow grew brighter and brighter, sending a cascade of light and shadow across his evil countenance. The screeching was so loud now that it filled his ears, drowning out his subordinate.

So close. It was getting so close now, the monstrous black engine threatened to demolish him to shred his stolen vehicle into nothing more than unrecognizable scraps of metal. He was on the verge of passing out. If this was indeed his time to die, at least it would be a quick death.

No, he couldn't think like that. The Reich required his courage now more than ever. He had to be resolute. His mission had to succeed, but it wouldn't succeed if he were to fail in his next move.

"RAHHH!" he roared, stomping down on the gas pedal as he wrenched the steering wheel to the right. The police car bucked over the rails, kicking gravel behind it as it managed just the narrowest of escapes.

"It seems that today wasn't your day to die after all. You were lucky," the German in his ear said with some astonishment. Baldwin made a relatively smooth U-turn and was now following alongside the slowing row of cargo covered in spray paint.

The emergency brake would take about another minute to completely stop the train, but at least he was finally able to breathe.

"Luck? No, it was fate," he said.

When the train's wheels let out one last squeal, Baldwin crossed the rails in front of the locomotive and parked along the right side where the engineer sat. Another *Polizei* car pulled up beside his. It had four men inside and was followed by another man on a Vyrus 987 motorcycle. They'd planned the operation so that the train would have to stop in the middle of a vast field, where there would be no witnesses to the events that were about to take place.

Baldwin approached the man sitting idly on his bike. "Off," he said, motioning with his hand for the rider to remove himself. "What, you think it's yours now?"

"It almost was," the man said, his response echoing in Baldwin's earpiece. He was of course referring to the near-death experience that Baldwin had just had. But before he could receive a response, the engineer's door opened and a silhouette of a man peered down at them.

"What's going on, officers? For a moment there, I thought I was a dead man."

"You thought right," Baldwin said as he raised his gun and shot the engineer straight through the heart. The conductor was executed in a similar manner, though he was considerably heavier than the engineer, so it took two of Baldwin's men to toss his lifeless body onto the field below.

Phase one now complete, they congratulated each other while filling the cab with a variety of weaponry. The hijacked train was just a means to a greater end. A train carrying dozens of hulking M1A1 Abrams tanks, the likes of which no one had seen back in 1943, was scheduled to be traveling along a parallel track up ahead. They were being relocated from a U.S. base to a German proving ground for training purposes.

The blond took over the controls of the train, while the four men from the other *Polizei* car pulled ski masks out of a duffel bag and slipped them on so that they were covered from head to toe in black clothing. They then moved to the rear of the cab, each carrying a sniper rifle equipped with a suppressor.

Baldwin eyed his own duffel bag. He'd discreetly placed it in the shadows in the corner of the cab, thinking the explosives would do well there.

Once everything was in place, he picked up a satellite phone and connected to an open line.

"*Poison My Eyes* is a go," he said, and with only a single tone in response, the connection was terminated.

Next, he activated a crate which had been hefted onto the locomotive from the stolen police car. It was a high-powered radio and signal jammer. It would jam frequencies, even rotating ones, except for the very specific one that Baldwin and his team had set up.

Outside, Baldwin's Vyrus was waiting for him. He gave a nod to the team aboard the freight train, mounted the bike, and then sped off toward the parallel track. His plan was to cross it, and then set himself a safe distance away so that he'd be unseen by the oncoming enemy. Meanwhile, high above in night sky, there flew a Tornado fighter jet. When the captain received the single tone signal that he'd been waiting for, he immediately wrenched back on the stick and maximized the throttle. The G-forces caused by the sudden ascent pressed him back hard into his seat and threatened to crush his chest. In front of the Tornado's nose was an array of infinite stars encircling the great void—the same stars that had given his cause their greatest gift.

"Captain, what is happening?" his navigator asked, clueless of their true path and mission.

"Your job is to prepare the payload as instructed," he said, speaking of the missiles they were carrying. "I suggest you concern yourself with the task at hand while I fly the plane."

"Jahwol."

The Tornado was exceeding its service ceiling, and the twin engines thumped, choking from the lack of combustible oxygen. Still in a steep climb, the radio towers below tried calling out to them, but the signal came through as little more than an unrecognizable garble.

"Ready the EMPs," the captain ordered.

"EMPs ready. Target zones identified and locked."

"Release."

The jet rocked as one of its anti-satellite solid rockets screamed into the black void of space with its twin immediately following.

The sight was breathtaking. The pilot watched in wonder as the missiles sped off toward their target, painting a sharp contrast against the starry sky.

The engines sputtered and cockpit alarms rang out for attention, yet the captain did nothing. Their momentum continued to carry them higher, but then eventually, just for fraction of a second, they reached the highest rung on their sky ladder. Two brilliant white explosions occurred with a crackling of electricity and a haze of lightning.

A satisfied smile stretched across the captain's face, for he'd lived to see the completion of his mission. Massive holes had just been punched into the modern world's observation systems, as satellites for hundreds of miles had been completely destroyed by the EMPs' powerful blast.

Now was the time for those on the ground to work their magic. Their mission complete, it was time for he and his navigator to disappear. The instrumentation of the Tornado went completely silent as the EMP shock wave overtook the aircraft, allowing them some semblance of peace as the aircraft fell from the sky and carried them to their doom.

Down below, tanks swept through the night like phantoms, soundless except for the low moan of the locomotive that was carrying them to their destination.

Baldwin crouched lower in a frost-coated field, peering through his binoculars at the oncoming train. The Americans thought they'd secured their machines by shipping ammunition on separate carriers, but that was nothing more than a simple inconvenience, easily bypassed. This was a mission that would change the world, and not even the two NATO soldiers guarding the tanks could stop it.

"I see them. They're on schedule. The guards are equipped with M16s and simple sidearms. Be ready to move," Baldwin said into his mic, and one by one, each member of his team responded that they were ready.

Once the train had passed, Baldwin got to his feet and bolted for his bike.

The freight train coasted at approximately 40 miles per hour, with the NATO train fast approaching. Baldwin's men lay still atop the various cargo cars, blending into the night with their black-gloved fingers ready on their triggers. Their instructions were simple—shoot to kill. It would be a challenge, however, once the two NATO soldiers on each of the flatbeds armed themselves and started firing back.

Baldwin raced behind the NATO train, his jaw clenched tightly as the wind whipped at his face.

The freight train sped up to match the pace of the NATO train. The soldiers guarding the first of the flatbeds never knew what hit them. Both were shot with such precision that they immediately fell over without a fight, their groans obscured by the pounding sounds of the two trains as they raced alongside one another down the tracks.

The men moved their sights to the next flatbed, and with the help of their laser sights, managed to take those two soldiers out as well. However, they weren't so fortunate with the third, as the soldiers had spotted their lasers and taken cover. Shots were fired in return from automatic weapons, peppering the rusty cargo and zipping overhead.

Hearing the shots, Baldwin yelled to his men, "Stay down! Take them out!"

His bike bolted forward as he snuck along the left side of the NATO train. No one would notice him since all the action was happening on the other side. "We're going to die out here!" a scared voice said in his ear.

Baldwin would have given the man a hard smack on the back of the head if he weren't busy hijacking the enemy. He pulled his custom Glock from a thigh strap. As he passed one of the soldiers, he shot him in the back, dropping him to his knees.

Keeping a firm grip on his gun, he quickly aimed at another unsuspecting target and fired. His wrist jerked as he pulled the trigger, and another soldier went down.

Speeding along from one flatbed to the next, soldier after soldier fell to his steady hand and keen eye. In his mind, the soldiers were tumbling off the flatbeds as if in slow motion. It was a beautiful scene that would have been well suited to a classical music accompaniment, but his moment was abruptly interrupted when one of his men cussed loudly into his earpiece. He was dying and began sobbing at the realization that his life was coming to an end.

"You've died for a great cause!" Baldwin snapped, pausing his shooting. "Go with dignity!"

The moaning cries continued to grow louder and louder until Baldwin had finally had enough. According to the plan it would be premature, but he wouldn't leave the rest of this mission to babies.

Baldwin ripped his earpiece out, and the air stung his face. He was traveling at more than 100 miles per hour in his calculated attempt to advance to the front of the NATO train. Fortunately for him, his bike was more than up to the task.

Hunched low on his machine, his speedometer continued to climb. When he got close enough to the engine, he reached for a grab-iron stepladder, and once he had hold of it, he pulled himself up, letting his motorcycle slip out from between his legs. It wobbled a bit, and then veered off to the right and fell over in a heap, sliding along the ground for some distance before it finally came to rest. He hated parting with it, but he'd be able to afford a dozen of them if he reigned victorious in his mission.

As he climbed the side of the locomotive, the ping of a bullet ricocheting near his neck made his ear ring. Not missing a beat, he snatched his handgun out of the thigh strap, flung his arm toward the enemy behind him, and fired. He heard the man groan as he fell against a tank. It was another close call, but he was getting used to them tonight.

He climbed higher on the ladder of the engineer's cab, thinking about how he could get inside with the least amount of effort. Suddenly the door cracked open and gave him just the opportunity he was looking for, or it would have, if not for the short, shiny barrel that was pointing at his forehead.

A man in camouflage clothing glared down at him and said with a snarl, "*Wilt u sterven?*" Do you want to die?

Baldwin cocked a brow. "*Het hangt er van af.*" It depends.

"*Die u gezonden?*" Who sent you?

"Hitler," Baldwin said.

The man looked perplexed, but not for long as Baldwin gripped the grab-iron tighter and threw up a sudden kick, knocking the surprised soldier's gun out of his hands. He then lifted his own gun and fired.

Another man within the cab yelled out something indiscernible as his comrade hit the floor. The door stayed wedged open as the soldier's limp body hung halfway out of it. Baldwin climbed a little higher, and then forced his entry into the cab by stepping over the body.

The engineer surrendered the controls and was about to take off through the cab's back door when Baldwin snatched him by the back of his collar like a misbehaving child and ordered him to sit.

"You know how there's a junction coming soon?" Baldwin asked, his handgun pressed tightly against the portly man's temple. "Answer me!"

"I know where it is," the engineer said nervously.

"We're going to leave the main track and head south. Do you understand? South?" he asked as he shoved the gun even harder into the man's temple, just to add emphasis to his threat.

"I understand."

"Good. You make any other moves, and you die. You obey, and you live. It's simple, yes?" Baldwin asked. The man halfway nodded, the rolls of his neck jiggling with the effort. Satisfied with his response, Baldwin put his handgun back into its strap. He then spoke to his team through the radio. "It's time for the bunny hunt."

Through the engineer's side window, Baldwin watched as two of his teammates launched grapples, and then successfully swung over to the NATO train. Their job was to sweep the remaining flatbeds for any survivors. The last sniper was stalling however, overly cautious in making the leap.

Their objective of stealing dozens of tanks from the future had been accomplished. Now there was just one last thing.

Baldwin pressed the button on his remote detonator, and the explosion was magnificent. Blowing up his remaining teammate wasn't part of the plan, but the Reich needed true believers. If they were not willing to make a leap of faith, then they were of little use. After all, there wasn't any room for lukewarm followers.

"For *Der Führer*," he said, smiling to himself as he watched the flames billowing up in the distance.

PART ONE:

LEGACY

1

480 B.C.

Low Earth Orbit

Arhegus, the Engarian captain, sat at his central command station, checking for incoming messages after he'd been awakened from stasis. He pressed a yellow button on his glittering console, and yet all he received in response was complete and total silence. Unfortunately, that could only mean one thing. Their communication receivers had been damaged, on purpose.

The rest of the crew remained asleep in their stasis chambers, so he was left to check things out on his own.

Still stiff from his confinement in the stasis chamber, he wandered over to the viewports to have a look at what was outside the ship. The viewports were large, and completely encircled the bridge. On one side, a small, blue planet was suspended peacefully in the glow of its sun. On the other side of the ship there hovered something foreboding. It was the size of a moon, with weapons extending like tentacles from its carbyne-studded hull.

He immediately recognized the ship, thanks to the stories and rumors that had been passed from one intelligent species to another, but he never expected that he'd actually come face to face with a Bwain ship. Now he had to think fast, not only for his own sake, but for the sake of his crew.

He knew that the mostly likely reason for their presence was that they wanted distortion spheres, and unfortunately, that made his ship the perfect target. He'd just reloaded his spheres, his ship had minimal weaponry, and only one person from his home planet knew where he was.

The Bwain's weapons were preparing to fire, and with limited options available to him, Arhegus called out a series of commands that brought up a tactical display in the viewport in front of him, and in no time at all he knew exactly how the enemy ship operated and where to target his weapons for maximum effect.

Unfortunately, the Bwain ship's hull was powerfully magnetic, so shooting it would ultimately result in his own ship being hurled backward, directly toward the planet's surface.

He had no time to make phase calculations before the larger ship fired. The direct hit to his ship caused no movement within. All the sub-controls flickered and went dark, the shielding from the distortion spheres dissipated, and an almost tangible whiteness flooded the interior of the ship. He could see nothing but white space, and the main controls in front of him. Fortunately, they were still functioning, so he ordered the ship to make one last desperate distribution of power.

The shot that emanated from his vessel brought about the destruction of the Bwain ship and caused an explosion the likes of which the primitive humans down on the planet had never seen before. The resulting flash of light in the sky would inspire legends of gods, and of fire, from both Heaven and Mars on the planet below.

The Engarian captain could only watch helplessly as his smooth, seed-shaped ship passed through the atmosphere of the blue planet. Met with surprisingly little resistance, it planted itself deep within the base of a massive mountain. The concussive blast that resulted from the impact flattened every tree within a 100-mile radius. The ship's automated systems tried to release its occupants, but none survived the impact, and so it rested there beneath the mountain. Over time, all traces of the incident were wiped away. The thick layers of dirt, ice, and foliage that built up over the centuries wiped away all evidence of the impact site, and of the incident itself.

It took several weeks for the Engarian home world to realize that the ship had disappeared. They had no idea where to look. According to the unusual readings they received from the ship immediately before takeoff, it appeared to have been headed through a remote and desolate sector. A tracer probe was dispatched, but when it found no trace of the ship using the prescribed search protocol, it was called back home.

* * *

November 1944

Bad Tölz, Germany

"This isn't beer, it's piss!" Professor Steiger said to the barmaid as he wiped the sour taste from his lips with the back of his hand, then pushed his stein back across the bar. A seemingly endless week of grueling, useless surveys through the mountains had put him in no mood for the thin water that was masquerading as lager in the glass before him. The girl behind the bar reddened, half-dropping into an embarrassed curtsy before she caught herself.

"My deepest apologies," she said as she wiped up some of the thin beer he'd spilled when he pushed the stein away. "With all the rationing that's been going on, I'm afraid we've had shortages, and ..."

"I know all about the shortages!" the professor said irritably. "In fact, that's exactly why I'm here. Tell me though how you could possibly consider something that utterly disgusting to be worthy of serving to the men of our great Reich?"

The girl paled. Her eyes flitted over Professor Steiger's shoulder to where three Waffen-SS cadets sat under an arch in the low stone room. Candles lit the Metzgerbräu *Keller*, their flickering light glinting off the silver insignia that peppered the three *Junker Untersturmführers'* black uniforms. The pub was full, but a defeated hush hung over those who had braved the town's blackout to quench their thirst. They were mostly miners and farmers—men too old to be marched into Hitler's losing battles. They were those like the young men behind him from the town's *Junkerschüle*, who'd be rushed through their graduation and sent to the Eastern Front without enough training or ammunition to make even the slightest bit of a difference.

The Reich needed iron to make its weaponry if it were to have any chance at of defending itself, but unless Professor Steiger could locate an ore source in Bavaria to replace the mines the Russians had taken in Czechoslovakia, their defenses would collapse even more quickly than he'd previously feared.

"There's no charge, sir," the red-faced girl whispered. "Again, my deepest apologies."

"Here now," a voice said at Steiger's shoulder. "What seems to be the trouble?"

The professor turned and found a rather squat man sitting there on the stool next to him, peering at him from under a pair of bristling gray eyebrows. White powder coated the man's hair and shoulders, and strange red lines like streaks of sunburn zigzagged across his fleshy face.

"The beer here is terrible," Steiger said flatly.

"Of course it is, but we all have make our sacrifices for *Der Führer*, do we not?"

"Yes, of course we do," the professor sighed. He opened his wallet, pulled out a few *Reichsmarks*, and laid them on the bar for the girl.

"There now, that's a gentleman," the man said. He took a long sip of the thin beer, his throat churning in an even rhythm as foam tunneled out from the corners of this mouth. Setting his stein on the bar, he signaled to the girl that he wanted another, and then leaned over so that he was almost resting against Steiger's shoulder.

"I know who you are," he said. His breath reeked of sour mash, and his bloodshot eyes struggled to focus around the broad bulb of his nose. "You're the geologist from München who's been looking for iron up there in the hills."

The barmaid returned with another stein full of weak beer and set it down in front of the old man. Stuffing the *Reichsmarks* he gave her into the neckline of her blouse, she smiled at him pleasantly and then went back to serving her other customers. Steiger watched her go, and then he offered his hand to the man.

"Professor Hans Steiger, from the Technical University."

Fingers like stumps of hard knuckle and scar tissue gripped Steiger's hand with a heavy strength.

"My name's Steffan. I'm a—" the miner managed to get out before he interrupted himself with a belch. "Oh, pardon me. I'm a prospector here. I know these mountains better than anyone, and you, my friend, are indeed fortunate, for I'd like to invite you to bear witness to my findings."

"You've found the iron ore I require? That would be an absolute godsend! If you own the land, the Party will lease your claim for a very fair price, especially if the hematite is high grade."

"*Ja, ja,*" the man said, waving his hand dismissively. "And what if I were to give you something better?"

"Better? I don't understand. Unless it's milled steel, how could it be better?" Steiger asked.

The man only smiled and took another sip of his beer. "I report directly to Albert Speer," Professor Steiger said. "Is this a name that's known to you?"

"It is."

"Then you know my task is of utmost importance to the Reich. Anything that could aid the war effort would be of great value to *Der Führer.*"

Steffan set down his mug and then turned the glass in a tight circle between his rough hands. His eyes met the barmaid's, and after she made a quick glance over Steiger's shoulder, she nodded tightly. Professor Steiger twisted around in his seat to see what she'd been looking at and found that the SS that had previously been sitting behind him in the dark corner of the bar were now gone. When he turned his attention back to Steffan, the older man's glassy eyes bored into his own.

"You're a man of rock and stone, are you not Professor?" the miner asked. "You study the creation of these things?"

"Yes, of course. I have a master's degree in tectonics."

"I don't care about degrees," Steffan said. "I care about someone that can explain a mystery from God himself."

"A mystery from God? I'm afraid I don't understand," Steiger said with a confused look.

"Meet me here tomorrow morning, and it will be my honor to answer all of your questions," Steffan said, slurring his words as he spoke.

The barmaid set yet another of the insipid beers down in front of Steffan, and as the miner curled his hand around the stein and drank deeply from it, the strange burns on his face seemed to redden. The barmaid swept a rag over the bar top as he drank, doing her best to clean the white powder that the miner had shed all over the scarred wood of the bar.

"Do you have an ore claim or not old man?" Steiger asked. "What exactly is it you want me to see?"

Steffan finally set his glass back down on the bar and slipped off his stool in a sloppy, drunken stupor. He wobbled for a moment on his thick legs, and then patted Steiger on the shoulder before he turned and headed for the darkened bar's exit.

"I have only my suspicions to go on, of course, but I would hazard a guess to say that what I've discovered could quite possibly be a gift that will make *Der Führer* smile."

2

He found the miner seated on a bench outside the tavern. His eyes were closed, and he had a cigarette dangling from his lips.

"Steffan?" the professor asked, but the man seemed fast asleep. Reaching out, he nudged the man's shoulder a few times. "Steffan, wake up."

The cigarette's ash fell off the end and landed right where the cloth of his shirt had buckled open between two buttons. As soon as its burning sensation penetrated his alcohol-induced haze, he burst awake, howling in pain as he coughed and spat the cigarette out into the gutter. It hissed for just the briefest of moments and then grew dark. Levering himself upright, he patted himself down to make sure that his shirt hadn't been singed by the embers.

"Oh … *Guten Tag*," he said as he glanced up at the professor. "You look as though you're ready for an expedition."

"If this is an important find, I'll need to take samples," Steiger said.

"Nothing in that bag of yours will be of any use to you," the miner said, smiling to himself as he got to his feet. Steiger knew he was holding something back, but he didn't know what it was. Just to be safe, he'd slipped his revolver into his trouser pocket before he came out of the tavern.

"Where are we headed?" the professor asked. "I have a car with me if it's near a road."

"We're heading to The *Zitternberg*. It's a few kilometers southeast of here. The road will take us part of the way. After that we'll have to continue on foot."

"Very well," Steiger said as he led the miner to the two-seat Volkswagen he'd parked outside of the Bad Tölz Inn.

"They pay professors this well?" Steffan asked as the professor ground the car's gears and turned the wheel south.

"The car was a gift from *Herr* Speer."

"Ah, a gift. I wonder what gift you'll have in mind for me."

"The gift will be commensurate with the value to the Reich," Steiger said.

"Good, good. It suits me to have no restrictions, Professor. It's important for you to keep an open mind," Steffan said drowsily as he smiled and closed his eyes. "The road will end at a footpath into the hills. Wake me when we arrive."

* * *

Bad Tölz's stone buildings grew ever smaller behind them as the road carried them far into the foothills. Steiger drove under a clear blue sky that kissed the gray mountaintops with sunlight. The evergreen forests were mixed with crisp glaciers high above them, and for a time the professor lost himself in thought. It was beautiful here. In fact, the whole of Germany was blessed with a strength and a majesty that was unmatched anywhere in the world as far as Steiger was concerned. The Reich had risen on strong foundations to become a pillar of progress in an uncertain world. It could not fail. He would not allow it.

The car's rattling engine labored as the dirt road continued to grow steeper. So much so that Steiger had to push his foot to the floor to keep moving.

After another kilometer, the road ended at a muddy turnaround, where he finally brought the car to a stop. The miner's eyes opened just before the professor shook him, and Steffan winked as he unlatched the door.

"It's my gift, Professor—being lucky with timing I mean," the miner said. "I once stepped out of the mine for coffee not 30 seconds before the shaft caved in."

"That was lucky," Steiger said.

"Indeed, as was your arrival. Years after I made my find, and on the very day that I finally decided to tell my story, you arrived on the train and decided to frequent my *Keller*."

"How far will we be going?" Steiger asked as he retrieved his pack from the Volkswagen's boot and placed his arms through the straps.

"Not far. Maybe two kilometers or so," Steffan said as he stepped forward to lead the way.

They crunched through the thin layer of snow that lay against the roots of the evergreen trees, following a footpath that overlooked the town's valley. Looking over his shoulder, Steiger could see a distant locomotive pull into Bad Tölz, its steam fading gracefully into the sky. If Steffan had in fact found ore here, it would be a simple matter to extend the rail spur up through the hills.

"We're not climbing?" the professor asked.

"No, no climbing. The mountain is that one there—the *Zitternberg*. We go in at its feet," Steffan said as he pointed just beyond the next hill to the base of a mountain that rose into a thin haze of clouds at its peak.

"*Zitternberg?*" Steiger asked. "Is that old German?"

The miner looked over his shoulder and smiled strangely. In the morning light, the streaks on Steffan's face were much more visible, and his pale blue eyes sparkled with his secret.

"*Ja.* It means *trembling mountain*," Steffan said. "The name suits it quite well, Professor, as you will soon see."

3

"This is your find?" Professor Steiger asked once they'd reached a small clearing at *Zitternberg's* base. Steffan had cut the pines away years ago, to make room for his tailings. The mounds of rock and dust lay in glittering white heaps on either side of a rough-shored tunnel entrance that was just wide enough for a broad-shouldered man to fit through. Behind them, the cliffside fell away in a sharp 15-meter drop before rejoining the forest.

"This is the entrance, *ja*," Steffan said.

Professor Steiger unstrapped his pickaxe, hefted it in his hand, and then crossed the clearing to enter the narrow shaft. The morning sun shone just far enough inside to reveal white stone on either side of the tunnel mouth, and his face soured. This was the powder he'd seen on Steffan yesterday. He should have known it was some sort of a trick, and now his morning had seemingly been wasted. However, since he was there, he needed to be sure. Tapping the stone with the point of his axe, he knocked away a bit of the material, placed his finger on the fresh cut, and then tasted the residue that clung to his skin.

"Sodium chloride. Thank you for your time, Steffan, but the *Führer* has plenty of table salt," Steiger said as he turned to go, but the smiling miner held up a palm to block his path.

"*Nein*, Professor. *Nein, nein.* This is just the entrance."

"*Iron ore*," the professor said firmly. "I told you I was looking for *iron ore* and you said you would take me. Now you've wasted half of my day and I need to report back to *Herr* Speer that—"

Instead of answering, Steffan squeezed his bulk inside the tunnel, pressing Steiger against the crumbling salt stone as he passed. A few paces further in, the miner picked up a lantern and lit the wick with a match he pulled from his pocket. An orange glow illuminated the featureless walls, revealing a straggling passage that led deeper into the *Zitternberg*.

"I never said it was iron, Professor. I said it was something that would make *der Führer* smile. Now, come along," the miner said as he jerked his head, turned, and then headed down the passage.

Steiger tried to calm his anger. He had no time for foolish secrets. There was a war going on, and the Reich didn't need to spend its time following the wild goose chases of eccentric old men. Still, he'd already made the trip and invested the time, so he might as well see it through to its conclusion. After all, how deep could a shaft dug by an old drunk possibly go?

His shoulders brushed against the stone as he followed the miner through the cramped tunnel. Wooden pillars and beams supported the ceiling about every ten feet, but the walls bulged and constricted wherever Steffan had grown weary or encountered resistance in the stone and lost his focus. Steiger studied the supports as they passed each one, and he was becoming more and more nervous about the soundness of the tunnel.

"I know ore is valuable," Steffan called over his shoulder. "I've been prospecting in these hills since the first war, so I knew it was salt here, but at least you can sell salt. After all, I have bills to pay, just like any other man. This shaft here I sank years ago, long before the war, so I thought, *why not keep digging and see if I get lucky?*"

"A fascinating story, but my patience is growing thin, old man," Steiger said. Steffan stopped a few paces in front of him, and then turning back so that he was facing the professor, he opened the glass door of his lamp and blew out the light.

"Your patience is about to be rewarded, Professor," he said through the darkness.

Steiger's hand tightened around his pickaxe. If the miner's plan was to rob him, then he'd defend himself with every ounce of his strength.

He could hear Steffan's breathing grow heavy in front of him and tried to pinpoint the miner's location, but he could see nothing. A few moments later, however, a new light appeared in the darkness, peeking out from behind the man's broad shadow.

"Do you see?" the miner asked as he clutched Steiger's arm, then shuffled forward toward the strange illumination. The tunnel widened as the light grew in intensity to the point where the professor could easily make out the grain of the rock, and even the stitching in his boots.

"What in God's name is this?" Steiger whispered as he stared in awe at what appeared to be a polished steel wall. The light it was emanating came from intense strips of blue illumination that mimicked the strange burn patterns on Steffan's face, and as he watched, the lights slid from their original positions and reformed into an entirely new configuration. Daring to step closer, Steiger pressed his hand against the shining metal. It felt warm, almost alive, and he could not escape the feeling that the lights were somehow beckoning to him.

"What in God's name indeed, Professor? I was hoping that you could answer that question for me," Steffan said. "I've been keeping this place a secret up to now, just waiting for the opportunity to meet someone like you. Someone who could understand the importance of it all. You know, I've come here often just to sit and watch the patterns—to listen to them."

Steiger traced the glowing letters with his fingertips. They burned more and more brightly until the agonizing heat seared his skin. Finally, he closed his eyes and stepped away. The wall darkened, and the script's afterimage slowly faded from his vision. All the while, he stood there smiling through the sunburn that had tightened his face.

"I was wrong to have doubted you, Steffan," the professor said. "This will indeed be a marvelous gift."

4

May 2014

München, Germany

Lightning burst through the windows, and then a few seconds later, thunder shook the house and startled the Steigers' maid. The tea service she was carrying rattled in her hands, and she quickly had to steady herself.

Looking down her hawkish nose, Maria Steiger shook her head at the Polish girl they'd found through the university placement service.

"Sorry, ma'am. I've not felt a storm like this in years," the maid said as she continued.

"Fear is for the weak, Elsa. You'd do well to remember that," Maria said.

"Yes, ma'am," she said as she set the tray on the coffee table. The tea service was polished silver and was rumored to have been stolen from the Soviets. Like so many other things in their mansion, the table and service were pre-war antiques. You could not find such craftsmanship anymore; it was such a shame how the world had changed.

"Will you take tea, Martin?" Maria asked.

Her husband stood at the window, watching the *Garchinger Mühlbach's* swollen current flow as watery light crawled down his shoulders.

"The old Bavarian tribes used to say that thunder was the king under the mountain trying to break out," he mused. "What do you think they'd have said if they'd have known the truth?"

"Will there be anything else, madam?" Elsa asked timidly.

"No, that'll be all Elsa. I think—" Maria said, but just then the front door boomed with the sound of someone knocking from the outside.

Martin turned, revealing dark blue eyes above the violet bags that scarred his upper cheeks. Consumed with his research, he rarely slept, and Maria woke to his pale blond hair floating away through the darkness more times than she could remember.

"See to the door, Elsa," Martin said.

"Yes, sir. Right away," she replied as she turned and quickly disappeared from the room. Maria set aside her tablet with her lecture notes and rose from the divan.

"Who'd come visiting on a night like tonight?" she asked as the door opened. The rain grew louder, and the sound of galoshes squelched on the hardwood floor of the entry hall before Elsa closed the door once again.

"*Herr* Steiger, Miss," a strange voice asked. "Is he in?"

"May I take your coat, sir?" Elsa asked him in return.

"I'm afraid I have little time," the voice protested.

"Elsa," Martin called. "Let the man in. A little water never hurt us."

Maria bent to pour a third cup of tea and watched as the steam rose from the dark silver. Just as she finished pouring, the thumping of the man's boots announced his presence in the room. He wore a dripping leather overcoat that shone with the oil of its tanning, and he'd topped his blonde hair with a fedora, which he swept off his head when he saw Maria. High cheekbones cast shadows down his long face, and eyes that shown with sharpness and intelligence scanned the room. His mere presence left them both with the impression that he was a man used to command, stiffened with a formality rarely observed the modern world.

"Please forgive my late arrival," the visitor said.

"Elsa, see to the gentleman's coat and hat," Maria said.

"Yes, of course, ma'am. Sir, if you please ..."

Their visitor looked back at the maid, then shrugged off his heavy coat. Underneath, the man wore what seemed to be a homespun shirt above gray tweed trousers held up with suspenders. He reeked of wet wool, and the heavily worn leather of his galoshes rose over his calves.

"Would you care for some tea?" Maria offered. A small smile flashed across the visitor's face.

"Thank you, madam. I was sure that in this home above all others, I would find such gracious hospitality."

"Come," Martin said. "Elsa will make a fire so you can warm yourself. While she does, perhaps you'd give us your name?"

The visitor took the tea from Maria with a thankful nod, and then he studied them both carefully for a moment.

"No," he said. "No, I think it is too soon for names. For now, let's just say that I'm an old family friend."

Elsa returned from the hallway, knelt by the marble hearth in the sitting room's center, and began stacking the fire logs.

"Are you with the university?" Maria asked.

The maid struck a match. Flame kindled in the fireplace, growing in intensity until its light reflected off the screen of Maria's tablet. It caught their visitor's eye, and he stared at it intently for a moment while Elsa got back to her feet and moved away respectfully while she awaited her next orders.

"I was working on my notes," Maria said when she noticed that he was staring at the tablet. "I'm scheduled to lecture tomorrow on the latest theories of dark matter."

"My dear, we don't need to—" Martin said, but the man interrupted him.

"My apologies, but may we have a moment of privacy?" he asked.

"Yes, of course," Martin said. "Elsa, if you please."

The maid nodded and withdrew from the room as the fire brightened, pushing back some of the night's chill.

"Now then," Martin said. "Would you do us the courtesy of telling us what this is all about? It *is* late after all, and as she mentioned, my wife has work to do."

The visitor set down his tea on the table as if he hadn't heard. He reached for Maria's tablet but then halted as his manners caught up with him. He looked up at her, smiling.

"May I?" he asked.

"Of course," Maria answered.

The stranger took the electronic tablet, hefted it in his hand, and then tapped a finger against its frame. The screen appeared, and a great smile spread across the man's face. Flames from the fireplace reflected from his eyes, and as he offered the device back to Maria, she had the impression of a wolf's anticipatory grin before it devoured its prey.

"I couldn't help but notice that this house is a wonderful piece of property," their guest said. "It's clear that you and your wife have both been very successful. Is it your salary from the university that has allowed you to amass such wealth, I wonder?"

"We have published several books as well," Maria said. "The royalties are—"

"That's not what he's asking, Maria," Martin interrupted. He set down his tea and stepped between the strange man and his wife. "Are you from the *Polizei*? The Central Tax Office?"

"There is no need for hostility," the visitor said.

"I have answered the Tax Office's questions repeatedly, and with honesty," Martin continued. "I will not keep subjecting myself to these—"

"With honesty?" their visitor asked, suddenly looking rather amused. "Well now, I find that quite interesting. Have you told your Tax Offices about the seed that your grandfather, Hans, planted, or of why he planted it?"

Outside, the storm growled and kicked. Rain bashed against the windows and spewed from the gutters. Martin glanced back at Maria, and a sudden tension filled the air, while behind them the fireplace crackled and smoked.

"I don't believe we need to continue this conversation," Martin said, attempting to hide the uneasiness he was feeling with a firm tone.

Their visitor scanned the room's vaulted ceilings, the massive panel of their television, the blinking security system, and the bright screams of color from the artwork that lined their walls.

"Though much of what surrounds me I do not understand, I do know it was purchased with gold from long ago. I haven't come here tonight to lay any claims upon that gold but understand that I am the one who was responsible for its placement, and I have come to ask you both one simple question."

"Martin," Maria said, gripping her husband's arm tightly with trembling fingers as a rush of adrenaline coursed through her body.

"Ask," Martin practically whispered.

"Does your loyalty still align with what lies under the *Zitternberg?*" the man asked.

Maria's skin flushed in the growing warmth inside the room. The silk of Martin's robe whispered like breath through her fingers, and she felt as though she might faint as the crushing weight of a lifetime of hope suddenly overwhelmed her.

"We never thought we'd live to see this," Martin said as sheen of sweat rose above his wide eyes. "My grandfather, the late Hans Steiger, told me it might not come for centuries."

"Yet all this time you have remained loyal to the cause, and now I have come," the man said.

The storm blurred the windows, shutting out the lightning-scarred world outside, while in their sitting room the air had grown taut and humid. Maria's husband brought his heels together as he stood at rigid attention. He lifted his right arm above his shoulder, and then flattened his hand into a blade.

"*Sieg heil!*" he cried from behind the Nazi salute. "*Sieg heil!*"

Maria joined her husband in the *Hitlergruß,* their voices rising to the rafters. Amidst their chants, their visitor smiled and sipped his tea while the fire burned with an ominous light.

"Perhaps my visit will be a longer one after all," the man said. "Allow me to introduce myself. My name is Kristock Keck, and it appears that we have much to discuss."

* * *

September 1943

Exeter, United Kingdom

"Able Company, on your feet!" Sergeant Bucknell's gravel voice growled.

Private Jim Thompson groaned as he lurched upright. Platoons of men lined the beach in jagged rows, while the rest of the infantrymen in his company dusted their hands and flicked their cigarettes into the wet sand as they got to their feet. A damp drizzle had soaked them to the bone long before they'd spent the afternoon slogging up and down the surf line, practicing their maneuvers. As Jim strapped on his heavy rucksack and felt it grind against his blistered shoulders, he let out a string of exhausted curses.

"Jeez Jim, listening to you makes me feel like I'm right back in Brooklyn," one of the other soldiers said with a breathy laugh.

"Bangalores on your shoulders!" Bucknell called as he jogged past. "No slacking now, men!"

Thompson squatted, wrapped his hands around the six-foot canister he'd dropped in the sand, and then hoisted all 85 pounds of it onto his shoulder. Bangalore torpedoes could be screwed together in as long of a line as was necessary to clear out various obstacles, like brush, mines, or barbed wire. The only problem was that they were hell to carry, especially when they were being lugged over the soft sand of a beach, where every footfall sank lower than expected, and the traction was less than stellar.

"I'm gonna airlift this thing straight to Hitler," someone called.

"I'm gonna jam it right up Bucknell's rear end," another laughed.

"You think they're trying to punish us?" a private two rows over asked.

"If they are, then the sergeant's gonna have to learn that I don't react all that well to discipline," Jim called back to him.

Staggering under the weapons' weight, they were all dead tired at this point, and more than a few soldiers were muttering about what was going on at the target, which for this exercise consisted of two concrete blockhouses behind 30 feet of razor wire about a mile down the beach. He could just see the Limeys manning the blockhouses, waving at them, and finding all manner of amusement in their suffering. This would be the tenth time the Americans ran their drill, and the Brits were having quite the laugh watching the Yanks run up and down the beach until they nearly puked.

Relations between the two allies were not exactly cozy, thanks to the billeting laws the British government had put into effect, and the Limeys had brought their resentment to the beach with them. Jim had already been mooned, spit on, and had his mother insulted, so he was in no mood for another go-round.

"Hey, Big Jim," Private Reynolds said as he turned to look back at him. The man's face sagged with exhaustion, and even in the gray daylight he looked washed out. "Listen, I'm not feelin' so good. Any way you could help me out when we get down there?"

"You got it, Teddy," Jim grunted as he continued to slog through the sand.

"All right you men, get down that beach!" Bucknell shouted at the top of his lungs.

Jim's calves burned as his boots sank into the sand to gain traction. Pushing his tired muscles as hard as he could, he charged down the beach right through the middle of his ragged string of men. The aluminum sleeve he was carrying bounced on his shoulder, and the sand that had worked its way into his boots and his uniform ground uncomfortably against his skin. He'd sleep for a week when they got back to the barracks, but not before downing a dozen or so of the English ales they served in the town pubs, because he had a score to settle with the Limeys tonight.

They'd only covered a few hundred yards when Reynolds began to stumble in front of him.

"No slacking now, Reynolds! Keep it moving!" Bucknell roared. "You think the Jerries are gonna care whether you have the flu?"

Reynolds had been to the infirmary three times since they'd arrived in England, and it *wasn't* for the flu. Back in the States, Jim knew that the smaller man had never been a shirker. Bucknell should have known that as well and not singled him out the way he did.

Jim picked up his pace, closing the distance between himself and the sick private. The light drizzle was mixing with his sweat. It stung his eyes as it trickled down his face, and his muscles continued to burn as he pushed them to their limits. His whole body was on fire, but the blockhouses were growing closer with every step, and that thought alone inspired him to push himself even harder.

As he pulled even with the smaller man, he reached out his free hand, grabbed Reynolds' torpedo, and rolled the extra weight up onto his left shoulder. Reynolds' gray face grimaced in thanks.

Sergeant Bucknell was hollering something at him, but at this point, Jim didn't care what it was. His whole world had narrowed to his leg muscles, his cramped breathing, and the damp air that was licking every inch of him.

His platoonmates fell behind as the blockhouse swelled in front of the dirty beach and the darkening sky. His pack pounded his spine and the weight of the Bangalores numbed his shoulder muscles. But he kept pushing himself, gasping for breath with each step. The razor wire glimmered, at first 50 yards ahead of him, then 20, and then 10.

He slid down in front of the obstacles, letting the torpedoes flop into the sand.

"Look at this 'ere Yank," he heard some cockney soldier shout as he arrived. "Thinks he can take on 'itler all by 'is'self."

Jim threaded the first torpedo into the second, and then shoved the 12-foot tube hand-over-hand under the wire. Now he was supposed to light the tube's imaginary fuse, and then take cover while he waited for the dummy Bangalores to explode. Once he'd given them enough time to do their job, he was supposed to get up and jog back down the beach.

"Oi! Yank! There ain't no medals for being the first to get shot."

"Look out!" another called. "Grenade!"

Jim looked up just as a bag of something that should have gone into the latrine hit him in the shoulder and exploded all over him.

"A direct hit!" one of the Limeys cried. Jim stood up and quickly scanned the barbed wire in front of him.

"Thompson! What in the hell do you—" Bucknell yelled from somewhere behind him, but Jim didn't hear the rest of it as he took off running toward the blockhouse along a path that led him through the winding coils of concertina wire.

"Wot's this?" one of the Brits called out in surprise.

"'E's a big fella, ain't he?" another asked mockingly.

"Thompson, get back here!" Bucknell screamed at him, but if there was one thing that Jim knew other than how to arm a Bangalore, it was when to stand up and fight.

A Limey chewing a big cigar greeted him at the rear of the blockhouse. The man still had tears in his eyes from laughing.

"'Ere now Yank," he said, wrinkling his nose at the smell. "Wot do ya—"

Jim broke the Limey's nose with one punch to the man's doughy face before he could finish. He felt hands grab at him and blows coming in from all directions, but his aching muscles shrugged them off as he continued to swing his fists, just like he'd done in those sweaty Brooklyn arenas where he used to fight. He'd always been a fighter. It was all he knew, and a fight was as good a way as any to finally end all those damn drills.

* * *

"You are one pug-ugly soldier," Captain Lathin said from a foot in front of Thompson's face. Jim could barely see the company's commanding officer through his swollen eye, and he was having trouble standing at attention due to a rib that he had a sneaking suspicion might be broken. "Oh, and why the hell do you smell like a sewer?"

"I believe that's British excrement sir," Sergeant Bucknell said. "The private here knocked four of the offending Brits out cold before they finally turned the tide."

"Private, am I right in thinking that you were a boxer back stateside?"

"Sir, yes sir," Jim slurred through his swollen lip. He felt a tooth at the front of his mouth wiggle and tried to improve his diction by pressing it back into place with his tongue. Hopefully he wouldn't lose it, but only time would tell. He'd just have to be extra careful with it for a while.

"Sergeant Bucknell here tells me that you've been a problem in your unit since the first day of basic. What do you have to say for yourself, Private?"

Thompson's eyes flicked to the burly sergeant. Bucknell had rolled up his sleeves to let the thick mat of hair on his arms dry in the captain's office. The sergeant hadn't liked him since basic when Jim had knocked another recruit out cold for rummaging through his footlocker.

"I don't believe a few brawls between friends are a problem, sir!" Jim slurred.

"A few brawls between friends?" Lathin asked.

"The man's stubborn as a mule, sir," Bucknell said. "I told him, one more fight and I'm sending him to the MPs for court martial."

"Is that right?" Captain Lathin asked as he scratched at his chin thoughtfully. Behind him, Jim could make out a blurry map of Europe. The red arrows that represented German units swung all throughout Northern France like a predator's claws.

"I understand that during today's exercise you came to the aid of one of the other members of your platoon who's been under the weather. You were carrying two torpedoes, and yet you were still the first man down the beach. Is that correct, Private?"

"Sir, yes sir," Jim said.

"Furthermore, I have received a letter of apology from the CO of the blockhouse, assuring me that his men have taken responsibility for the incident. Whenever they return to consciousness, those British soldiers you fought out there are gonna be disciplined," Captain Lathin said as he glanced at Sergeant Bucknell. For just the briefest of moments, Jim thought he saw a hint of a smile on the sergeant's face.

"Do you think it's the right decision?" the captain asked.

"I'll be sorry to see him go, sir, but yes, I think it's the right decision."

"Sir, permission to speak?" Jim asked.

"Denied, Corporal," Bucknell said. Jim's mouth hung open for a moment, but he kept his silence as he tried to process what he'd just heard.

"Son, you need to keep your temper in check, but you're also a natural born leader, and it just so happens that this army's got a place for pluggers like you," the captain said, and then he smiled as he reached out to shake Jim's hand. "Congratulations, *Corporal* Thompson."

Sergeant Bucknell stepped forward and pressed a double chevron sleeve patch and a set of orders into Jim's stunned hand. He squinted down at the paper, but he couldn't quite make out what it said.

"Thank you, Captain, Sergeant," he said, nodding appreciatively to them both. My eyes are still fuzzy though. I wonder if you could tell me what my new orders are?"

"You're to report to Carrickfergus, Ireland," Captain Lathin said. "We're putting together a new unit called the Rangers. There's gonna be lots of physical training, and lots of fights to get into. It's the perfect fit for someone like you."

He looked back and forth between Bucknell and Lathin, and a sense of pride swelled within him for the first time since he'd lost his fourth fight in a row back home, and then shipped out for the war without telling his disappointed father.

"I promise I won't let you down," Jim said firmly.

"We know you won't, son," the captain said. "Just do us all a favor and save the fightin' for Hitler. Now, you're dismissed. Go and see the medic about your injuries."

Jim snapped the tightest salute he could. His smile tugged painfully at his swollen face, but he couldn't keep it from spreading.

"Thank you, sir," he said. "Oh, and Sergeant—"

"Save it, Thompson," Bucknell growled. "Just do me and the captain here a favor. Make sure you burn that uniform before you transfer. We don't want you makin' a bad impression on the Rangers now, do we?"

"No sir. I'll be sure to do that," Jim said, snapping them both one more salute before he turned and headed out to find the medic.

5

July 2014

Berchtesgaden National Park, Germany

Yanis Miller paused to wipe the sweat from his face with his free hand, and then sipped from his Camelbak's warm plastic tube while he peered up at where the Blaueis Glacier's blue-green flow rose to a saddle between the two peaks of the Blaueisspitze and the Kleinkalter. Beyond lay a small valley in the Hochkalter Massif that was the both the glacier's front, and Yanis' destination. He wouldn't get there if he didn't keep moving though, so he kicked the crampons on the edges of his boots into the ice and then drove his axe into the crystal overhead. He'd come here to push himself, but so far, the Alpine warming had presented other ideas.

The warm summer sun had reduced much of the glacier's mass to a thin sheet of glass and snow that was choked with boulders, and the going was steep but not that challenging. He was able to walk for long stretches, making his way past trickling water that was flowing toward the glacier's source. Summer ice climbing made the process trickier, but with a heavy teaching load coming in the fall, and the possibility of tenure at the university in the next year, this was the only time he had to pursue his hobby.

There were many back in Jerusalem who would have called an ice climbing trip the opposite of relaxing. This was also the case in Germany no less, a land still associated with maliciousness for many of his people, but few Israelis understood him. It was hard to strike up a conversation about cryptology with anyone other than the few academics and mathematicians who shared his passion, and he'd given up on finding anyone who understood his drive to explore. After living in his mind for so long during the school year, he relished the opportunity to flee to Germany for a while, so he could once again experience the thrill of exploration.

The only technical part of the climb came when he reached the glacier's saddle. He pulled an ice screw from his bag and drilled it into position on the cool blue lip of ice. A second followed, and then he paused with his hand on his line.

His phone switched from the playlist he had selected, over to shuffle, resulting in an instinctive eye roll. He was *so* not in the mood for the song that was playing, so he pulled his phone from its protective pocket and attempted to swipe to the next song. Unfortunately, he didn't have much luck. His new and impervious waterproof case wasn't the problem. The problem was the fact that he was wearing gloves, and the touch screen wouldn't respond to his commands no matter how many times he swiped. Frustrated, but recognizing that this was probably the worst possible place to get in a fight with his phone, he stuffed it back into his pocket.

Surprisingly, even though he hadn't been in the mood for that song, it didn't take long for Yanis to lose himself in the music. So much so in fact, that he even started singing along with it.

"Her name is Rio, and she dances on the sand," he sang awkwardly, and then he laughed when he suddenly remembered what a horrible singer he was.

The vertical part of the climb wasn't even two meters, so it was relatively simple. He paused for a moment with his breath fogging against the ice. Again, better to be safe than sorry, he thought to himself as he anchored his line to the screws, double-checked the knots, and then seized a screw in each hand. Driving his crampons into the glacier, he lifted himself in a pull-up until his chest was over the ice. Freeing one of his hands, he drove his axe into the plateau, and then pulled himself over the edge.

Air blew cool and refreshing against his face. He lifted his sunglasses to study the crisp blue sky and the damp gullies that had worn into the sides of the mountain from centuries of water flowing down during the summer melts.

Three peaks rose at the end of the ice bowl a few hundred meters from him. He visually traced the route ahead, looking for the safest path. The bowl wasn't too deep, and he reckoned he had little to fear from crevasses that would have been more of a menace in the thicker Canadian glacier fields.

Reaching below the saddle, he untied his safety line and looped it at his waist before he set off across the gently sloping plateau. For a time, he heard only the wind's whistle and the crunch of his boots.

He closed his eyes as he walked, enjoying the sun's warmth and the feeling of peace that came from being alone in the mountains. He knew he shouldn't climb alone, but since few others shared his love of both natural and mathematical mysteries, he preferred the solitude.

His mind drifted toward his work. Integer factorization, discrete logarithms, and information theory all seemed far separated from this place, and yet, somehow, they also belonged, like mysteries that fit into the ordered ruggedness of nature. His thoughts were soon interrupted, however, by a shifting groan that shook the glacier beneath him.

His eyes flew open and he looked around wildly, trying to discern if there'd been any change in the snow and ice around him. The glacier shuddered once more, throwing him from his feet. He grabbed at the ice and felt it slip from his gloved fingertips. The glacier was giving way, and there was nothing he could do to save himself.

He screamed as he fell, but there was no one to hear him as he slipped into the widening crevasse. Desperately, he swung his axe and kicked out with his crampons, trying to somehow get a grip on the walls that were little more than a blur as he fell. But it was all for naught. Ice scraped and clawed at him, ricocheting him through the crevasse. His screams echoed off the dim chamber walls until the unseen bottom rose to strike him, and his consciousness fled.

6

Yanis woke up in a heap on his side and blinked a few times, trying to get his eyes to focus. He tried to sit upright, but dizziness and nausea quickly forced him to lie back down as shards of ice from the widening crevasse continued to clatter against his helmet and parka. He didn't know how long he'd been lying in the dim chamber, but he thanked God for his survival as he stared up at the blurred streak of blue sky above him.

Slowly, he wiggled his hands and feet, and then carefully lifted each limb. It was beyond him how he'd managed to survive the fall, much less that he survived it with no broken bones, and no real pain aside from the headache that was currently pounding away at the inside of his skull.

His climbing had gotten sloppy, and incredibly so. It was a miracle that he still lived, so when he finally felt well enough, he struggled to his knees and offered an informal Birkhat HaGomel to thank God for preserving him.

As the last Hebrew syllables faded, he got to his feet and attempted to assess the situation. It was then that he realized that something else had joined him at the bottom of the glacier.

As his head cleared, the massive brown and green blur in front of him slowly resolved into a recognizable shape. Years of shifting ice had revealed long gashes of rusting metal between what remained of its camouflage paint. Yanis traced the cylindrical form back to where it emerged from the melting ice, sucking in a breath when he reached a black and white cross glimmering at him from just under the glacier's surface.

Anyone would recognize the *Luftwaffe's* insignia from their history lessons. The Nazi plane must have crashed here in the Alps during the war and lay buried under decades of snow and ice until he'd finally stumbled upon it. He stepped back, toward the crevasse's far wall, so he could take it all in and get a better sense of its actual size. Ice still held the front and rear of its fuselage, but the exposed section before him ran nearly ten meters.

At roughly the midpoint, an angry swath of torn metal revealed where the crash must have torn the wing away from the fuselage, and below that stood the oval outline of a door.

He turned away from the wreckage and had to fight off a sudden wave of dizziness when his blurred vision took a moment to catch up. He closed his eyes for a moment, and then reopened them once he'd steadied himself. In front of him was a wall of ghostly blue ice that composed the far boundary of the crevasse. He tapped on the wall with his axe a few times to test the hardness of the ice, and then he leaned back to study the sparkling white of the glacier's opening 15 meters above him.

He tugged on his safety line and was relieved to feel that it was still secured. The ice looked sturdy enough, and since all his equipment had fallen with him, climbing his way out of there probably wouldn't be all that difficult. At least it gave him a chance to explore a bit before he moved on.

He shrugged off his pack and unclipped his harness. Freed of all the weight and extra bulk, he pulled the flashlight from his belt and anxiously pressed the switch. He half-expected it to be broken, but its beam shone brightly against the aged body of the plane.

Making his way to the hatch, he ran his glove across the frozen metal, causing what was left of the paint on its surface to flake off like dust under his palm.

The handle on the door screamed as he put all his strength into opening it. Once the handle finally gave way, he held it tightly and pushed hard against the rusted weight of 70-year-old hinges. The sound of groaning metal filled the crevasse, but eventually he managed to get it open just enough for him to be able to squeeze himself inside.

A damp, rotting smell met him from the plane's interior. He stopped with his hand still on the door handle and glanced up through a hole in the fuselage at the bright sliver of sky above him. His pulse was racing, and as he wiped the sweat from his face, a part of him wanted to start his return climb immediately. These weren't just movie Nazis after all. There was very likely at least one Nazi corpse sitting up there in the cockpit, possibly more. These were the genuine article, the embodiment of pure evil, and he was here alone with them in their tomb.

For a moment, it all seemed impossible. But while his innate curiosity drew him forward, disgust and fear held him back. He wondered for a moment if some sort of a head injury was causing him to have delusions, a scenario that seemed more plausible than the current reality.

Another tremor suddenly shook the crevasse, so now he had a decision to make. He'd come to test himself against whatever challenges the mountain could provide, so he planted his boot on a torn strut, took one last breath, and then climbed into the fuselage.

He nearly gagged on the sour odor of cold metal and rotting leather as his flashlight swept across the rusting deck plates. Metal ribs that were spaced roughly a meter apart supported the cabin, while empty jump seats jutted out from the metal walls. Between the seats, small windows looked out upon on the surrounding ice, while the glass that had once sealed them was strewn about in scattered shards on the deck. He'd planned to start with the plane's rear, but the crash had shorn off the wreck's tail five meters from him and replaced it with a wall of blue ice.

Glass and ice crunched under his boots as he turned toward the cockpit. He raised his flashlight and slowly traced the beam along the shattered windows until it reached the pilot's station. In front of the headrest, he saw the remains of a rotted wool cap held in place by the rusting clasp of a headset.

Yanis' crampons screeched across the deck and the wreck groaned underneath him as he made his way forward. His progress was halted, however, when his foot caught on something that his flashlight had missed. He cursed loudly and stumbled forward a few steps before he finally managed to regain his balance. Quickly, he swung his flashlight back around to see what he'd tripped over.

The offending object seemed to have been a heavy black box that was maybe a foot and a half square and lashed to the deck. Kneeling, he fingered the rusting metal of the latches for a moment, but there was something else exerting a far greater pull on his consciousness, for he could feel the pilot's presence there in the cabin with him.

He'd read of Otzi, the remarkably preserved Neolithic man discovered in the Swiss Alps, but what would he see up in the cockpit? Would he see the well-preserved face of a criminal staring back at him? He didn't know; but, driven by a curiosity that was almost out of his control, he stood and left the crate behind him as he made his way to the cockpit. The glacier had burst through the cockpit's windscreen and was filtering in just enough light from the outside to make out the co-pilot's station, the shattered instruments, the gray sleeve of the pilot's jacket, and the tattered glove at the end of that sleeve that was dangling toward the ground at an odd angle.

The crash had driven the pilot's control yoke into his chest, which undoubtedly killed him instantly. He wore the remains of a rotting gray trench coat trimmed with a gold knot and silver studs at the sleeve and shoulder.

Yanis could see vague remnants of flesh and sinew as his flashlight climbed slowly, and he let out a gasp as a pair of empty eye sockets returned his gaze from behind their wireframe glasses.

The dead sockets seemed to follow him as he turned away. All he could think about was getting out of the plane and climbing his way out of the crevasse as fast as he possibly could. In his haste to escape, however, Yanis' foot again struck the box on the cabin's floor hard enough that it broke free of its rotten lashings and went skidding toward the hatch.

It struck him that the box seemed to be heavier than a case of that size should be, which piqued his curiosity tremendously. Fighting his desire to leave the dead man in peace, Yanis approached the box and knelt, wondering what secret the long-forgotten Nazi in the cockpit had risked died trying to protect.

***

December 1944

Bad Tölz, Germany

Sturmbannführer Kristock Keck watched the cabin burn with a cold satisfaction. His *Totenkopfverbände* wrestled with one of its occupants as the man tried to rise from where they'd forced him to his knees in the winter slush. Screams pealed from the house's broken windows, while its black smoke billowed up into the darkness.

"*Meine Frau!*" the prisoner screamed as he tried to lunge forward toward the house.

"Hold that man!" Keck ordered, but the desperate husband broke free of Keck's guards and sprinted for the burning doorway. Keck drew his Luger, aimed with his left hand behind his back in the dueling position that his father had taught him, and then fired a single shot. The man staggered, clutching at his back, and fell to the ground with his head and chest just across the threshold. Smoke rose from his body as the fire consumed first his hair, and then his coat.

"An excellent shot, *Sturmbannführer*," his aide, *Rottenführer* Taschner, said.

"Taschner, see that those two men are disciplined for losing control of the prisoner," Keck said as he holstered his pistol. Then he turned from where the charred house lit the night sky and met the sullen eyes of the scattered ring of townspeople who surrounded the house.

"This is all of them?" he asked.

"All who could be roused at this hour, *mein Herr*," Taschner said, handing his superior a report. Keck scanned it, then frowned as he stomped through the mud to address the townspeople.

"These are the consequences of polluting our Aryan bloodlines with Jewish blood," he said, loud enough so that everyone could hear. "You know that Bavaria is under my control, and that we live by the Nazi laws. See to it that you understand them and act accordingly. Now go back to your homes and remember this night."

As Bad Tölz's residents turned and headed back to their homes, Keck slipped on his kid leather gloves. It was a chilly night, and he was quite looking forward to returning to the *Junkerschüle* for a warm brandy. There were other reports of sub-human sympathizers in the region though, so he knew that he had to maintain a constant state of vigilance.

"*Mein Herr*," Taschner called as Keck climbed back toward the stone road and his waiting car. "*Mein Herr,* you have guests." the *Rottenführer* said as he trotted ahead to open the coach door. Keck entered the vehicle and found two men already seated inside.

The first was Horst Vogle, a Gestapo parasite whose incompetence continually hampered his efforts to cleanse Bavaria of the Jewish threat. The second was a weathered man in a white shirt and blue tie with streaks of sunburn across his face that Keck had never seen before.

"What have you brought me this time, Horst?" Keck asked as his driver got the car underway. "A pig farmer grown too friendly with his stock?"

The secret policeman's moustache stretched in a grimace.

"This man came to our offices asking to speak with someone who could authenticate his discovery. It seems he has exchanged messages with Berlin, and his … *humor* was not appreciated. He had been operating under the orders of *Herr* Speer, but it appears that his travel papers have been revoked."

"I fail to see how this concerns me," Keck said dismissively.

"Please, *Herr* Keck," the burned man said in a hoarse voice. "This man would not understand, but you—"

Keck held his hand up to stop the man. The air in the car was frigid, and he could see steam puffing from Vogle's nostrils.

"It was a difficult shot, was it not Taschner?"

"*Ja, Mein Herr,*" his aide said from beside him.

"I have dedicated my entire life to ridding this country of weakness, such as the filthy Jewish vermin that plague our lands, and the Gestapo sees fit to burden me with a straightforward case of expired papers?" Keck asked, and as he turned his attention to Vogle's guest, his expression became deadly serious. "What is your name?"

"The name is Steiger. Professor Hans Steiger," the man said.

"Professor Steiger, what is your opinion on the progress of our great struggle?"

The academic turned to Vogle, but as the car bounced along the town's stone roads, the secret policeman offered no solace. Steiger swallowed and ran his hands along his thighs. "I'm afraid I wouldn't be here if the war were going well, *Herr* Keck."

"No, it's not going well at all," Keck agreed. "And every single day, despite my supreme efforts to cleanse our Vaterland of filth and vermin, the rot continues to creep its way in. So please, do enlighten me, Professor Steiger. What could possibly be so important that it would keep *Herr* Vogle or myself from executing you for traveling with revoked documentation?"

"A mysterious power, *Herr* Keck. I'm afraid I don't understand the discovery myself, but it could prove to be of great value to the Reich. *Herr* Speer would not understand, but you, the SS—"

"What do you think, Vogle?" Keck asked.

"He brought a miner with him—a drunk who spends most of his days in the Metzgerbräu *Keller*. The man had the same markings on his face and corroborated the story. It sounded as though there may be some validity to it, so I brought him here to speak with you directly."

"I'm a Party member, *Herr* Keck, loyal to my very bones. If you would only send a man with me to the *Zitternberg*, you'll see—"

"Enough," Keck said sharply.

The *Sturmbannführer* studied the man in front of him. He was used to citizens shrinking from his glare, but even though he'd been interrupted and threatened, the man who was sitting before him only sat taller. He was nothing like the sniveling animal that Keck had dispatched earlier that night, so perhaps he might be of some use.

"Driver!" Keck called forward. "Take us to the *Zitternberg*."

"Yes, *Sturmbannführer*," the man replied.

"Oh, thank you! Thank you!" Steiger gasped, but Keck simply grunted dismissively as he pulled out a few reports and placed them on his lap. Taschner held a light for him as he began studying up on their next series of targets. After a few moments, however, Keck looked at the man, and spoke in a voice that was cold and emotionless.

"Save your thanks until after I've seen what you have to show me, for if you've wasted my time on a fool's errand, then I swear to you that you shall not be returning with us."

* * *

Keck found the frigid mountain air invigorating. Ahead of him, Professor Steiger scurried along under Taschner's watchful eye, while the *Sturmbannführer* walked beside Vogle through the pines. An owl's solemn call echoed from the heights, while here and there a burst through the undergrowth betrayed some nocturnal creature's bower.

"That man you killed tonight?" Vogle asked.

"Consorting with Jews," Keck said casually. "A tragic story really. He'd been a cook at the *Junkerschüle*, and a quite talented one at that. We'd been planning to serve his roast pheasant at our Christmas banquet, but one of my men found his mother-in-law's original name in our records. Her name was Goldstein."

"A great tragedy indeed," Vogle said, and as their boots crunched through the snow, Vogle shivered underneath his fur collar.

"Does the cold bother you, Horst?" Keck asked.

"It's going to end soon enough, Keck," Vogle said. "The Americans are nearly at the *Rhein*, and the Russians are in Austria."

"And that is why we must be ever more resolute," Keck replied.

"I've been making certain … *arrangements*," Vogle whispered. "The Argentinians have been very kind to the Reich throughout the war, and their weather is not so different from the weather here in Bavaria."

Keck pondered the thought of escaping to Argentina for a moment, but then his thoughts were suddenly overtaken by silent disdain for Vogle.

Up ahead, Steiger had stopped at a small clearing, where a faint blue glow could be seen drifting out from a small hole at the mountain's base.

"This way," the professor beckoned. "Please, follow me."

Keck looked to Vogle, then drew his Luger for the second time that night. "Just in case our friend here is planning an ambush, I'd like you to remain here, Taschner."

"*Jahwol*," Taschner said as he snapped to attention.

"Now, Professor," Keck said as he waved his pistol toward the mine. "Forward if you please and stay where I can see you."

He passed into the mine with Vogle at his back, while Steiger remained a few paces ahead. The blue light grew stronger and was soon accompanied by a strange heat that filled the narrow passageway.

"All I ask is that you consider it, Keck, for I don't think that history will be kind to us in the end," Vogle whispered, but Keck's attention was somewhere else. His entire focus was on the peculiar place where the professor had just halted.

The light in front of them had brightened with considerable intensity. Keck stepped forward and joined Steiger in a small chamber that had been carved out from the soft rock. Steiger stepped aside as he approached, revealing a strange set of glowing blue markings that were unlike anything Keck had ever seen.

"If you but touch it, *Sturmbannführer*, you will understand the importance of this discovery," Steiger said.

Keck raised his hand and pressed his glove against the strange metal before him. He trembled as its heat filled him, and a feeling of hope for the Reich's future suddenly erupted in his chest. It was a feeling he'd tamped down long ago, but now, *now* he had a reason to feel hope once again.

With tears welling, he turned, raised his weapon, and shot a stunned Vogle right through the heart.

"You see, *Herr* Vogle?" he said as he stepped over and looked down into the dying man's eyes. "You were wrong to doubt the Reich. The Vaterland always rewards its most loyal, while disloyalty has its own consequences."

7

June 2014

Bad Reichenhall, Germany

The man who burst through the hotel's door wore a tank top that stretched tightly over his hard musculature. Tattoos that ran like blue blood across his arms tensed as he scanned the group that had gathered under the lobby chandelier's dim lighting. He held up a clenched fist, showing all who cared to look that the letters H-A-S-S, which means *hate* in German, were tattooed across his knuckles. With a bit of a grunt, he threw a wadded-up piece of paper onto the table.

"I want to know who is saying such things," the man said irritably. "I want to meet this *King Under the Mountain* person who thinks he knows so much."

Sharp eyes that revealed an unsettling amount of nothing stared back at him, none of them bothering to respond to his demand. Many of the shadowed figures seemed to be either active or ex-military, but there were others here that he just couldn't fathom. They had the look of academics who'd be more at home behind a microscope than they would be wielding a pistol. One man near the head of the table had an academic's tousled hair, and a crimson ascot knotted at his throat.

"Ah, Baldwin," the man said as he swept a gracious hand toward an open chair. "Please be seated, and all will soon be revealed."

"Who are you to give me orders, eh?" Baldwin demanded.

"My name is Martin Steiger. Up to now I have been your caretaker, although you wouldn't have known this until tonight. I am continuing the mission my grandfather, Hans Steiger, began. For all intents and purposes, you may consider me to be The King's emissary," Martin said. "Now, please be seated. There are still more coming."

Baldwin stared hard at Martin for a moment before pulling out the closest chair. He'd spelled the letters E-N-D-E, the German word for *termination*, in swollen ink on the knuckles of his other hand. Bottles of wine and spirits filled the center of the table, but so far, no one had partaken. The reception desk stood empty, and no one spoke as the night's blackness deepened like curtains falling across the windows.

"I could have been in bed," Baldwin finally muttered. "Instead, you drag me all the way out here to this miserable flea trap."

"The time for sleeping has passed," Martin said. "And as for our accommodation, you must all become used to such extreme discretion."

"I want to know about that letter, Steiger," Baldwin said. "You all got one?"

Heads nodded around the table. Some looked embarrassed, while others appeared proud. *Had they been gathered to be blackmailed?* Baldwin had come unarmed, just as the letter had asked, but he imagined that every one of the thirty or so people in the room had their associates waiting close by, as did he.

"That's enough, Baldwin," Martin said firmly. "We will speak no more until—"

The lobby doors suddenly swung open, and Baldwin turned to see two women enter. They were slightly older and growing thicker in the midsection, which suited him just fine. He'd always appreciated the way women filled out a bit as they aged. Both women wore simple black dresses that were accented with dashes of gold jewelry, and they both seemed quite startled by the number of people before them.

"Well now, things are finally looking up," Baldwin said with a sleazy grin, but the women only sneered as they passed him.

"Ah, the sisters. Now that everyone's here, we may finally begin," Martin said as he rose from his seat and circled the table, his smile growing wider with each step. Finally, he walked over to the wall and turned off the lights. "One moment please."

"What is this?" Baldwin asked suspiciously.

"I have men waiting if I don't return," another voice said in the darkness. "They are quite heavily armed."

"I can kill you with my bare hands just as well," Baldwin said.

"If you will all please just calm yourselves," Martin said. "As I mentioned before, discretion is of the utmost importance. We have not brought you here to harm you, so please be patient. It will be only a moment longer."

The protests died down, leaving only the sounds of the old hotel to fill the stale air. Floorboards creaked under someone's weight, and wind whispered through the cracks in its mortar.

A few tense moments later, the hotel's doors opened once more. Baldwin turned in his chair to see who it was, and momentarily caught sight of a tall man who appeared as little more than a silhouette against the darkness of the night's sky. Seconds later, the doors closed once again, placing the room back into a state of complete and total darkness. The new visitor's boots snapped against the floorboards with an almost metronome-like precision as he passed.

"Have you brought my bags?" Baldwin asked. A few weak laughs could be heard around the table, but then everyone suddenly grew nervous and fell silent once again.

"It is good that you make jokes," a new voice said from the darkness. "After tonight, you will have little time for merriment—*if* you have any time at all."

"Why are we here?" Baldwin called out. "Who are you?"

"You each received a letter from me that brought you here. I believe that makes me your pen pal, so to speak," the man said, chuckling to himself lightly.

"Well, Your Majesty," a voice said rather sarcastically. "Could we please turn the lights back on now and get to the point of this whole thing?"

They heard the footsteps arc around, toward where Martin had been sitting.

"You said you had a business proposition?" one of the sisters asked.

"That is the truth, but first I must understand if those of you that have gathered here are the right partners. In my letters, I told each of you some truths that you have worked very hard to keep hidden from both the law, and the world at large. Would you not agree?"

Baldwin nodded in the darkness, and then felt rather stupid for nodding when no one could see him anyway.

"*Da*," a Russian-accented voice called. "But how do you know of such things?"

"Those of you whom we've assembled here deal in the types of activities that I will require. You have done so for some time, just as your fathers before you, and your grandfathers before them. You'll not have been told who funded these efforts, or why they were funded, until tonight."

"Just what are you up to then?" Baldwin asked.

"For the greater part of a century, the beliefs you harbor in secret have been looked upon as criminal, but these ideas are both pure and right. Millions died fighting for them and a war was lost, but the great struggle has not yet ended. Millions more must now join in the fight, and I have come to muster you all to your duty. The time has finally come for you to fulfill the promise you made to your ancestors."

"We have called you all here, because the time has finally come to establish the Fourth Reich," they heard Martin say from across the table.

Baldwin stayed silent as gasps and whispers filled the darkness around him. His memory raced back to his aging father's basement, and the wall that had slid back to reveal a night-black uniform shining with silver *Totenkopf,* and the single slash of a blood-red armband.

"This was your grandfather's," Baldwin's father told him as his hand shook on his cane and the fog of age clouded his eyes. "Does it bother you?"

"Nein, Vater."

"Das ist gut, *because I am aging now, and there will be a time when a man will come to speak to you of your heritage, so that our family will no longer be ashamed of what we were."*

"And what is your proposal?" Baldwin asked as he brought his focus back to the present. The boots stopped their pacing, and the strange man's voice pierced the darkness once more.

"I want weapons. As many as can be found, and as heavy as can be found. The Reich's fight begins tonight, and I ask you to be its armory."

"But I'm a scientist!" a voice protested.

"And we deal in art," one of the sisters added.

"Yes, we're well aware of that, but fear not. Those of you with legitimate businesses will prove quite useful to us," Martin said. "We have a number of assets that will require liquidation, and an interesting scientific endeavor to begin."

"I don't understand," someone said.

"I'm sure you have many questions right now," the unidentified voice said. "Before any more of our plan is revealed, however, I would ask those of you who lack the proper commitment to our cause to leave the room. You have not seen my face, and you will learn no more about our plans."

For a moment, no one moved. Footsteps passed Baldwin's chair. He strained to make out what was happening but could see nothing in the darkness. Then, a dim light flooded the room, revealing that Martin Steiger was now standing next to the open door.

"Well, I've had enough of this nonsense," the man beside Baldwin said as his chair squealed across the lobby floor. "I thank you for your patronage, but I have other clients to attend to who aren't so theatrical."

Five others stood to join him, avoiding eye contact with everyone else as they headed toward the door. When the first reached him, Martin slammed the exit shut and flipped on the light. A pistol rang out six times, and those that had dared to leave fell gasping to the floor.

Baldwin reached for the gun that the letter had warned him not to bring, though he only succeeded in patting the naked spot against his hip where the weapon would have normally been resting. It was simply a reflex on his part, and not an unexpected response for an arms dealer such as himself.

As things fell silent once again, he smiled and relaxed as he scanned the faces of those remaining at the table. Their expressions were impassive, even understanding. These were people with whom he could do business. These were people who understood the need for sacrifice.

"Now," said the man standing at the head of the table as he holstered a smoking Luger that looked quite similar to Baldwin's own. "If there are no more doubters among us, we shall begin our planning."

* * *

July 2014

Bad Tölz, Germany

"Professor!" Miriam called from the door of her bed-and-breakfast.

Yanis greeted the innkeeper with an exhausted smile and an apology as she held the door open wide to help him through. She wore a thick robe over her nightgown, and he could see her spotted ankles peeking out above her slippers.

"It's nearly three in the morning, Yanis," she said. "What happened?"

"I did a bit more exploring than I planned," he said with a grunt as he stepped past her. Just inside the hallway, he thumped down the heavy box he'd carried from the wrecked plane. "I'm sorry I woke you."

"What's this?" Miriam asked as she squinted at the box. Will it stain the carpet?"

Sighing, Yanis squatted and lifted the box from the rug. After strapping the box to his back and then climbing back out of the crevasse and down the glacier with it, the thing already felt as though it weighed somewhere in the range of 200 kilos, and that number grew every time he had to pick it up and move it.

The case had been constructed of a sealed hardwood, and its edges had been reinforced with what was now a rusted metal banding. Just visible under the patina of mold and rot, a swastika that had been burned into the wood was clearly visible in the light of the hallway.

"It looks ancient," she said, but then her hand rose to her mouth. "Yanis! What are you doing bringing something like this into my house? A Jew of all people should not have such things!"

"I found it inside the glacier," he said.

"I don't care where you found it! My family—" she said, but then her voice cracked, and she had to pause for a moment. Her curls snapped from side to side as she shook her head. "You don't know what it's like for a German Jew to see something like that."

"I meant no disrespect, Miriam. Really, I didn't," Yanis said. "I just thought that it might have some historical value, that's all."

"You want to profit from another generation's suffering?"

"What? No! No, I just want to study it. Not the suffering. I mean the box. I want to study the box," he fumbled. *Why was he so awkward with women? It seemed as though he was always saying the wrong thing, even to this kindly, gray-haired woman who'd packed him a lunch from her own kitchen to take with him on his climb.* "I promise, I'll tell you all about it tomorrow, but I almost lost my life when I found this box buried in the glacier near Berchtesgaden, so I want to—"

Her eyes were wide now, and focused intently on his hands, which were resting almost protectively on top of the box.

"Was it Hitler's?" she asked, her voice hushed, as though she dared not even ask the question.

"I haven't opened it yet, but if you don't like it being here, then I promise I'll put it back in the car and take it away first thing in the morning."

The innkeeper squinted at him, then reached past him to close the door. She could see the anticipation in his eyes. He was such a nice man, and he'd been through so much to bring the box back home that she didn't want to disappoint him.

"All right, I'll put the coffee on. You look at that thing tonight, and then tomorrow you take it away. I don't want anything like that in this house. My grandmother would turn over in her grave if she knew I kept something like that in the same house where she hid our people during the war."

Yanis smiled at Miriam's cantankerousness as the innkeeper turned and swayed toward the kitchen. The old woman might be tough, but underneath that stern exterior, he suspected that she enjoyed a good adventure just as much as he did.

* * *

The coffee tasted rich and only slightly acrid from sitting too long in the pot. Yanis drank it black and rubbed his eyes for a moment before returning to the case that he'd set down on his room's wooden desk. He felt he should make some sort of a record of what he'd found, so he used his phone to take pictures of the box at various angles. As he did, he was continually haunted by the empty eyes of the dead pilot that seemed to bore into his very soul.

He set down his phone and rested his hands on the softened wood, trying to fight off the shiver that suddenly wormed its way through him. Maybe Miriam was right. Maybe he shouldn't dig into old wounds that history had sealed, but it was not in his nature to accept ignorance. His stubbornness and determination were the reason he'd crossed the globe as a single man, while all his colleagues seemed to take vacations to the beach with their wives.

The women that his fellow professors had tried to set him up with in the past had been more interested in talking about various new appliances and the life and times of children than they were in discussing the mysteries of mathematics and the world as a whole. He'd resigned himself long ago to the fact that he'd likely conduct his explorations in solitude for the rest of his life. It wouldn't have been his first choice, but it was better than settling for a relationship with someone that he had nothing in common with.

The case's metal catches crumbled as he opened them, leaving a bloodstain-like rust on his fingers. He rubbed the grit between his thumb and forefinger as he stared out the dormer window at the pitch-black night beyond. In the distance he saw a lone set of headlights tumbling down the hillside road, and it brought back memories of the yellow smear of his flashlight as it illuminated the dead pilot's face. He'd been through so much to retrieve the box, and he was glad that he did, for this was a mystery that should not have been left to rot in the ice.

Gripping the box lid, he lifted it from the base and set it aside on the floor at his feet. Underneath, he found a machine that looked like a typewriter with two sets of keys, a row of lamps above a series of levers, and a set of dials at the top right.

"It can't be," he whispered.

The machine had been bolted to the bottom of the case and appeared to have suffered no damage in the crash. He'd only ever seen a machine like this in pictures, but he knew everything about it from his studies. It was an Enigma. A pristine example of the device the Nazis had used to send their secret messages, and the very device that had kindled his interest in mathematics and cryptography.

He gave a tentative tap to the letter "Y." The key sunk down with a soft click that he could barely hear over his own heartbeat. Running his hand over the Enigma's metal casing, he felt the layer of oil that had protected the machine from the elements.

Lifting the lid from the floor, he looked underneath and studied the plush lining that had prevented moisture from seeping past the casing. The machine hadn't been the only thing the box had been protecting.

With gentle hands, he pulled a 70-year-old envelope from where it had been wedged into the lid's lining. The envelope was thick, made of tanned oilcloth that appeared just as remarkably preserved as the machine it was meant to be used with.

He set the envelope down on the desk and reminded himself to breathe as he pulled out his pocketknife and teased open the flap.

Three yellowed index cards slipped into his palm, followed by a bound pamphlet labeled *Signalbuch*.

The cards bore lines of handwritten block letters that were grouped into sets of five characters each. At first glance, they appeared to be gibberish: "XYEHN, SLPWQ," and so on. However, these were the last encrypted messages the pilot had seen. He held in his hands the message that sent the pilot to his death, and he had the code book that could be used to decipher that message sitting right there on his desk. What was so important to the Germans that a pilot had to give his life trying to deliver it to its destination? Hopefully, that's just what he was about to find out.

8

"Why would you need wiring and pliers?" Miriam asked.

"I'll show you in a moment," Yanis called on his way up the stairs from his trip to the local OBI store.

As soon as he got back to his room, he sat down at the desk, pulled the wire from the Enigma that once led to its battery, and separated the positive and negative ends. Then, he stripped the crumbling cloth from the copper, twisted the wires onto the new extension cord he'd purchased, and plugged the machine into the wall.

Sitting back, he studied his makeshift power supply for a moment, unsure if what he was about to do was safe. If it blew the breaker or started a fire, he'd lose his deposit, and the last thing he wanted to do was to take advantage of Miriam's kindness.

"Only one way to find out," he said as he flipped the switch on the side of the machine. Fortunately, no sparks flew from the outlet, and billows of smoke didn't fill the air. In fact, nothing happened at all. Straightening in his chair, Yanis raised a finger and pressed the "Y" key.

"Oh my God," he said, staring at the letter "M" that had lit on the panel above the keyboard.

Excited by his success at restoring the Enigma's power supply, he pulled up the procedure for decrypting a message on his phone, and then set the device on the desk in front of him.

Carefully he wedged the first card into the top of the machine. It read:

EXP ESX ALCUE NDHYX NEYDH DNIEH HWYRM XLOSJY SHUEHG QPLUD AXYWL EOCUY XNHDU EXHSP IEHXY WSOKX EIJDN CHFUR TYGHP QALZK HFJDK IWOQP NXBCV EDCVF HNJKI PLMKO

Following the instructions on his phone, Yanis turned the three rotors at the top of the machine to the letters EXP, and then he typed ESX. The letters IVM lit, so he turned the rotors to the IVM position, and then typed ALCUE. As he did, the letters XBNEI lit in succession on the lamps. He spoke no German, but he knew those characters couldn't possibly spell the beginning of a message.

Opening the code book's onion skin pages, he carefully flipped to the back of the book. The dates ran into the 1950s, which displayed an impressive optimism on the part of the Germans. He turned back to 1945, and started on the day the Nazis surrendered, May 7.

In the code book, EXP corresponded to SLO, so he clicked the rotors to SLO and typed ESX once more. The lamps for OYC lit up. He then turned the rotors to OYC and typed out the first character set, which produced even more gibberish.

He sighed as he glanced down at the code book once again. This was his least favorite part of mathematics—the blunt trial and error required to get to a solution.

Fumbling for the last of Miriam's coffee, he twisted the rotors to the initial cipher for the 6th of May and started again.

* * *

Down in the kitchen, Miriam was mixing dough for *lebkuchen* cookies. She'd just popped a piece of the ginger-infused dough into her mouth when the strange Israeli came pounding down the stairs.

"Miriam!" he cried. "Miriam!"

"In here, *liebchen*," she called.

Breathless and pale from lack of sleep, the professor ran into the kitchen holding a scrap of paper in front of him.

"What?" she asked. "What's this? It's nearly suppertime, and you're still messing with that thing?"

He pressed the scrap of paper into her palm.

"Please Miriam, I can't read German. Would you be able to translate this for me?" he asked.

"*Ja, ja,*" she said, trundling out of the room as she wiped her flour-covered hands on her apron.

"Where are you going?"

"We are not all so young and energetic," she said as she rejoined him and balanced a set of reading glasses on the bridge of her nose.

"I'm sorry. I know I've kept the box here longer than you asked," he apologized.

"It's all right, dear. Now, let me see here. It says, '*Der Krieg ist verloren. Sie sind der letzte, der unser Geheimnis kennt. Finden Sie Keck. Alle hoffnung liegt jetzt in Der Dom.*'"

"Can you read it? Does it make any sense?" he asked.

"I can read it, but I don't understand what it means."

"What does it say in English?"

"It says, '*The war is lost. You are the last one who knows our secret. Find Keck. All hope now lies in the dome.*'"

"The dome?"

"Wait … no. I don't think that's the right translation. We often say *Der Dom* when we mean *Kathedrale*, so I believe it says, '*All hope now lies in the cathedral.*'"

* * *

December 1944

The Zitternberg, Germany

As Keck watched, the eyes of one of the mineworkers rolled up into his skull. The man stumbled before collapsing in a tangle of sallow skin and bone. The other workers that Keck had ordered brought in from Dachau merely stepped around their fallen compatriot as they carried buckets of rock and debris to dump down the side of the mountain. They'd been well-trained in obedience. He'd have to send the camp commandant a note of congratulations.

A man emerged from where a double file of workers passed in and out of the widening hole in the mountain. He spotted Keck and greeted him with a smile.

"Hans! Professor Steiger!" Keck called out to him.

"I didn't know that you'd be coming to the dig today," Steiger said. Strange patches of deep tan ran across his face, and he'd stripped down to his undershirt in order to cope with the warmth inside the tunnel. A shiver ran through him, and he began to rub his arms vigorously as December's chill closed in on him.

"I would not have come, but I received word that you've made incredible progress, so I wanted to see it for myself," Keck said.

"Oh, we have, and I can't possibly thank you enough for your assistance."

"These?" Keck said as he gestured toward the stream of workers. "These people are nothing, but what lies inside that mountain—"

"Would you like to see?" Steiger asked as his smile grew wider.

Keck looked back to the fallen worker. Beyond the body was the Isar Valley, which sparkled under a freshly fallen blanket of snow. He'd heard that morning that the Russians had taken Prussia. His ancestral homeland was now under the control of the godless communists. He did not know what the professor's excavation of the strange energy source had revealed, but the feeling of immense power that had stayed with him ever since he'd touched the shimmering lights was unforgettable. It just had to be something of significance… something that could help the Reich turn the tide of the faltering war. The alternative was simply unthinkable.

"By all means," the *Sturmbannführer* said. "It's been far too long since I've received any good news."

The two men shouldered their way past the laborers who were working with pickaxes and shovels to widen the tunnel. Keck had ordered them to dig a clearance wide and tall enough for two *Radschlepper*

Ost trucks to drive through, and the workers had nearly completed the task. With more of the salt stone removed from in front of the strange wall, its eldritch blue light poured through the domed tunnel. It caused the sweating workers' faces to glisten and painted the normally white walls a sky-tinted hue.

"As you can see, the work is moving extremely well," Steiger said. "In another few days, I believe we will reach the required height and width, and then …"

The professor trailed off as another of the workers sagged under the weight of a basket of rubble. As Keck passed, one of his *Totenkopfverbände* shouldered his rifle, bent down, and lifted the worker up by his armpits. The man swayed, shook his head, and returned to work.

"That's all very well, Hans, but I am most interested in knowing what lies *beyond* the wall," Keck said. "A dead-end tunnel does nothing to help us win the war."

They'd stopped at the end of the tunnel, staring at the twenty square meters of wall the workers had freed from the stone. The strange barrier shone before them like the crisp metal of a newly forged knife, and its exposed portion showed no sign of any seam or curvature. Keck closed to within a meter of the glowing letters, and then stood there watching them as they changed and curled over the wall's length. He felt like there was a pattern to it, like it was a language he'd once known. Something right on the edge of understanding, if only he studied it long enough.

"The same happens to me," Steiger said.

"I beg your pardon?" Keck asked. He shook his head, blinked a couple of times, and then turned to face the professor.

"Here," Steiger said as he handed a pair of dark-lensed glasses to Keck. "They're polarized."

Keck placed the sunglasses on his face, and as the light dimmed, the patterns seemed even closer to revealing themselves.

"I'll come here to study the wall in the morning, thinking that I'll only spend an hour or two sitting here. When I go to leave, however, it will always be midnight, or even one in the morning. Time here doesn't pass the same, and I have no explanation for it," Steiger said.

"What progress have you made in breaching the wall?" Keck asked.

"I've tried everything short of explosives, and nothing so far has even left a scratch."

"Then you shall have explosives," Keck said.

"We'll need to reinforce the tunnel first. Blasting of that type—"

"I do not care for the details, Professor. All I care about is the urgency of this project. If what lies beyond that wall can help our efforts—" Keck said, but he fell silent when the sound of a bell rang forth from the mouth of the tunnel. "What is that?"

"It's the lunch bell," Steiger answered.

All around them, the exhausted workers set down their tools and stood in a ragged line, while several *kapos* assigned by the camp to supervise the labor began passing out bowls of porridge to them.

"*Das is gut, ja?*" Keck called to a nearby cluster of miners when the *kapos* reached them. One of the workers lifted a skull that looked swollen above his thin neck. He nodded with what looked like the last of his strength and struggled to form a smile.

"*Ja,*" the man whispered.

Beside him, another Jew at the end of the line closest to the wall staggered. This one was older, with tufts of gray hair ringing his scalp, and a permanent stoop worked into his shoulders. The man mumbled some guttural pig's language before his legs finally gave out. The Jew who'd spoken to Keck tried to catch his friend's sleeve but was too late. The old man fell toward the glowing blue wall, and at the last instant his weak arms rose to keep himself from falling. His dirty palms slapped against the wall's lettering and broke his fall, but he slid to the ground and started coughing as the dust filled his lungs.

"Get that filth away from the wall!" Keck screamed.

Keck's *Totenkopfverbände* ran to the man, seized the Jew's ankles, and then pulled him backward. The prisoners had been under strict orders not to touch the wall, and they had long experience with how Keck's men punished disobedience at Dachau.

"Have that man shot," Keck ordered one of his *Totenkopfverbände*. The *Schütze* rushed forward, lifted the Jew from the stone, and carried his half-conscious form down the tunnel. Changing his mind, Keck drew his pistol and started after his guard, intending to handle the matter personally.

"*Herr Sturmbannführer!*" Steiger called from behind him.

"I will be with you in a moment, Professor," Keck called over his shoulder.

"No! You must look!" Steiger called again.

Irritated, Keck turned to where the professor stood, and the angry retort that was about to escape from his lips quickly faded, only to be replaced by a look of wonder. Above the spot where the worker had placed his hands, a hole had appeared in the wall. The opening continued to widen, letting more and more of the warm blue light escape into the tunnel, until even with his sunglasses on, Keck was forced to look away.

From the corner of his eye, the *Sturmbannführer* saw Steiger reach the entrance and peer inside.

"What do you see, Professor?" Keck called.

"I see the future *Herr* Keck," Steiger said, though he was so stricken by the experience that his voice came out as little more than a whisper.

9

"*Mein Gott,*" Keck whispered. The *Sturmbannführer* stood beside the professor in the strange room on the other side of the metal wall. The chamber appeared limitless, stretching as far as his eyes could see with neither walls nor supports of any kind. The blue light that had saturated the tunnel was fading, replaced with a rainbow of hues from shards of flickering color that glowed above them like stained glass.

Squinting toward the top of the room, Keck thought he could make out hovering images—views of distant vistas like the old master landscapes that lined his estate's walls in Prussia. The likenesses collapsed back into the shifting colors before he could make them out, and he found himself wondering if they'd ever been there at all.

Turning back, Keck studied the oval entryway that led back into the tunnel. His mind knew that the wall of the chamber ended at that portal, but his senses told him that no wall existed. The chamber seemed to extend beyond the entryway, as if the door hung in blank space. He could see the astonished faces of two of his *Totenkopfverbände* through its oval, and beyond the white salt stone, the workers froze with their cooling porridge in their hands.

Keck ran his hand over what would have been the door jamb, feeling a warm, almost living texture, but his eyes recognized only the faintest hint of a barrier. It looked like a waterfall of glacier blue water, less than a millimeter thick, flowing silently over the entryway. The warmth of it spread through his hand though he couldn't feel its touch.

"*Sturmbannführer*," one of his *Schütze* called from the tunnel. "Is everything in order?"

"Yes," Keck said. "Yes, it most definitely is. Remain outside."

"*Herr* Keck!" Steiger called.

Kristock Keck turned away from the entrance and found the professor standing about two dozen meters away in the featureless room.

"How did you get there?" Keck called.

"I ... I don't know. The dimensions here are quite strange."

As Steiger walked, he seemed to recede into the room and slide meters to Keck's right. There was no sense of perspective or distance on the other side of the barrier—only the faintly throbbing shards of light, and each step the professor took seemed to move him in multiple directions at once.

"Where are you going?" Keck called, an unusual tenor of uncertainty in his voice.

"Kristock, I see something!"

Keck took a few hesitant steps after the scientist, trying to acclimate himself to the white spongy surface underneath his boots that made no sound as he walked.

"*Sturmbannführer,* we've lost you!" one of his *Schütze* called. The man's voice seemed distant, muffled. Keck looked back toward where he remembered the entrance to have been, only to find the portal thirty meters behind him to his left.

"Professor," Keck called. "I suggest we do a more thorough examination before we—"

"It's here! I see it!" Steiger exclaimed. His voice was quite close, and when Keck turned to see where it was coming from, he found himself nearly on top of the professor.

"But I didn't move," Keck whispered, dumbfounded by what had just occurred.

"Look, Keck!" Steiger said as he pointed at the blue lettering that had appeared in the air before them, floating at head level in the cream-colored emptiness. As Keck watched, the glowing material contorted itself into a ball, then reformed as a familiar shape, but with five thinner extensions jutting out from the central core.

Before he knew what was happening, Steiger extended his arm from his shoulder, straightened his palm in the *Hitlergrub*, and touched the shape of a human hand that floated before them.

"It cannot be," Steiger said.

A small orb of barren space appeared before them, and its blackness swelled to reveal itself as another entryway. The *Sturmbannführer* forced his way through the strange disorientation of stepping instantly from the center of one massive room to another.

Steiger had known from the first moment he'd seen the strange lettering skitter across the metal under the trembling mountain, that the world—the universe itself—was much bigger than the Reich, or anything else that he ever could have imagined. The gods had chosen to reveal themselves to both he and Kristock Keck, and it was German destiny, the destiny of the superior race, to respond to them in kind.

There in the chamber before them lay the bodies of what must have been the alien ship's crew, all except for one that appeared to have collapsed at its station. The strange gray of their skin and tall, spindly limbs glowed ethereally under the lights of their eternal cathedral. If anything, they resembled the chattering underside of a crab, with their torsos split into jointed segments, and tendrils of filaments that hung limp along their forearms and calves.

However, as with the ship, the *Sturmbannführer* found it difficult to assess exactly where their bodies began, and where they ended. They seemed to blur at the edges, and when he tapped one with his Luger, he had the impression that it moved in several directions at once.

Keck strode among the corpses and the shimmering lights of their instruments, squatting down to study the wrinkled band of eyes that ringed one of the limp creatures' heads. Then he looked up and met Steiger's eyes with a smoldering glare.

"Well, Professor," Keck said. His voice seemed to boom through the alien bridge, and he felt an incredible surge of possibility rise within him. "It seems that they have come a long way to deliver us this gift. Now we must figure out how to make use of it, before it's too late."

* * *

July 2014

München, Germany

"Fancy a cuppa, Jillian?" Harry asked as the junior Interpol officer shook a steaming thermos in front of her, startling Jillian Qualmes out of her thoughts. She'd arrived at the Quittenbaum auction house early that morning to give herself time to review the threads of what she knew would become a case. Still, she had to get some evidence before the Financial Crimes head would give her approval to commit any resources to the investigation.

"No, but thanks Harry," she said without looking at him. "I don't take caffeine."

"Oh, right," her subordinate said as a flush wove its way through his freckles. "I'm sorry, I shouldn't have asked. They told me that about you back at the Home Office."

She turned and studied the flame of Harry's hair against the predawn morning. The Scot tottered from a great nervous height as he looked for a sill where he could put her unwanted cup.

"So, what exactly *do* they say about me in London?" she asked.

"Oh, ah … nothing really," the junior officer said. He smiled awkwardly and then sipped at his thermos. Unfortunately, he burned his lips on the hot liquid and pulled back, sputtering as he wiped his mouth with his sleeve. Jillian handed him a tissue from her jacket, and he mumbled a quick thanks to her as he took it.

"If you need me, I'll be down the hall," she said as she turned and slipped into the auction room.

She wondered if she'd unintentionally given Harry the cold shoulder. He was just out of training and trying desperately to make a good impression, and she knew that she should probably be doing the same.

Back in London, they all said that she was too wrapped up in the work. *Ball buster* was the exact term they'd used, if she remembered correctly. But stopping criminals in these days of thefts that could literally occur within a millisecond was a job that required a great deal of focus. It mattered to her that she did her job well, just as her grandfather would have wanted.

Her mind drifted a moment. A stern, disciplined man to the end, her grandfather's time in a German prison camp, though brief, had not cut the kindness from his heart, but had refined it. He taught her how to be both kind *and* smart, even when the stakes were high. He taught her discipline. He taught her not that good *could* be done, but that it *must* be done. She often found that the lessons on being smart were far easier than those on being kind.

People started entering the hall and forced her to refocus her thoughts on the matter at hand. "All eyes forward!" her grandfather would say. Friends and a social life were a small price to pay if it meant that she wouldn't lose her edge.

Considering the crumbs of information that she'd come to Munich to trace, another agent might not have made anything of the incredibly large volume of gold bullion that had suddenly come onto the EU market, and they could have been forgiven for that, seeing how careful the seller had been to dispose of the gold in small lots and coins at auctions throughout Europe. However, in aggregate, the sales were 3,000 percent above the *Deutsche Bundesbank*'s normal gold transaction volume.

So, where had such a huge hoard of gold come from, and why was its seller taking such precautions to remain hidden? Over the years, Jillian had learned that sophisticated criminals nearly always practiced extreme discretion. She had a hunch as to the gold's likely source, but she still needed proof before the investigation could proceed. This was why she'd come to Munich.

The auction house's hall held fifty seats, but only a few purchasers had filtered in here and there. Most of the transactions these days were handled electronically, which made her job both easier, and more difficult at the same time. It was easier to find abnormal patterns, but harder and harder to track down a human being who'd claim to know anything about them.

At ten minutes to eight, the black-suited Quittenbaum staff filed into the hall. They'd man the computer and phone stations for the anonymous buyers who'd vie for a piece of the treasure that was seeping out all over Europe.

"Ah, *Herr* Wollsnacht," Jillian said as the dapper German who ran the auction house appeared at the end of his line of employees.

"Ms. Qualmes," he said, offering her a thin smile on the way to his trading dais. "Have I not answered enough of your questions?"

"Not until you tell me where this gold came from," she said.

"You've seen the terms of the confidentiality agreement we have with our client, so you'll understand that I have very little ability to help."

"I'll be paying a visit to the judge as soon as he's in his chambers," she said.

"The agreement was signed in Switzerland, Ms. Qualmes. Were you planning to visit Bern on this trip as well?"

"You know the account," she said. "You know exactly where the money is going, so you can tell me now or you can wait for the search warrant, but either way I'm going to find out."

The auctioneer's eyes darted to the few in-person buyers, the row of employees, and then to a polished grandfather clock that read 7:57.

"This is a legal sale," Wollsnacht said. "We have broken no laws, and yet you threaten me here in front of my customers."

"Look, Klaus, I know you haven't broken any laws," Jillian said with a faint smile, the first bit of warmth she'd ever shown him. "Nothing here is illegal, and you run a fine business. I'm simply asking you to consider what you're doing. The Bundesbank has never heard of a quantity of gold this large. If it entered the country legally, then EU customs would have a record of it, and they don't. That only leaves one source, and I don't think you're going to want any headlines about how much profit Quittenbaum made from the sale of looted Nazi gold."

Wollsnacht's lips pursed, and then he snorted to clear his nose while seizing his gavel at the same time.

"Meet with me after the auction," he said, and then he cracked the mallet down on its block. Finally, her chase had begun.

* * *

Back in her hotel room, Harry dropped his sport coat on the bed while Jillian got on her laptop and logged into Interpol's secure system. She then logged her request with the Swiss Financial Market Supervisory Authority to track the transactions and value of the account that Klaus had given her.

"You think FINMA will give it to us?" he asked.

"The Swiss aren't as proud as they used to be. They understand that they can't keep secrets buried forever," she said as she stared at her screen with great anticipation. "Aaaand … there we go."

She clicked the link in the message she received, and it opened a window that showed her the account's deposits and withdrawals.

"Bloody hell," Harry whispered.

There, sitting in front of her, was 30 billion in euros that had been deposited from auction houses and gold brokers all over Europe.

"There has to be something here, Harry," Jillian said. "It fits all the patterns of organized crime."

"But what can we do now?" Harry asked. "There still hasn't been any crime."

"Someone who mysteriously starts selling this much gold is doing it for a reason, and if it's Nazi gold as I suspect that it is, then that reason isn't gonna be very legal now, is it? All we have to do is to wait and see what happens next."

"Well, right then. Feel like a bit of a celebration?"

Her hands froze on her keyboard. She looked up at the junior inspector, one eyebrow raised and a frank expression on her face. It was a look that brought an embarrassed flush to his face once again.

"I think we're close now, Harry, so I'm gonna keep watching. The next move is gonna happen soon. I can feel it," she said. Her superiors always said that she was tremendously intuitive, and she had a deep-seated feeling that this time she was onto something bigger than even she had previously suspected.

"All right then," he said as he picked up his jacket. "Enjoy your evening, Officer Qualmes."

"Goodnight, Harry," she said as he stepped out the door and closed it behind him. Now it was all just a waiting game, she thought to herself as she turned back to the glow of her laptop. She couldn't allow herself to be distracted, not when there was so much at stake.

10

January 1945

Berlin, Germany

Heinrich Himmler's hairline had receded to the crown of his scalp, and the bunker's flickering lights stained the flesh of his face a sickly green color. Keck sat across from the SS *Reichsführer*, while Hitler's second in command studied the report on *Der Dom* that Steiger had helped him compile. Himmler closed the folder with care and unstrapped his glasses. The wire caught for a moment behind one of his narrow ears before releasing, and after carefully setting them on the table, he pinched the bridge of his nose and let out a heavy sigh.

"So, Keck, you think you've discovered a tool to help our cause?" the *Reichsführer* finally asked. Here in his cramped office, the powerful voice that Keck had heard so often on radio broadcasts now seemed rather thin and defeated.

"*Ja, Mein Herr,*" Kristock said.

"You have not even the slightest idea of how to activate this ... *craft,* if that is indeed what it is. You have no photographs, no evidence at all other than your word and the testimony of men subordinate to you."

"Sir, *Der Dom* does not appear in photographs. We do not yet understand why this is, and I cannot risk revealing its location to those not loyal to our cause. You are the only other to whom I've given the coordinates. I would be happy to arrange a visit if you wish."

A dull thunder drummed overhead, and dust from the concrete roof sifted onto the *Reichsführer's* desk. The lights dimmed under the bombardment for a moment, and then quickly recovered.

"Our cause," Himmler said, letting out a soulless laugh that gave the impression of a man in despair. He put his oval glasses back on, and then his bookish eyes met Keck's. "Shortly I will be leaving to take command of Army Group Vistula, tasked with attempting to keep the Soviets from reaching the Vaterland."

"A great honor sir."

"A useless one, Keck. Bismarck himself could not force even a draw at this point. Will your project make fuel? Does it give us more soldiers to send to the front, or bullets for their weapons?"

"No *Reichsführer.* I'm afraid I must confess that the scientist working with me does not even know the craft's full capabilities. He has managed to activate only a few of its systems, but the possibilities …"

The medals pinned to Himmler's chest rattled as the *Reichsführer* pushed away from his desk and stood.

"Kristock, you are a good man. A fine Aryan specimen, bred true back 150 years. Your intelligence, your courage, your record in Bavaria have all been exemplary. However, whatever you have found, it comes too late. This war was lost in the factories years ago. Return to your post and continue the preparations for the *Volkssturm* and our final solution. If you feel your discovery can help in these efforts, then use it as best you can. The Nazi ideals may yet survive, but they will not do so from within German borders."

"*Mein Herr,* I cannot believe that. We are building a Reich to last a thousand years. We have purged every trace of rot and sub-humanity that we have found, and nothing stands in our way—"

"*Sturmbannführer,* the war is lost," Himmler said. "The only thing that would help us is if we could go back in time, and I ended our futile research into that avenue long ago. Now, if you'll excuse me, I must see what can be done about the Eastern Front."

* * *

Kristock lifted his compartment's blackout shade and studied the Berlin suburbs under the gossamer moonlight as his train ran south. Air raid sirens squalled from the battered capital, and he could just see the city's futile searchlights combing the sky behind him. Anti-aircraft tracers split the night, their tiny flares disappearing in the voids between the clouds as the American and British bombers came to unleash their fury on the once-mighty Reich.

The rails below him thumped and squealed as his darkened train fled through desolate ruins. Here and there a pinpoint of lamplight struggled to pierce the night. A horse-drawn fire brigade scrambled to save a burning building, while a group of nurses tended to the wounded. He passed a stretch of homes where the elderly lived in half-destroyed floors, their blankets and stocking-covered feet fluttering as the train blew past. Then there were the factories. Once the backbone of German industry, now they were little more than endless rows of crumbled brick and twisted steel that could not be restored.

Everywhere he looked, Germany was in ruins; even the founder of the SS himself had lost his faith. The *Schutzstaffel* had done everything it could to purify the race, but the hard truth was that it had failed. Keck had failed, and he rode with a sickness in his stomach because of it.

Bombs fell behind him. Keck saw each flash of white on the horizon throw shadows over a ravaged land that he no longer recognized. As his countrymen died around him and the sirens blared futilely, he vowed to himself that he would not let the Reich fail.

He slapped the blind closed and then unholstered his Luger and began cleaning it. He'd need to be prepared when Steiger finally helped him unleash the machinery of the gods. He only prayed that *Der Dom* could contain his fury.

* * *

January 1944

Carrickfergus, Northern Ireland

Jim's muscles burned with exhaustion. The frigid wind battered him as it swung his shivering body and his 80-pound pack against the Irish cliff face, and numbed his hands as he climbed, inch by inch, up the rope that was made of thick hemp. He kicked out a boot, found a toehold in the crumbling chalk, and hauled himself upward.

The cliff top hung just five feet above him, and then with a little more effort, five feet turned into four. Sweat curled down into his eyes, but he blinked to clear his vision and then refocused on his goal. Suddenly a hand appeared above him. He reached up, grasping the man's forearm while holding the rope tight in his other fist. Then, digging in his boots, he walked himself up and over the crumbling ledge of disintegrating chalk.

He collapsed onto his stomach, gasping as the muscles in his shoulders and back slowly started to recover. There were other men behind him that would need his help though, so he allowed himself only a moment to rest.

As he rolled himself over, Jim met Captain Dickson's clear blue eyes. The commander's lips and nose were red from the cold, and he'd outfitted himself for the field the same as his men, with a sidearm, rifle, and pack.

"Sir," Jim called as he scrambled to his feet and saluted, "Sir, thank you, sir."

"At ease, Thompson," Captain Dickson said. "Finish the drill."

"Yes sir," Jim said. Slipping out of his pack, he first checked the security of the grappling hooks his platoon had fired from their landing craft. After ensuring that the heavy iron cleats were holding where they'd dug into the rock and earth, he followed the strained ropes and peered over the cliff. It was a rare cloudless day, and he could see the sweat of each man's face sparkling in the cold sun as they crawled up the ropes.

Far below, the frothing water of the Irish Sea churned in the wake of the landing craft that were slowly making their way south to the port.

How would his platoon ever do this under fire? The Germans would slaughter them all.

Reaching down, Jim helped Private Ellis up over the lip. Ellis gathered his breath, and then stumbled over to the next rope to help the next man up. Soon, a hundred Rangers lay sprawled out and exhausted on the top of the coast's white cliffs.

"God almighty, Corporal," Private Ellis said to Jim. "Without you there, I wouldn't have made that climb."

"You can say that again," another private said as he rubbed the angry rope burn on his palms. Jim smiled and passed his canteen among the men of his platoon as they sat on the cold, hard ground. He'd been doing nothing but drilling and training since his transfer to the Rangers, but he felt a change in himself because of it. His rebelliousness drifted away as a new sense of duty and purpose filled him. It was something he'd never felt growing up on the hard streets of Brooklyn. The men of his platoon were his family now. They were his brothers, and as their corporal, he was responsible for them.

Captain Dickson walked among the men, offering a back slap here, a cigarette there. Their CO was a good officer who was driven but fair, and Jim could look up to a man like that. Maybe he'd even become one someday. It would sure beat breaking other men's faces for a fistful of cash.

"Well boys," the captain called from where he stood in the middle of his men. "For a unit that didn't exist six months ago, I'm proud to say that D Company, Second Rangers is the meanest group of men I've seen in a long time."

The company unleashed a ragged cheer. Jim joined in and pumped his fist in the air, but he winced as the pain from his abused muscles set in.

"You've learned how to scale cliffs, live off the land, and kill Jerry six times with your bare hands before he hits the ground. As such, it is my great pleasure to inform you that your training is now concluded. This was your last exercise," the captain said.

This time the Rangers roared their approval.

"We'll be moving back to England in a few days," the captain continued. "From there, we'll wait for orders that I've been told will be coming soon enough. For right now though, just enjoy the rest. You've certainly earned it."

"I swear, Corporal, I'm gonna sleep for a whole day at least!" Ellis said from beside him. The men were smiling and clapping each other on the back, but Jim was watching the captain. Their CO was studying his men with a pained look that somehow felt worse than the steel wind that scoured the cliff.

"I want each of you to understand that the next thing we'll be doing is going to war, and I expect our illustrious leaders to ask Dog Company to lead the way," the captain said. "Non-coms and officers, we'll have a meeting at 2000 hours tonight to go over the details. Dismissed."

11

D Company had been billeted in an old wool factory. It beat sleeping in tents in the middle of winter, but Jim still wore his overcoat, muffler, and gloves as he walked through the drafty stone building to meet with the captain and the rest of the company officers. The enlisted men he passed were getting ready for a night on the town. Some were polishing their shoes, while others were climbing into their dress uniforms. Still others were attempting to shave by candlelight, a tenuous proposition at best. It was a kindness to let men who'd worked so hard celebrate, and Jim most certainly approved.

"Big Jim! Hey there, Corporal, are we gonna see ya tonight?" one of the men called to him as he passed. He stopped, smiling at Privates Ellis, Mitchell, and several of the others from his platoon.

"You're all gonna be face down on a pub table in an hour, so you better hope you don't see me tonight," he said with a laugh.

"Hey, we won't be any trouble for you at all. Now as for the women—" Mitchell said. The men all laughed, and Jim laughed with them for a moment before he gave them all a wave and then left them to their primping.

The captain had set up his office in a small room that must have once served as the foreman's quarters. Jim reached the old door, and then rapped on it a few times with his well-worn knuckles. The captain opened it seconds later, and then stood aside to allow him entry.

"You're the first to arrive, Corporal, as always. Take a seat."

The captain's office had a typical trunk-like field desk. It sat on a folding table, and consisted of a typewriter, a telephone, and a neat ream of paper reports. A map of Europe had been tacked to the back wall with red and blue arrows marking the various force deployments. Red arrows studded the entire European coastline from France to Norway, each representing German divisions that would fight like hell to keep Allied forces from making a beachhead.

"I don't think I'm *always* first, sir …"

"That's bullshit, Jim. Every drill we do, your lieutenant tells me that your hand is always in the air to volunteer before he's even finished explaining what you'll be doing. Even when he doesn't ask for volunteers, you're always at the front of the line anyway. A polar bear would have frozen out there today, but you got to the top of that cliff in record time. There are a whole lot of men who feel much safer at the back of the line during wartime, but they see someone like you, who's always right there front and center, and it elevates their performance."

"Well, thank you, sir. It's an honor to serve," Jim said. A ghost of a smile appeared on the captain's face.

"So, tell me, Corporal, just what kind of crazy streak makes you do what you do?"

"I just happened to have been born bigger, sir. God gave me a sort of a natural strength, so I was always a fighter. I used to fight a lot before the war, and I even got into a few scrapes after I joined the service. Now I just feel like I'm supposed to do whatever I can to make things a little easier on the other men."

"You think about the enlisted men a lot, don't you?" the captain asked.

"Of course I do, sir. I mean, they're my responsibility, after all. I just wanna make sure they're taken care of."

Captain Dickson's smile finally broke across his face, and the officer extended his hand. Jim shook it without any understanding what was happening.

"You know, Thompson, that's exactly why I think you'll make a perfect sergeant in Dog Company. Congratulations."

"Sir, I—"

A knock pounded on the other side of the door. The captain stepped around Jim to open it, and a group of the other non-coms and officers shuffled inside.

"At ease, men," the captain said. "I was just telling Big Jim here the good news."

Smiles erupted all around him as the rest of his company's leadership slapped him on the back and shadowboxed with him in congratulations. For a struggling brawler who'd never felt like he'd fit in anywhere, it felt good to be surrounded by a group of men who'd become like brothers to him.

The captain stepped behind his desk and retrieved a bottle of scotch, which he held up for all to see.

"Now, let's celebrate the end of all these horrible exercises. Drink up, men!"

* * *

Jim held his liquor better than most, but later that night he was still tottering down the hall of the wool factory on the way to his bunk. Sergeant McLean propped him up on the right side, while Corporal Barcroft held him up on his left, and the three of them staggered their way through the darkness with muffled laughter.

"There ya go, Sarge," Barcroft sighed as Jim and McLean helped him into his bunk.

"At ease, Corporal," McLean whispered. Jim guffawed, slapping McLean on the shoulder before collapsing into his own bed.

He watched the factory's thatch and mud roof twist above him while he tried to get comfortable against his mattress' straw ticking. As he lay there, the captain's words ran through his head over and over again. They were uttered in a moment when he'd been staring at the map behind his desk, and the bottle of scotch was two-thirds gone.

"They're gonna send us onto the beaches," the captain had said. "They're gonna send us onto the beaches, and there's gonna be hell to pay."

He picked up the bottle, took another swig, and then wiped his chin as he looked around at them all.

"You all keep those men safe. You do that for me," he said with a seriousness that sucked all the joy out of the room.

As Jim's eyes closed and his consciousness faded, the last thing he wondered was how a loner like him, who only ever really knew how to fight, could ever be responsible for keeping the men in his charge alive in the middle of the hell that was coming.

* * *

July 2014

München, Germany

The first withdrawal since they started monitoring the gold account happened three days later. At two in the morning, Jillian had been typing up a memo to the Home Office on the status of her preliminary investigation. Just as she hit send, an alert popped up on her screen. There were numerous transactions in the recent account history, as varied in amount as they were in branch location. Suddenly she found herself staring at a record of a cash transfer of 30 million euros to a Banca Intesa account in Serbia. Without hesitating, she fumbled for her phone.

"Hello?" a tired-sounding voice asked.

"Konstantin?" she said urgently. "Listen, I need your help."

"Jillian? It's ... what time is it exactly? What happened?"

"I'm tracking a transfer to Banca Intesa that just went through. It's scheduled to post tomorrow morning. I'll send you the information, and I need you to watch the account for me to see who comes for the money."

The Eastern Europe attaché let out a groan that almost sounded like a snore.

"That is, until we can get there," she continued. "Konstantin, your jurisdiction here is tenuous at best. I don't suggest you go flying in and making waves. Serbia is applying for EU membership and typically plays nice. But they don't like to be pushed around."

She waited anxiously for him to respond, but first he released a huge yawn.

"You know, Jillian, just once I'd like you to call me for something other than work. Any time, day or night, you decide."

"Konstantin, please!" she begged. "This is important. There's something major happening."

"I get it," he said exhaustedly. "Tell me what you can."

Her screen flashed. "Just a moment," she said, reading quickly. "An internal post from the branch just updated."

"That's strange. What do Americans say? Banker's hours?" Konstantin said in an aborted chuckle.

"It said there will be an early morning withdrawal and that the branch should prepare the transaction in 500-euro notes."

"So?"

She calculated quickly in her head. "It means you're looking for someone, likely a man, a strong man. With two large duffle bags or large, hard-shell roller suitcases."

"What? How did you get that?"

"Moving cash has significant volume and weight. Like a million dollars US takes up about a full briefcase of space. So, to move that much money, they'd need to have it issued in ultra-high currency notes—like 500-euro notes. Or, if they just wanted to get tricky, they could do 1000-Swiss franc notes. Based on the volume," she recalculated, "two large bags just about sixty pounds each. Likely on roller wheels—"

"I get it," he said. "I'll alert the locals and see if we can get this guy just as he leaves the bank."

And I'll look into who authorized the transfers internally in the bank. Most banks don't just have millions of 500-euro notes hanging around. So, someone on the inside must be facilitating that. Thanks, Konstantin."

"Fine, all right, I'll do this for you. I never really have a choice with you, do I?" he asked sleepily.

* * *

"Here's your man," Konstantin said over a secure video chat the next afternoon. Jillian hunched forward to study the other man in the room with him.

This was no 30-million-euro criminal.

The suspect was just a boy, with a slash of stubble over his lip and distant eyes that glared at her through a mat of hair clinging to his forehead. He wore stained jeans and a t-shirt with a gold chain that looked as if it had come from a pawnshop.

"What did you do with the money?" Jillian asked.

Konstantin looked sheepishly at Jillian in the video chat window. "Bad news," he said to her in English. "The local investigators didn't catch him until after he transferred the money."

"What?!"

"Yes, it seems they contacted the bank and learned the transfer would happen at 11 a.m. But the subject came early, and the local guys were caught off guard. Especially because he looked younger. I mean, look at this kid. He'd already transferred the suitcases to a taxi, and it was driving off when they stopped him."

Jillian couldn't help a frustrated exhale. Desperate to salvage what she could, she said, "Alright. Ask him what he did with the money."

While Konstantin translated her words into Serbian, she watched the boy's body language. He was fidgeting, unable to look away from the computer or the one-way mirror in front of him. When he spoke, his tone seemed to be cooperative.

"He says a man approached him in the street," Konstantin said as he stepped back in front of the camera. "The man gave him the account numbers, security passcodes, and two empty suitcases. He told him he'd get a percentage of the money once he dropped it off. All the boy had to do was make the withdrawal and put the suitcases in the taxi."

"What did the man look like?" she asked.

"I asked him that already. He says he doesn't know. He wore sunglasses and a hat. All I can tell you for sure is that he's white, he's in decent shape, and he spoke terrible Serbian."

The boy said something behind Konstantin, who translated it for her.

"Oh, he says the man had a German accent," the attaché said.

"What about the money? Were you watching it?"

"That's another story all together," Konstantin said. "The taxi driver was approached in the same way, most likely by the same man. He was paid 500 euros to pick up the suitcases and drop them into a manhole."

"Can you contact the sewer authority?" she asked.

Konstantin shook his head.

"That particular manhole led straight to the ancient caves under the city that were dug before Roman times. By the time my men got to the manhole, the cases were already gone," he said.

Jillian massaged her temples and growled quietly to herself in frustration. "Did the cab driver know anything else? Please tell me that we didn't just let 30 million slip right past us."

"The driver knows nothing. He's an old Serb and used to not asking questions, but our boy here's too dumb to know any different. He asked who the money was for, and do you know what our mystery man said?"

"What?" Jillian asked.

"He said it was for *The King Under the Mountain*," Konstantin said. "The way the boy understood, the money was some sort of a down payment for his, uh, *sta si rekao?*" the attaché asked. The boy mumbled something, and then Konstantin turned back to face the camera once again.

"What did he say?" she asked.

"Well, I'm not sure what it means exactly, but he said it was a down payment for his cathedral."

12

February 1945

The Zitternberg

"I've already told you, we don't know how the creatures died," Professor Steiger said in a frustrated tone.

"Were they suffocated? Did they starve?" Keck asked.

"I'm not a doctor, Keck, and any you send up here from Dachau wouldn't even know where to start."

"It's been *months,* Professor, and you have given me nothing!" the *Sturmbannführer* shouted.

"What would you have me do, Keck?" Steiger asked. "This technology is thousands of years more advanced than ours. Just to understand the concept of how this machine is powered could take lifetimes."

They'd been sitting there arguing in the car for quite some time at the end of the dirt road that led to the *Zitternberg.* They were supposed to be climbing the trail to *Der Dom.* This would be Keck's first visit since he'd returned from speaking to Himmler, and he was highly disappointed at the lack of progress.

He stepped out of the car, slammed the door, and then stared down at the valley where Bad Tölz's buildings still stood. The Russians and the Allies were but a distant thought, for here they had a chance.

The other car door opened, and boots crunched through the snow until the professor stood beside him.

"What happened in Berlin, Kristock? I have a right to know."

"We are losing the war, Professor," Keck said flatly.

"Yes, I'm well aware of that. It's why I came to Bavaria in the first place, and you almost had me executed for trying to help. Remember?"

Keck didn't respond to the professor's question. He just clasped his hands behind his back and let the cold mountain air numb his nose and ears. When he finally spoke, it was as if the words had been churning in him for days.

"I refuse to let our vision die," the *Sturmbannführer* said. "We are in possession of alien technology here, Professor. It's a great tool of immense power, if we could but learn how to use it. Germany is indeed stricken, but it could yet recover. We may be able to sue for peace and maintain our ideals if we show that we are not weak and that we still have strength enough to fight."

"Keck, I have spent weeks in that machine, and even now I barely understand how to open its doors. You've seen it the same as I. You know how strange it is to our minds. If you brought me more scientists and gave me the freedom to ask questions, then perhaps I would make more progress, but you've stuck me here on this mountain with nothing but three hundred Jews and your SS guards. I'm a geologist, for heaven's sake! This is *not* my field of expertise!"

"No one else may know, Hans. The secret we possess here is far too great to risk it falling into the wrong hands."

"Look, Kristock, I want to save the Reich as much as you do," Steiger said. "I'm working as hard as I can to learn the secrets of this technology just as fast as is humanly possible. But simple truth is that we may never learn how to use it, or even what it actually does. For the moment, all we have, for lack of a better word, is an immense alien warehouse, and I don't see how that in and of itself will help us in the war."

For a long moment, Keck stood in silence. His face had paled from the cold, and a vein throbbed in his forehead. The possibilities churned in his mind, however, so any other discomfort he was feeling was simply pushed aside.

"I will not give up," he said finally. "Even if it takes my entire lifetime."

"Then what now?" Steiger asked with an exhausted sigh. "What would you have me do?"

"You will continue your work," Keck answered as he marched back to the car. "For my part, I will begin to make use of your *warehouse.*"

He started the car without another word, and then ground the gears and sped away, leaving Professor Steiger standing there alone, buffeted by the gathering winds.

* * *

That night, Professor Steiger fumbled awake from his cot near the entrance of *Der Dom.* A horn had sounded, and the *Totenkopfverbände* began rousing their companions. Steiger padded down the length of the 10-meter-wide tunnel in his slippers and found a line of workers under close watch from the SS marching up the mountain footpath toward him. The laborers carried crate after crate into the widened tunnel and stood to be patted down by their guards after depositing each load against the salt stone walls. The boxes appeared thick and extremely dense, with two and sometimes three Jews straining under each one.

Professor Steiger wrapped his robe more tightly as he stepped out into the chilly night air and followed the line of numb-faced workers back down the mountain. There he found a column of trucks, and at their head was Kristock Keck, overseeing the entire operation.

"What is this?" Steiger asked as he approached Keck.

"Preparations," Keck said as a group of exhausted workers reached over a tailgate for their next punishing load.

"Preparations? For what?"

"Why, for your success, of course, my dear Professor," the *Sturmbannführer* said, smiling to himself as he watched the Jews labor under the heavy box they'd just removed from the truck.

* * *

July 2014

Bad Tölz, Germany

"You spend too much time on that typewriter," Miriam said, scolding him like a worried mother. "You spend all day locked away, trying to dig up the past. Who spends their vacation in their room?"

Yanis had just come downstairs for his fourth cup of tea, and a sudden yawn froze his response. He rubbed his eyes and felt the stubble that had grown out since the last time he shaved. He let out a heavy sigh, and then offered his innkeeper an exhausted smile.

"I'm a professor, Miriam, you know that. We academics love a good mystery."

"You told me you were going to call the museum and get rid of that thing," she said.

"I plan to," he said as he poured hot water from the kettle. "The thing is, there's nothing online about this *Der Dom* place that I can find, and I can't give it up when I know so little about it. The way they reference it, it sounds like it was really important to them. There's something more to all this Miriam, and I'm gonna figure out what it is. You mark my words."

"You should go outside and enjoy your life, Yanis. Maybe you'll even meet a nice German girl," she suggested.

Yanis blew into his steaming mug, his face growing red hot at the innkeeper's reference to his personal life. He'd always hoped he could meet a girl that would share his love of mystery and adventure, but he'd practically given up hope of that ever happening.

"If it would make you happy, Miriam, I'll call the museum tomorrow."

"*Gut, gut.* Now, it's time for supper, and—" she started to say, but then she fell silent for a moment as fists banged against the inn's front door.

"Now who could that be? We're already fully booked," Miriam said as she shuffled from the kitchen. Just as she was about to reach for the knob, the door suddenly burst open.

"What? What is this?" Miriam demanded.

A woman stepped into the hallway, followed by a tall redheaded Scot and a half a dozen other *Polizei*. Their walkie-talkies blared as they fanned out through the inn, knocking on the doors of all the guests.

"Here now," Miriam said. "Who are you people? There's no need for that!"

The woman's piercing eyes looked over Miriam for a moment, and then switched over to Yanis. This was not a nice German girl, but in spite of himself, Yanis smiled at her. She was quite fit looking, with brown hair that fluttered against her shoulders and a focused look of concentration that he recognized from his own photographs. He couldn't be sure, but he thought the woman's gaze lingered on him for a moment before she took a badge from inside her jacket and showed it to Miriam. Suddenly he flushed with embarrassment when he realized that she'd probably been looking at him like that was because of all the stubble on his face, and the fact that his thick, black hair hadn't been brushed in days. He was on vacation after all, but still, no man wants to look unattractive in the presence of a beautiful woman.

"Sir, ma'am," the woman said. "I need to ask that you and all the residents of this inn come with me for questioning."

"Why? What's this all about?" Miriam asked.

"My name is Inspector Qualmes. Someone here has been searching for topics that are currently related to an ongoing Interpol investigation, and I'm here to find out what they know."

* * *

"I promise you, I never even heard of *Der Dom* before two days ago," Yanis said truthfully.

"You heard about it from the Enigma machine that we took from your room," Inspector Qualmes said as she paced in front of him. She'd pulled her long brown hair into a severe ponytail before the interrogation. This was clearly not a woman who'd shy away from leading a chase. If he was going to place his mystery in anyone's hands other than his own, at least hers seemed to be competent. Besides, he'd always had a weakness for green eyes, and he found hers to be particularly enchanting.

One eyebrow shot up as she leaned forward, and now those green eyes that he'd been admiring were clearly communicating to him that she expected an answer.

"Yes, that's correct, and please be careful with the machine. It's an antique that's in almost perfect condition, and I'm sure it's quite valuable," he said with genuine worry in his voice.

A hint of a smile at his eccentricity fluttered at the corners of Inspector Qualmes' mouth, but there was not a moment to be wasted, so she quickly returned to the matter at hand.

"How did you know how to decode the messages? Do you have a military background?"

"I'm a math professor at Jerusalem Polytechnic who just happens to enjoy puzzles. Cryptology is a special interest of mine."

She had the typical reaction to his revelation, which consisted mostly of a blank stare. He knew what she was thinking too. She was probably thinking that he was just another Indiana Jones wannabe. In truth, Jillian was wondering how she could find out what cryptology was without having to admit that she was absolutely clueless. Even with a three-day shadow and unkempt hair, she could see the intelligence in his expressive brown eyes, and for some reason she couldn't quite explain, it mattered to her that he not view her as someone of lesser intelligence. As such, she'd just bypass the question and educate herself about the subject later when she was alone.

"Other than your web searches, you've had no contact with anyone else about *Der Dom?*"

"No, I haven't. I already told you that. What is this all about exactly?" he asked.

The woman sighed, and then sat on the corner of the desk. A part of him wanted to reach out to her, to take her by the hand so he could lead her up the Blaueis, or anywhere else she wanted to go, but he pushed those feelings aside. The last thing he wanted was for his awkwardness around women to creep into the conversation and taint her view of him. Normally he wouldn't think much of it, but with her it was different.

"I believe you, Mr. Miller," the inspector said after she rolled it all around in her head for a moment. "Your background doesn't fit the suspects we're looking for, and your story matches the evidence my colleagues at the NSA provided to me. You're free to go, but if you find anything suspicious in your searches, anything at all, please ring me at the number here," she said as she handed him her card.

He took the card just as the door to the interrogation room opened and the tall Scottish inspector stepped inside to escort him out. Yanis stayed in his seat, however, which caused Inspector Qualmes to cock her eyebrow at him.

"Is there something else you'd like to add?" she asked.

"I understand you can't tell me what's going on, but maybe I could help you," he offered, flashing her a hesitant, yet disarming smile. He was stepping out of his comfort zone here, and even though he was sure it showed, he didn't care in the slightest. Jillian didn't respond, however. In fact, she was a little bit irritated by the effect he seemed to have on her.

"And how would you be helpin' us?" Harry asked.

"One of the messages I decoded had the coordinates for *Der Dom* attached. I could take you there if you want. That is, if you think it'd be helpful, Jillian"

"Inspector Qualmes," she said, tersely correcting him, and suddenly his hopes fell.

"I'm sorry," he said. "I'm sure it's nothing and I didn't mean to be forward. It was silly of me really. I mean, after all, what would an old Nazi message have to do with anything?" he asked, but he realized then that Inspector Qualmes was staring at him, intrigue lighting her face. He recognized at that moment that she might just possibly be a kindred spirit, at least where curiosity was concerned.

"I suppose it couldn't hurt to check it out. Can you take us there today?" Jillian asked.

"Of course," he said. A warmth suddenly flushed through him as he realized that this might just be the closest he'd ever come to getting a date.

* * *

Three more *Polizei* cruisers and an armored van joined them outside the village. Their convoy flew south as Jillian used her phone and radio to coordinate with other members of the task force. Everything was taking shape, and Yanis watched the mountains swell in front of them as they drew ever closer. A nervous chill ran through him as he grew more and more anxious about just what they would find up there.

"You know, I still don't know what this is about," he said from the back seat. "I didn't realize that this would be such a significant operation."

Inspector Qualmes clicked off her radio and glanced over at her red-haired partner behind the wheel.

"We've been investigating a series of black market arms purchases made on behalf of a man who calls himself *The King Under the Mountain*," she said. "We know the transactions are happening, we know the weapons are being taken somewhere called *'Der Dom,'* but it's a sophisticated operation. Every time we think we have a lead, it turns out that we've only captured a runner who doesn't know anything."

"Arms dealing? What do they want?" Yanis asked.

"We don't know. Up until we found you, we hadn't been able to track down a single solid lead. I really can't tell you how grateful I am for your help."

"It's nothing, really," Yanis said, smiling to himself as he suddenly realized that he'd never been so happy to have had a climbing accident.

"Yes, it's quite lucky that you were on holiday when you were," Harry added.

"You're from Israel, you said?" Jillian asked.

"I am, yes."

"What made you want to come to Germany of all places?" Harry asked.

"It's a beautiful country," Yanis answered. "The mountaineering and climbing are incredible. It reminds me of my hometown in Montana."

"And you felt safe here?" the inspector asked.

"Well, not when I was falling into the glacier, but other than that I haven't had any issues. Why do you ask?"

"No reason," the inspector said. "I, uh … no reason."

"Are you trying to ask why a Jew would come to Germany on a vacation?" Yanis asked. The inspector had turned back to face the road ahead of them once again. He could see from her reflection in the glass that she was blushing.

"I didn't mean it like that," the inspector said.

"It's all right. At home they asked me the same thing before I left," Yanis said. "What happened seventy years ago is all just ancient history to me. It's a different time now, and no one knows that better than the Germans. The people here have shown me nothing but kindness. To be honest, I don't think there's much Nazism left in this country."

Inspector Qualmes and her driver shared another glance, and Yanis suddenly realized that he might have overstepped his bounds with that comment.

"I'm sorry if I made you uncomfortable talking about all this," he said. "I'm afraid I can be somewhat blunt at times."

"No, you're fine," the inspector said. "The truth is that I'm the same way, really. I just hope you're right. All that stuff from the past needs to stay in the past, right where it belongs."

13

Helicopters thumped overhead as their convoy rose into the mountains. The pilots' voices buzzed through Inspector Qualmes' radio, and as Yanis listened to the chatter, he realized lives may very well be on the line. The Scottish driver wound them up toward the ski resort that crowned the mountain indicated in the coordinates Yanis had translated, but as they neared, Yanis saw the resort was closed for the season and stood empty.

The inspectors turned into a resort parking lot stuffed with vehicles. Dozens of German GSG counter-terrorism operators leaped from the armored trucks and sprinted toward the deadened lifts. Yanis opened his door and felt the sudden rush of cool mountain air against his skin. He quickly joined Inspector Qualmes as she wedged an earpiece into her ear and tightened the straps on the bulletproof vest she'd slipped on over her jacket.

"What should I do?" Yanis asked.

"Stay here with Harry and the car," she said. "If this goes well, I'll be back soon."

"I will," he said. "Be safe."

There was that smile again. She wondered to herself for a moment if he even knew he was doing it. No time for that now. All eyes forward, as her grandpa would say.

"I'm sorry," Yanis said. "Was there something else?"

"No," the inspector said, shaking her head slightly. "No, it's just that … no one's ever said that to me before."

102

"Inspector? It's time," one of the other agents called. Qualmes nodded and then jogged to join the rest of her team.

"You know, I wouldn't have believed it if I hadn't seen it myself," Harry said after she was gone.

"What's that?" Yanis asked.

"I think she likes you, and here I was starting to wonder if she actually liked anyone at all."

* * *

Yanis waited with Harry while the helicopters circled, and the sun burned a pleasant swathe across the mountainside. An hour passed. Then two. The radio on the dash crackled with the same report every few minutes.

"*Hier nichts,*" the *Polizei* called. "*Klar.*"

"Nothing here," Harry repeated each time. "Clear."

The helicopters grew low on fuel and withdrew. As the reports continued, Harry fell into a sour mood.

"You know, I told her this was ludicrous," he said after the GSG reported that the mountain's base had no entrance. "This isn't a bloody film. You don't get mysterious Nazi codes telling you where to go."

"I was just trying to help," Yanis said.

"I know that, but the inspector, she's so desperate to solve this one that she's not thinking clearly."

"Why is this case so important to her?"

Harry glanced at the tree line, bright green against the deep sky. They couldn't see any of the officers.

"That's just who she is. You'd have to know her to understand."

Yanis *thought* he understood her, but it was the mystery—the frustrating draw of the unsolved that fascinated him so. It was why he'd chosen academia, and why he'd spent two days awake with the Enigma.

As the hours stretched on and a growling rose in his stomach, Yanis' sense of foreboding grew. The voices over the radio grew more frustrated and tired with each passing call, until finally he heard Inspector Qualmes herself.

"There's nothing here," she said. "It's done."

One by one, the *Polizei* trickled back to the parking lot. The GSG operatives appeared as if from nowhere, carrying slumped, annoyed looks on their faces as they marched back to their transport. Inspector Qualmes was the last to emerge from the resort's gates.

"Ooh, this isn't gonna be good," Harry said as soon as he saw her.

The inspector walked toward the car with a stiffness that looked as though she were trying to keep something inside. She slipped into the front seat without a sound, and then slammed the door behind her. Tense silence filled the vehicle as she sat there staring straight ahead.

"I'm so sorry," Yanis said. If there had been a more annoying response possible, Jillian couldn't think of it.

"Start the car, Harry," Qualmes said without any hint of emotion. "Let's get back to the hotel."

"You didn't find anything at all?" Yanis asked.

So there *was* a more annoying response. She took a short breath and then said quickly, as if trying to spit out the words, "Those helicopters were using ground penetrating radar. The GSG covered the entire mountain. This entire operation probably cost a million euros."

"The Home Office is not gonna like that," Harry said.

"But you'll find them, right?" Yanis asked. "You won't give up, will you?"

She stared at the mountain road as its greenery flashed past them. Yanis saw the frustration and embarrassment she was feeling and wracked his brain for something he could do. A Nazi had died trying to deliver a secret message about *Der Dom*. It had to mean something.

"Maybe we could try—" he said, but she quickly interrupted him.

"Let's have some quiet in the car now if you don't mind, Mr. Miller," Jillian said. "I'm sorry I ever involved someone like you in this investigation. It was a mistake."

"Someone like me?"

"An academic," she said. "Someone who plays with history instead of facts."

"You really don't know what cryptology is, do you?" he asked. She didn't answer. She simply sat there, staring out the window in silence.

* * *

March 1945

The Zitternberg

Keck paced the strange dimensions of what they'd come to call the bridge with tension tightening his face. Steiger had replaced the deceased aliens with notebooks, chalkboards, and a cot with two oil lamps. These few human artifacts seemed pathetically crude here, where the colors and shapes seemed to hint at unreachable wonders. A place where the very dimensional fabric seemed to flex and bend for unknown purposes. Keck found himself turning at a wall that he had not seen a moment earlier and circled back to where Professor Steiger sat on a white ledge that appeared to be floating in mid-air.

"The war is lost, and we are fumbling with the key to the Reich's last hope," Keck said.

"This again, Kristock? Your threats have no bearing on my progress, you know."

"It is not a threat, Professor. It's simply an acknowledgment that we must discuss preparations for the inevitable."

"Maybe it's best if we just re-bury this blasted thing," the professor said. "Hide *Der Dom* from the Allies before it's too late."

"That is treason!" Keck shouted. Professor Steiger's defeatist attitude was the last thing he needed to deal with at such a dire time. "I have killed many for far less insolence."

"Yes? And what of it, Kristock? We brought our discovery to Heinrich Himmler himself and he didn't believe us. What else are we to do?"

Tears rose in Professor Steiger's eyes, the frustrated anger of a man who'd given his every waking moment to the Party and to the cause.

A man who hadn't seen the sun for days because he was wasting away here trying to discover the secrets of another race.

"The *Reichsführer*'s vision has failed him," Keck said flatly.

"And if his has gone, then how many others are feeling the same?" Steiger asked.

"What are you saying, Hans?"

"The German people are a great people, Kristock. They will live on, but what do you plan to do in the meantime? Are we to simply hide ourselves in the hills and wait for the Americans to leave? We could have won this war without the meddling of an inept corporal."

"YOU WILL NOT SAY SUCH THINGS ABOUT *MEIN FÜHRER!*" Keck screamed as he lashed out with his hand and hit the wall. His fist made contact with a hard panel that had not been there a moment before, and as he pulled back his throbbing hand and attempted to shake the pain from it, a white flash lit *Der Dom's* bridge. The flash was almost blinding at first, but then it slowly calmed until it matched the same blue glow of the script that played about the exterior of the ship. The light didn't emanate from the craft's ceiling, however. It came from another portal that Keck had revealed with his angry outburst.

"I can't believe it," Steiger whispered, his lower lip trembling slightly. "Kristock, do you see?"

"Oh yes, Professor, I see it clearly," Keck said as he stepped through the portal with Steiger following close behind.

They stepped into a new chamber that was more fully shaped than any that had come before. A slender tube that was just larger than the width of a man's shoulders rose from the center of the room. It seemed to be made from some kind of a pulsing glass, and its top flared out where it met the ceiling, giving it the appearance of a fluted, multicolored vase.

The air in this room tasted strangely metallic, as if a great power were held in check, and the walls of the chamber crackled with rapid repetition of the same blue script found on *Der Dom's* outer walls. Surrounding the strange tube, ordered in what appeared to be a series of concentric rings, thousands of objects glittered and shone in the eerie blue glow. Near the portal, they appeared to be made of glass, metal, and other strange materials that seemed to absorb the light.

Steiger rushed past him, picking his way through a field of objects toward the chamber's center point. Keck followed with caution as he tried to make sense of what he was seeing, while at the same time pushing away the ghostly afterimages that seemed to plague his vision here in this hall of relics.

"Kristock, look!" Steiger said excitedly. He was several rings closer to the glass tube and was standing there holding up a brass helmet. The plume was a rough brown and probably made of horsehair. The helmet's cheek guards curled under its eyes like long daggers and were separated by another blade of metal that would have served as a nose guard. He knew the shape from his textbooks. It should not be here, but it was.

"That's a Greek helmet," Kristock said in astonishment.

"Yes, it is! It's at least three thousand years old. Look over here!" Steiger said as he set down the helmet and then ran to a mound of gold serving ware. He picked up one of the spoons and examined the engraving on it.

"My God, Kristock, this is the Habsburg seal!" he cried. "Five hundred years old, at least!"

"This ship must have been under the mountain for a very long time," Keck said.

"Perhaps—" Steiger whispered as he came to join Keck in his ring. Once there, he squatted down and picked up yet another object. "Or perhaps not. What do you make of this?"

Keck took the small piece of glass that Steiger handed him and felt its smooth lightness in his hand. Just out of curiosity, he pressed the single button at its base. The glass lit, showing him a picture of a woman's face, and a word in English.

"It wants a password," Keck said in shock. "And this language is English. Professor, what is this place?"

** * **

The find galvanized Steiger, and he redoubled his efforts to discover the secrets of the alien technology. Three days later he summoned Kristock once more to the *Zitternberg*, so he could reveal his findings.

Leaving Bad Tölz behind for the climb up the mountain, Kristock closed his eyes and felt the rattle of the car underneath him. The Russians would reach Berlin in a matter of days, and he knew the German people would suffer immeasurably under the Communists' bitter retribution. Whatever the professor had found, it was more than likely that the time of its usefulness had already passed.

Workers continued to fill the tunnel that led to *Der Dom* with the last of the heavy crates they'd been working for months to move. The Jews were tottering, thinned by the lack of rations and the heavy loads. The vermin were still needed for the moment, but they wouldn't be available for much longer, so he needed to make sure they maximized their output.

His *Totenkopfverbände* were another matter. The loyal *Schütze* had seen much, and he'd not yet decided what to do with them. However, these were decisions for another day. As for today, however, his only plan was to share one last moment of enjoyment with the professor before everything came crashing down around them.

Keck found Steiger inside of *Der Dom's* newly revealed room, standing at what looked like a series of glowing wheels that hung in the air next to the shimmering tube.

"What is it, Hans? Your message—" Keck asked, but then he fell silent as Steiger turned to look at him, a smile stretched across his scarred and peeling face.

"Kristock, may I see your watch please?" he asked.

"Of course," Keck said as he unfastened it from his wrist and handed it to him.

"Excellent," the professor said. He rested Keck's Glashütte on his arm, then twisted his own watch's winding. "Both at 10:14 on the nose, *ja?* Now, let's see here—" he said as he scanned a collection of artifacts that had been brought closer to the tube. He selected a piece of Chinese porcelain decorated with cranes in flight, placed Keck's watch inside of it, and then set the vase inside the tube.

The cavity was tall and narrow, apparently designed to fit one of the alien creatures they'd seen on the bridge. Its interior glowed with a bright cyan, and a brutal heat cascaded from the opening with such intensity that it was only a matter of seconds before Keck started sweating.

Steiger exited the chamber and returned to the glowing rings. He rested his palm on the fourth dial from the left, and the control ring flashed a bright orange. Then he raised the ring just slightly, with a small, nearly imperceptible motion.

The tube's portal closed like an iris, and a sound like tearing paper suddenly filled the room. Steiger pulled Keck's sleeve toward a rising walkway leading through the rings that he hadn't noticed before.

Professor Steiger's lips moved as they walked, but Keck shook his head. He could not hear anything above the tube's monstrous noise. The professor gripped Keck's shoulder, and he turned him toward the rings of artifacts so that he could witness the discovery.

The tiers on either side of the walkway filled with a steadily increasing white light, and in the space of a breath, the glow flashed impossibly bright, blinding them both. Once they could finally see, Keck found himself staring at an empty room. He spun back to the tube and saw the chamber sitting open, just as it had been before. It now glowed with the same mysterious blue light it had been emitting when he first entered.

"You'll note that we sent the two objects at exactly 10:14," Hans said as he held out his wrist so that Keck could see his watch.

"What happened to the artifacts?" Keck asked.

"I'm not exactly sure. In my limited understanding, I believe that this room is somehow connected to time. My first insight was that the rings surrounding the chamber align with these controls here. I must say, it took some amount of courage to make an attempt at using them."

"How many rings are there?" Keck asked as he scanned the room.

"That's another mystery I'm afraid. You know how strange this place is. I find myself setting out through them in a straight line, but somehow, I end up curving when I turn to gain my bearings. I have not been able to make an accurate count. But your glass device lays two rings after the vase that I transported. The vase was produced in China just prior to the war. Of that I am sure."

Suddenly, the tearing sound returned. Keck winced and squeezed his eyes shut as the lights brightened. Steiger gripped his arm once more and bade him to look as the painful illumination faded. Keck saw that the objects around them had returned, spreading as far as he could see through the fantastic chamber.

"Come with me now, and see what has happened," Steiger said as he jogged back to the tube. He bent down for a moment, and stood back up, smiling as he held out the vase for Keck to see. "Take your watch and place it back on your wrist."

Kristock retrieved the watch from the vase and strapped it back onto his wrist, just as Steiger had requested. Once he'd done that, Steiger held out his own wrist, so that Keck could compare the time between the two watches. Steiger's watch read 10:27, while the gears of Keck's watch were just pushing the minute hand to 10:15.

"I don't understand, Hans. What are you showing me here?"

"I'm showing you time," Steiger said, smiling excitedly as he looked down at the watches once more.

14

October 2014

München, Germany

"Ms. Qualmes, at this point I'm not even sure you're still the right inspector for this job," Deputy Director St. Pierre said as his flat stare bored into her through the secure video chat screen. Behind him, she could see a flurry of activity going on at the Home Office, and she was glad she didn't have to face him in the middle of all that confusion.

"But sir, we've identified the pattern. We know the arms sales are happening. The emails we've intercepted have all been in code, and the transfers are always preceded by calls from single-use cell phones that were purchased with cash. Also, Vasily thinks—"

"Yes, I know what the FSB thinks, but my concern lies with you. In six months, the only action you've been able to take is a raid on a ski resort that cost this department nearly 800,000 pounds. Tell me again what you were thinking when you decided to waste our precious resources on a raid that turned up nothing?"

"Sir, it was a lead that I thought was worth pursuing," she said, trying to sound confident, even though she wasn't exactly feeling that way.

"Why? Because a mountain climber found an antique from the Second World War? You must have found his story very persuasive, Inspector."

Jillian closed her eyes, trying to force away the embarrassment. She'd never returned Yanis' calls because she'd become concerned about the feelings they raised in her. The case was what was important here, not her interest in a mountain climbing mathematician who'd only wanted to help.

"Please, sir," she pleaded. "Vasily believes the anti-aircraft artillery is crossing the border to Austria as we speak. The satellite photos I forwarded to you show the crates being loaded into trucks, and no less than fourteen of those trucks are headed to Germany right now."

"You're asking me to approve a second action based on Russian military inventory discrepancies, and money that you believe is being spent by a mysterious Nazi sympathizer who may or may not exist?"

"Those billions of euros are going *somewhere,* Director, and these arms sales *are* happening. Someone is trying to arm a military and intercepting this shipment could be our only chance to find out just who's behind it all."

St. Pierre turned to stare out an unseen window and tapped his fingers against his chin for a moment while he weighed the pros and cons of his decision.

"Most of my other inspectors trade in facts, Ms. Qualmes. They perform their duties, and then they go home. They don't manufacture cases just because they want one to exist. They have families, other interests—"

"Sir, I—"

"I'm authorizing this raid because of your impressive track record, Ms. Qualmes, and because there are other governments that are growing quite concerned with your findings. However, unless you can make some tangible progress on this wild goose chase that will help calm our allies, then your role in the investigation will come to an end. Am I understood?"

"Yes, Director, understood, and thank you," she said.

"Don't disappoint me, Jillian," he said, not waiting for a response before he closed the call.

"I'm sorry about that, Inspector. He shouldn't have—" Harry started, but Jillian already had her coat and radio in her hand and was heading for the door

"Those trucks aren't stopping for anyone, Harry. We need to move out *now!*"

* * *

Drizzle blurred the sedan's windshield as the German *Polizei* driver whisked them down the E60 toward Salzburg, where the trucks they pursued were just now crossing the border.

"Confirm," Harry said into his radio. "We'll pick up visual."

Jillian studied the traffic as their driver worked his way through the lanes. Up ahead, there were no checkpoints or gates. There was nothing but an unimpeded flow of vehicles that had made her efforts to track the weapons shipments on their way through Europe so very difficult. However, these trucks were headed to Germany, and *Der Dom* was German, so she was convinced that she had to be close.

"There," she said as she jabbed her finger at a line of white trailers about a kilometer or so ahead of them. They were driving in a convoy formation in the slow lane.

"We have visual," Harry shouted excitedly into the radio. "I count thirteen, no, fourteen white Mercedes Antos headed westbound on the E60 in the right-hand lane. The operation is go. I say again, the operation is go."

Dozens of red and blue lights flashed to life around the tractor-trailers as Jillian's net of unmarked *Polizei* and Interpol cars revealed themselves. Civilian traffic slowed and came to a stop along the shoulders, while her own driver slammed on the brakes and fishtailed their car around to form a roadblock. Jillian stepped into the wet blare of sirens and horns, loosed her badge and pistol, and then waited for the first truck to reach them. The drenching mist felt cool on her skin, and her breath clouded the air. Harry and the *Polizei* officer joined her as they watched the oncoming trucks, and the excitement they were all feeling was palpable. She had them now. After so many false leads and missteps, she finally had them.

The first Mercedes swelled larger and larger as it approached. She couldn't make out the driver's face from behind his windshield wipers, but she heard him grind the vehicle's gears and feed more fuel to his engine.

"He's not going to stop!" Harry shouted.

A helicopter churned somewhere in the clouds overhead. A loud-speaker from one of the *Polizei* cruisers blared for the truck to pull over, but the driver only accelerated.

"Get back!" Jillian screamed. She pulled the two men into a sprint across the slick asphalt, heading for the drainage ditch beyond the shoulder.

Once she reached the roadside, Jillian stopped, aimed her Glock at the driver's rain-glazed windshield, and fired.

The Mercedes smashed into their car, crushing the sedan as if it had been made of little more than paper. Glass burst out in all directions and bounced along the road as the metal of the vehicles tore with a wrenching squeal. Tires exploded like grenades, and for a moment she thought the truck might just brush their barrier aside and escape, but that was not about to happen. Her bullets had all gone through the cab's windshield, and the truck's front wheels shredded down to nothing more than rubber flaps. The vehicle was slurring right and drifting off the road as it passed her. She immediately got to her feet and ran after it as fast as she could.

The Antos roared into the drainage ditch thirty meters beyond them, listing farther and farther until it toppled onto its side and skidded across the wet mud. The truck finally came to a stop another twenty meters farther down the road. The other trucks in the convoy slowed and came to a stop, cowed by what had happened to their leader. The *Polizei* closed in around them cautiously as Jillian and the two men approached the crashed truck.

Harry drew his pistol, screaming at the truck's driver as the man struggled from the cab's opposite door and dropped to the ground. Harry and the other officer were on him in an instant, and quickly had him secured. Once that situation was handled, Jillian turned to make sure the other trucks had stopped, and that their drivers were being arrested as well.

Panting, she retraced her steps back to the rear of the trailer. Its doors had sprung open when the frame warped in the crash, revealing a smashed crate that had tumbled loose of its moorings. Finally, after so many months full of failure and disappointment, Jillian smiled at what she was seeing, for right there in front of her was the black muzzle of a Russian anti-aircraft gun.

Holstering her Glock, she pulled out her mobile and called the director. Now that she had her evidence, it was finally time to solve the mystery.

15

"Who were you working for?" Jillian demanded. The Russian translator shouted her question loudly into the driver's face, but he only shrugged, and then winced at the pain it caused in his shoulder where the bullets had hit him. He'd shaved his head down to stubble, and sweat caused by the strain of his injuries was starting to glisten on his scalp. Finally, he let loose with a stream of Russian that was directed at the translator.

"He says he doesn't know. He only works for the trucking company. All he knows is that the loads were not to be stopped. He figured that whatever he was carrying must be valuable, and that we were thieves trying to steal it, so he panicked."

"Thieves with police lights?" Harry asked from beside Jillian.

"Tell him we're going to charge him with three counts of the attempted murder of a police officer and that he'll be in jail for decades if he doesn't stop with the lies and tell us what we want to know," she said angrily.

Russian flowed back and forth between the pair for a moment, and then the translator turned back to face her once again. "He says, why would he lie? We can check his records and see he was clean."

"Where was he going?" Jillian asked. "Where were the weapons being taken?"

"He doesn't know. He was to leave the truck and keys in Bad Reichenhall, and then wait for the company to pick him up."

Unable to contain her anger any longer, Jillian stepped in front of the driver, slammed her hands down on the table, and shouted at him.

"I know what you're doing, and I know who those weapons were for! If you don't start being more cooperative, then you'll never see your home ever again!"

The driver spread his hands and looked confusedly at the translator. Then Jillian spotted something on his wrist that she hadn't noticed when they first brought him in, and it confirmed exactly what she'd been thinking all along.

"No more questions. Maybe some time in a cell will make him feel a bit more chatty. Lock him up," she said as she burst out of the interrogation room, desperately trying to contain the tightening in her gut.

"Inspector?" Harry called down the hall after her, but she was already passing through the duty room, and was now quickly making her way out of the police station.

The gray day had darkened into night. Cold wind caused the fallen leaves to swirl around in seemingly endless drifts. She was being toyed with by a power far larger and more dangerous than she'd ever thought possible. She'd have to be cautious, ruthless even. She'd have to redouble her efforts, but she knew that her suspicions were right.

"Ma'am, if you don't mind me asking, what was that all about?" Harry asked when he suddenly appeared behind her.

"You didn't see it, did you Harry?" she asked.

"See what Inspector?"

"The swastikas on his wrists. Tattooed right over the tendons."

"Oh my God, he's guilty, isn't he?"

"There's no doubt about it," she said.

"What the hell are the Neo-Nazis planning to do with all those weapons, and where were they going?" Harry asked.

"Well, that's the question now, isn't it?" Jillian said. It was more of a statement than a question though. She turned the details of the case over in her mind for a moment. She had a lot more questions for that driver, but a strange sense of foreboding had settled over her.

As the chill of the evening grew, she found her mind once again turning to Yanis, a Jew who was searching for something that appeared to be incredibly important to the Neo-Nazis. It felt strange to actually admit it, but she was really worried about him now, and her hunches were rarely wrong.

* * *

April 1945

The Zitternberg

"But *Herr Sturmbannführer,* we are not ready!" Professor Steiger cried. He was running toward where Kristock stood behind his *Totenkopfverbände* along the mountain path. The SS had lined up the Jewish workers at the edge of the forest, facing the Isar Valley. Birds chattered, and the bright green buds of spring lit the trees that marched down the side of the steep cliff.

"Aim," Keck called.

"The chamber has not been fully tested. There may be grave consequences to—"

"Fire!" Keck shouted.

The staccato roar of MP 40s was almost deafening. The Jews shuddered, screaming as they fell over the side of the mountain. Many tried to run at the last second and were cut down by snipers. Others stood rigid, their courage or pride forcing them to face their end with what little dignity they could muster as bloody holes erupted through their gaunt backs and skulls. Keck wondered occasionally about the different ways that members of the inferior races chose to face their end, but he had little time to waste pondering the fate of such animals. There were far more important matters at hand.

In a few seconds, the hundreds of Jews who'd excavated *Der Dom* and loaded it with supplies lay either dead or writhing at the lip of the trail. Their pale skin shone in the spring sunlight, their dead eyes now staring at nothing.

"Finish them, then meet me inside the tunnel," Keck ordered his *Schütze*.

He turned to Professor Steiger as his men drew pistols and bayonets. The SS simply booted the dead over the side of the mountain. Those who still lived first received a mercy shot or blade across their throat before following their brethren. The professor stared, his scorched face frozen in astonishment, hands clutching tight to his notebook.

"Their usefulness has come to an end," Keck said. "Now, as to yours, what have you got to tell me?"

"I don't understand how to go backward yet. There is no experiment that can validate the procedure. If we—"

"Such an experiment exists, Professor," Keck said as he stalked toward *Der Dom's* tunnel. "I will be its observer. As for time, the American Third Army is less than a day away. You may take the issue up with them if you wish, but my *Totenkopfverbände* will be watching you, and they are quite skilled at punishing treason."

"Stop talking like that, Kristock. You know as well as anyone that my loyalty is true. If I only had more time—"

Keck stopped in the tunnel and turned his piercing gaze toward the professor.

"You have given me all the time in creation, and I intend to make great use of your gift. Will you join me?"

"*Herr Sturmbannführer*," one of the *Schütze* called from the tunnel entrance. "We await your orders."

"Excellent. Bring the detachment inside, along with my supplies," Keck said. The soldier clicked his heels and trotted away as Keck turned back to the professor. "Now, Professor, would be so kind as to indulge me with a brief tutorial?"

* * *

Keck stood at the glowing chamber controls as the professor recited the instructions he'd put together in his notes.

"I've verified that each control ring corresponds to what appears to be an era of history," Steiger explained. "As near as I can tell, the artifacts in the rings on the floor will give you a rough sense of where you're going. You need just a slight push upward for minutes, a harder one for hours and days. I haven't yet tested for weeks, or years, so I don't honestly know what will happen if they're pushed beyond where I've already tested."

The *Sturmbannführer* nodded, and then raised his hands so they were hovering just in front of the controls.

"And everything in this room will come with me?" Keck asked.

"Everything in the ship, except for what rests on that walkway," Steiger said.

The sound of equipment rattling caused Keck to turn around to see what was going on behind him. His astonished *Totenkopfverbände* were just entering the chambers that had been forbidden to them for so long with an extreme sense of caution. Three of them set down Keck's traveling trunk within the first ring outside of the tube, along with a pile of rations and ammunition. Two more carried a generator, fuel, and a jackhammer.

"So, we're ready to proceed then?" Keck asked, turning his attention back to Steiger for a moment.

"Ready enough to make an attempt, though I do wish we had more time for testing."

Nodding, Keck turned back to face the men under his command. He scanned each of their faces in turn. Despite their actions outside moments before, and the strange setting they presently found themselves in, they carried no doubt or hesitation whatsoever. They were his best.

"You have all performed your duties to the utmost, and for that you have my eternal gratitude. Now, here in *Der Dom,* I must provide your final orders. Berlin—nay, the Reich itself—will fall at any moment. I will use this alien machine to travel to the future to bring back the knowledge and weapons we'll need to bring our Reich back from the ashes, but I will not be able to accomplish this task alone.

"Along with Professor Steiger here, you men must serve as the Reich's emissaries between now and the time when I make my return. I ask you now to abandon both your uniforms and your outward loyalty to the Party. Instead, I want you to carry it in your heart for all your days. The professor here will be leading you in your underground efforts to restore the Reich, and to that end he has received quite a large deposit in his Swiss bank account that will keep you and your descendants very well-funded. That money will lay the foundation for my return, and in exchange for that I would ask for your absolute loyalty throughout the years. As long as it will take, you and your progeny will remain loyal to our noble cause."

The men clicked their heels together and raised their hands in salute.

"*Heil* Hitler!" They cried along with Steiger.

"*Heil*!" Keck responded. "Now, the Americans will be here within a day, and they must never learn of our discovery. Your last act under my command is to wire this tunnel with explosives. See that the entrance is closed before nightfall. No one must ever know of this discovery until my return. Professor," Keck said as he turned to Steiger. "Is there anything else?"

"How will we, or our descendants, know that it'll be you upon your return?"

Keck paused as he was about to step into the tube and cocked his head in thought for a moment. The first thing that came to mind was a story that his father used to tell him in the firelight. It was a story about the strength of the German people, and of their ancestral might that would rise once more.

"Tell them to wait for The King Under the Mountain," he said, and then he stepped into the chamber and nodded to Steiger. "Now, take me to the time of this device."

Professor Steiger's last view of Kristock Keck was of the *Sturmbannführer* holding up the strange glass rectangle with the single button at the bottom as the tube sealed itself around him.

"With me," the professor called to the SS men. "Stay within the pathway."

The *Totenkopfverbände* crowded around him, their faces still filled with awe as Professor Steiger reached up to adjust the controls, and once again felt the alien power surge through his body.

16

Professor Hans Steiger walked down the trail from the tunnel entrance surrounded by Keck's *Totenkopfverbände*. Behind them, dust from the tunnel explosion choked the blue sky with a gray haze that would soon settle, wiping away a whole year of his life.

But this was the future, Hans thought to himself. Despite the great wealth he now possessed, the responsibilities that had been placed upon him were overwhelming. So much could go wrong. If Keck survived and was able to push himself through the collapsed tunnel to arrive at whatever future time existed, what would he find there?

Steiger ignored the few pale limbs and torsos still showing from the undergrowth beside him. The world had already shown that it wasn't ready for democratic socialism, and for the greatness of the thousand-year Reich, but its ideals were still right and true. Now that the responsibility for resetting its foundation lay with him, he pondered what such an effort would require. Much would be asked of him, and he wondered if he was up to the challenge.

Boots crunched up the trail toward him. The *Schütze*'s hands fell to their weapons, but it was nothing more than a lone figure that came into view as he rounded a bend in the trail. The man weaved up the rocks and dirt, hiccupping and murmuring quietly to himself. The guards looked to Steiger for his orders, but the professor reached out a hand to stay their aim.

"Steffan?" Hans called to him.

The miner shambled to a halt, and then squinted at Steiger.

"Hans!" he slurred. "I haven't seen you all winter, and it got me thinking about what you were doing up here."

"You received your payment, did you not?" Steiger asked.

"*Ja, ja.* I've got thousands of Reichsmarks that will all be worthless just as soon as Berlin falls. You damned Nazis care only about your purity, not the people you ground down for your godforsaken war. What am I supposed to do now? I'm broke Hans! Washed up!"

Steiger held out his palm to the soldier at his side, and suddenly felt a heavy weight settle into it.

"I gave you the greatest gift, Hans," Steffan said ruefully. "I gave you everything I had."

The professor raised his arm, pointing the pistol directly at the drunken old man.

"I'll tell the Americans! I'll tell the Soviets! At least they'll have the decency to pay me in real currency! At least they'll have a heart!"

Steiger fired. The miner fell, grasping at his chest. As the professor neared him, he lurched, spewing up crimson blood that stained the soil a deep brown color.

"Whether you believe this or not, I am truly sorry Steffan," Professor Steiger said. "Unfortunately, your service to the Reich has reached its end."

He returned the pistol to the *Schütze*, and then continued down the trail. It was a new era now. The era of building the Fourth Reich, and it was his duty to erase the past.

PART TWO:

WRATH

17

February 1943

Berlin, Germany

Heinrich Himmler stepped out of the *Reichskanzlei,* and into the chill of the night. Moonlight reflected off the lenses of his glasses and sparkled from the silver leaves and wreath badges on his collar.

"Where is this man?" he asked the cloud of cigarette smoke that rose from his guards and aides.

"This way, *Herr Reichsführer,*" one of them called. The aide led him down a stone walkway toward where a tall shape stood amongst a cluster of barren trees in the darkness of the courtyard. They were only halfway there, however, when the air raid sirens began screaming.

"Sir," one of the guards called as men ran for cover. "We need to bring you into the bunker."

"Not until I understand what our visitor wants," Himmler said.

"I want only to preserve the Reich," the man said as Himmler approached him. The *Reichsführer* squinted at the strange, flaking scars the moonlight revealed on his visitor's face. Though the man looked young, streaks of gray wove their way through the blond hair underneath.

"Do I know you?" Himmler asked. "You seem familiar to me."

"We have met before, *Herr Reichsführer,* but in a different time. You would not remember me."

"The story you told my subordinates was quite convincing. I've been summoned from a meeting with *Der Führer* himself."

"Does he know of this meeting?" the man asked.

"No, and he will not unless he needs to. Many charlatans seek to profit from this war. One of my roles is to guard against them."

Breath blurred the night between the two men. Searchlights blazed through the dark like giant fingers grasping for the death that would come as the SS around them gripped their rifles and scanned the sky.

"That is why I've brought proof of my veracity," the visitor said as he held out a thick tube to the *Reichsführer*. Himmler hefted the device, which appeared to be a short telescope assembled in chunked sections.

"It's so light," Himmler said. "What's this material?"

"It's a type of polyethylene. In English, it's called plastic."

"And how will it help us kill the Soviets?"

"This isn't a weapon, *Herr Reichsführer*. It's simply a tool to allow you to witness the accuracy of my statements. If I may?"

At Himmler's nod, the visitor raised the tube to the sky and guided Himmler's eye to the soft rest at its base.

"What's this? I can see!" the *Reichsführer* said in astonishment. "The sky is as clear as day!"

When Himmler finally took his eye from the device, his guards caught glimpses of a tiny green screen that showed British bombers flying in a neat formation high overhead. Himmler considered the man before him for a moment, as well as the strange story his aides had relayed.

"If you are indeed telling the truth, *Sturmbannführer*, you will have a great future in the Party, and I will welcome you with open arms," he said as the bombs began to fall around Berlin. "Now, let us find a safe location where we may discuss your proposal."

✳ ✳ ✳

June 1944
Portland, England

Sergeant Jim Thompson followed the last of his men into the cramped landing craft underneath the churning, slate-colored sky. In total, he was carrying around one hundred and fifty pounds of weapons and gear down the ramp. Once he was inside, he turned to face the Limey dock master who'd offered his platoon cigarettes and chocolates for the voyage.

As the craft's pilot wheeled the ramp slowly closed, the Brit drew himself into a salute, and Jim snapped his hand to his brow in return until the hatch sealed off his view. The ramp clanged closed, and Jim reached forward to latch it shut, just as he'd done dozens of times when he was training.

They all knew there was no going back. If they were ever going to get Hitler, today was the day.

The craft's hull shook as its engines fired. Jim turned to his men as the craft trundled into the channel to join the massive flotilla gathering out there on the waters.

"Fourth Platoon, Dog Company!" he barked.

Tight, pale faces turned toward him. Many of them were clinging desperately to the guide ropes strung along the side of the craft, struggling to keep their balance under the weight of their gear and the heavy swells. There was no joking at all, and very little talk. Nervous cigarettes sprouted here and there to help men calm their nerves, while others prayed, or simply just closed their eyes and remembered their loved ones.

"All right, let's go over it all again. Ellis, how do we get off this thing?" Jim asked.

"The landing craft's gonna hit the beach, and then once it hits sand, we fire the grapples and drop the ramps."

"How do we identify our target? Illinois?"

The dark-skinned private panted with nervousness and struggled to meet his sergeant's eyes.

"We're lookin' for *Pointe du Hoc,* sir."

"Describe it," Jim ordered.

"White cliffs with about fifty feet of sand in front of 'em."

"And once we're up the ropes?" Jim asked. "Mitchell?"

"Sarge, we're, uh," Mitchell said, squeezing the words from between his trembling lips. "Up on top of the cliffs, we're supposed to locate the artillery batteries and destroy each of 'em with a thermite grenade down the barrel."

"Good. All right, men, just hang in there. Today's the day we make history," Jim said encouragingly.

Pushing toward the center of the craft, Jim balanced himself against the shuddering waves, as if the deck was the sweat-soaked ring canvas of his old life. He shook each man's hand, patted shoulders, and offered kind words until he reached the pilot's station at the craft's rear.

"Hold on, boys!" the British lieutenant called. "We're coming free of the harbor."

Jim seized a handle as the full force of the sea shook their craft. In front of him, Private Jenkins bent over and loosed his stomach on the deck. Jim patted the man's back, met the eyes of those watching, then stood on his tiptoes to peer into the fog-shrouded waters that surrounded the French coast. Hundreds of vessels of all shapes and sizes surrounded them. It was the largest amphibious assault in history, but he eyed the heavy waves with trepidation. This would be nothing like their training.

"All right, you men, listen up!" Jim called as he worked his way back through his troops. He wanted them facing him instead of what lay ahead. The Rangers tried to straighten and push away their nausea. They needed him now, more than ever, and he could not let them down.

"You've all received the best possible training that Uncle Sam's Army could provide, and you've been selected for this mission because you're the hardest, toughest SOBs in this entire war. Now I hope to the good Lord Jesus that I never see Carrickfergus again, but that cliff was taller than what we're gonna be up against here pretty soon, and we climbed that bastard until we could do it in our sleep."

He heard scattered laughter as a few men loosened up.

"As a lot of you know, I was a fighter back home, and I still am, I guess. What you learn as a fighter is that you're always afraid. Now, we don't know what's gonna be on the other side of this ramp, but you all know exactly what to do. You take that fear, and you use it to push yourself. You stay with me, you follow the mission and do everything you've been trained to do, and hopefully we'll all make it through this. Now, if you find yourself hiding somewhere because you got too scared to carry on, you just remember that your sergeant is gonna be out there front and center givin' those Krauts hell, and I can't do it without you. No matter how scared you are, you're just gonna have to swallow that fear and keep on goin', no matter what it takes. Now, are you with me?"

"Yes, Sergeant!" the platoon called.

"I CAN'T HEAR YOU!"

"YES, SERGEANT!" they roared at the top of their lungs.

The boat rocked and shook as the platoon readied themselves. As Jim made his way back to the front of the craft, swells splashed over the side and drenched his boots. Up ahead through the thick veil of fog he could just barely make out the dim shape of the French coastline. The navy's batteries opened full force, the thuds of their guns beating like fists against his chest.

"Now let's go get those Nazi bastards!"

18

October 2014

München, Germany

"And you're sure?" Yanis asked Erich across the table. "There was never anything mentioned anywhere?"

"A history professor could spend a lifetime publishing papers on the Nazis' ambitions and never cover them all," the older man said with a smile, "I've tried, believe me, and yet I've never heard anything about this *Der Dom.*"

"I'll just have to keep looking then," Yanis said with a heavy sigh.

The sound of silverware on plates filled the restaurant, while Yanis sat there reflecting quietly on what his next move should be. He chewed his codfish without tasting it and watched in awe as the sunset stained the distant Alps with hues of red, yellow, and orange. It had been a week since the embarrassment of the failed ski resort raid, and he couldn't forget Jillian's crestfallen silence on the ride back from Bad Tölz. All his online searching since then had been utterly useless. Erich had been his last lead, and now he was at a dead end. He was starting to think he should simply let the investigation go and head back home to Jerusalem, but the mystery of the desperate Enigma messages still gnawed at him.

"You know, Professor, that message was authentic. There's no doubt whatsoever that it was an official communication. A man gave his life trying to deliver it, so it had to be something of great importance."

"Oh, I believe you. If what you said about the circumstances of the find is true, then I absolutely believe you, but I can't tell you of anyone who studies Nazi history that has heard of this so-called *cathedral* before. Perhaps you should turn it over to the museum and let the experts—"

"You're saying I don't know what I'm doing?" Yanis asked. "You're saying it isn't important?"

"Heavens no! I'm not saying that at all—" Erich started.

Yanis irritably tossed his fork onto the plate, startling the other diners around them.

"I'm sorry," Yanis said after he took a deep breath to calm himself. He was used to numbers, where even unpredictability had an equation. This was a mystery that he just couldn't solve, and it involved real people—*his* people—and the one person who could help was unlikely to trust him again after the previous fiasco.

"What makes this find so important to you?" the old professor asked. "It's not even in your field."

Embarrassed, Yanis studied the remains of his dinner. His holiday time had nearly run out, and Jillian hadn't returned his calls. Miriam had told him that she was turning away other bookings so that he could stay longer, but also that she was happy to have him stay there for as long as he liked.

As the buzz of diners resuming their conversations swirled up around him once again, he listened to all the talking and the laughing, and gathered his coat more tightly against the chill that crept up from the river.

"It's just … somehow, I know that this matters, and I can't let go of the feeling that I was meant to find that plane," Yanis said.

"Well, you certainly are a very persistent young man. I made some inquiries after you contacted me. You've been in touch with every possible expert who could help you in this country, so I guess that trotting me out of my nice, quiet retirement was your, how do the Americans say it? Your Hail Mary? There is no shame in hitting a dead end, Yanis. You'll make a name for yourself in mathematics someday."

"But I want to know the truth. I'm not interested in making a name for myself …" Yanis said, but he trailed off as Erich tapped his napkin down on the table and got to his feet. Yanis followed the older man's eyes to the door where the host was just greeting a newly arrived couple. They both had sharp German features and were impeccably dressed. He was in a fall gray suit that was cut tight against his shoulders, and she was in a black dress that clung to a body that was well-toned, especially for someone in her forties. The woman's jewelry glittered as she held her husband's arm and smiled at the hostess.

"Martin! Maria!" Erich called to them. The couple turned toward Yanis' table, both breaking into a wide smile of recognition.

"Erich!" the man said as he came over and shook Professor Roth's hand, but his smile tightened when he turned to Yanis. "And who may I ask is this?"

"Oh, my manners!" Erich said. "May I present Yanis Miller? He's a math professor at Jerusalem Polytechnic. Yanis, these are the Steigers. They're my colleagues at the Polytechnic, and professors of theoretical and astrophysics, respectively."

Yanis smiled as he shook Martin's hand. Martin's grip clamped painfully over his, and the ghost of a flinch flickered at the edge of the man's narrow cheek.

Maria offered her hand, crowned with a pair of thick diamond rings, but withdrew her fingers before Yanis' lips could touch her knuckles.

"This is certainly a … pleasure," Maria said awkwardly. "Erich, we'd heard you were dining out tonight, and we hoped we might find you here."

"Ah yes, *bitte*, come join us," Erich said as he pulled a second table next to theirs. "The view is excellent, and Professor Miller was just telling me of a rare archaeological find."

"Are you sure?" Maria asked, almost in protest. "If Professor Miller would not mind?"

"Please," Yanis said. "I insist."

"*Wunderbar*," Erich said. "We will have beers. Yanis enjoys this part of our culture."

A glance passed between the couple, and they both sat like stiff mannequins. Maria even shifted her chair a few inches away from Yanis as the waiter set menus in front of them.

"Now, what's been keeping the two of you so busy lately?" Erich asked. The old man seemed oblivious to the tension within the couple. Martin snapped his napkin twice, and then swept it over his thighs. He still had barely even looked at Yanis.

"We have been working extremely hard," Martin said. "A new research initiative with a very tight deadline has come our way…"

"So, as you can imagine, we needed a night out to take our minds off the work for a while," Maria finished as the waiter approached. "A glass of wine please, and the rocket salad."

"The soup please," Martin said as he handed over their menus.

"Ah, a light dinner," Erich said. "The best at this hour. Who is working you so hard? Is it Bern again? Will their particle accelerator not wait?"

"No, it's not Bern. The client this time is … confidential," Maria said.

"Erich, we've talked of nothing but our work for weeks now," Martin said. "I am, however, most interested in hearing about your friend's find. Tell me Yanis, what brings a Jewish mathematician to Germany on an archaeological investigation?"

Yanis lifted the beer that had just arrived, took a long sip, and felt the crisp carbonation at the back of his throat. For some reason he just couldn't shake the unsettling feeling he was getting from these two. It almost felt as if he didn't belong at the same table with them, but he wasn't sure why.

"It was a hobby, actually," he finally answered. "I took the summer off to climb the Alps. Only, nature had other plans for me. I found a relic underneath the Blaueis glacier."

"Yes," Martin said. "Erich mentioned it to me the other day. A Nazi plane, wasn't it? With an Enigma machine?"

Yanis glanced at Erich, but the professor was too busy admiring Maria's bracelet to have paid much attention to anything else. He purposely hadn't shared the story of Jillian's involvement when he told the old man his story, so Erich would have had no idea how sensitive the information about *Der Dom* potentially was. It seemed a strange coincidence that this couple had suddenly decided to show up and inquire about what he'd found.

"I was just telling Yanis here that it's time for the Munich museum to take over, but he insists on puttering with the device," Erich said as he broke free of the bracelet's enchantment.

The waiter brought their food and set it down in front of them. Maria twirled her fork through her salad anxiously, though she didn't take a single bite. Martin didn't start eating either. He simply sat there smiling coldly, and Yanis was quickly growing tired of the discomfort it was causing.

"A person such as yourself must have already translated the messages, *ja?*" Martin guessed.

"Um, yes, I mean, the truth is that it's really quite a fascinating mystery. I turned to Erich for help, and—"

"And I've never heard of the code name *Der Dom,*" Erich said suddenly. "In all my studies about the Nazis, I've never heard of such a project. Oh, and the coordinates are now a ski lift. Isn't that what you said, Yanis?"

Yanis didn't answer. He was too busy staring at the tines on Maria Steiger's fork that had bent from her pressing them so hard against the plate.

"If you'll forgive me, I just remembered that there's a phone call I need to make," she said as she stood with a strange haste and quickly left the restaurant.

"Are you not hungry, Martin?" Erich asked. Professor Steiger glanced at Erich, but it seemed as if he had not comprehended the question. As soon as he noticed that Erich was looking at his soup, he realized what he must have said and lifted his spoon in such a mechanical way that it almost seemed rehearsed.

"My apologies. I'm afraid I was a bit preoccupied with something from work," Steiger said. He lowered the spoon and then brought more of the steaming soup to his lips, and then did it once more, as though he were making a particular show of eating his soup. This didn't escape Yanis' notice. Something was definitely wrong.

They ate and drank in silence, but after each sip of his beer, Yanis noticed Martin's cold glare slip away from him at the last second. Finally, when he couldn't take the tension any longer, he got to his feet.

"Leaving so soon?" Martin asked.

"If you'll please excuse me, I need to use the restroom," Yanis said as he turned and headed toward the bathrooms. As he maneuvered his way through the tables, he could feel Martin's eyes boring into his back like a pair of knives.

19

Yanis leaned over the sink and splashed some water on his face. He'd simply say he was tired and exit the dinner quickly. Erich's strange friends clearly had a problem with him, but that wasn't even the issue. They definitely knew something about *Der Dom*. As he stared at himself in the mirror and observed the water dripping down over his cheeks, he wondered if two astrophysicists could possibly be behind the plot that Jillian had described. They had to be involved somehow. But how?

He dried his hands and then paused at the door for a moment. He had to be smooth with his exit. He couldn't let them know his suspicions.

He threaded his way back through tables filled with diners chatting over their meals, relaxing with a beer, and enjoying a freedom that suddenly seemed all too dear. When he got back to his own table, he found that Maria Steiger had returned and seated herself in Erich's place. She was hunched close to her husband and whispering animatedly as he approached.

"Ah, Professor Miller," Martin said from behind a forced smile. "Erich offered his apologies. It seems that the beer has caught up with him."

"As has mine," Yanis said. "I'm afraid I have work to do as well. It was a pleasure meeting you both."

"Oh, but please, won't you stay for another lager?" Maria asked. "Bavaria has the best in the world."

"Of that I have no doubt, but I'm afraid I've had too much already this evening, so I'm going to head back now and relax a bit. It was a pleasure to meet you."

"The pleasure was ours," Maria said.

"Where are you staying, Professor?" Martin asked. "Perhaps we could offer you a ride?"

"I drove but thank you. I'm staying here in Munich for the moment, so it isn't far," he said. He shook both of their hands cordially and then after one final goodbye he left the restaurant. Even though he didn't glance back behind him, he could feel their cold eyes following him through the window until at last he was swallowed by the night.

* * *

He'd parked several blocks away and tightened his coat against the chill as he walked. It would be a long drive to Bad Tölz, and more than anything he needed some time to think about what had just happened. He was certain the Steigers knew about *Der Dom* and had come to find out just exactly how much he'd figured out. But he had no proof, and until he did, he couldn't call Jillian again.

Fog crept in from the river, dampening his footfalls and wrapping the streetlamps in wads of gauzed light, while azz music floated softly from someone's open window. He pressed forward urgently, eager to put as much distance between him and the Steigers as possible.

Approaching his car, he fumbled with his keys and dropped them onto the cobblestone pavement. Grumbling, he squatted to fetch them. When he stood, he found a rather tall man blocking his path. A scar bunched the man's lip, and he wore a black t-shirt under a black blazer.

"Are you Professor Yanis Miller?" the man asked.

"Yes, I am," Yanis said before he thought better of it. A light wind scuttled a scattering of leaves down the street between them. "What can I do for you?"

"The Steigers would like to extend you the courtesy of a ride home," the man said. He stepped to the side and gestured toward a waiting sedan with black tinted windows that hid its interior.

"That's very kind of you, but I have a rental."

"This is not a request," the man said.

"Why? Who are you working for?"

"I will be happy to answer your questions in the car."

Yanis' pulse thumped and the adrenaline began to flow as muscles honed by years of mountain climbing suddenly tensed. He considered the man blocking his path, and the certainty of what he was facing became all too apparent. The downed plane, the weapons shipments Jillian had been pursuing, and now the Steigers ...

Balling his keys in his fist, he sprung forward and swung at the thug's face. The punch connected, and the sharp metal of the keys slashed the man's cheek. As the hulking man howled with pain, Yanis tore open the car door, jammed his key in the ignition, and then floored the accelerator.

Bullets shattered his back window and battered the rear of his car as he sped away. He sank as low as he possibly could into his seat as he fled, praying with each passing second that none of the bullets would hit their mark. *Der Dom* was real. The Nazis were making a comeback, and he was the only one who knew their faces.

Even though his hands were shaking, he finally managed to dial Jillian's number. She didn't answer, as per usual, but he hoped she would at least listen as he steadied his voice and pieced together as much of the story as he could.

Later that night when Jillian heard the message, she was struck by the remarkably even tone of his voice. A typical civilian would have been falling apart in the face of this sort of danger. *Was he reliable? What kind of person was he really?* She knew so little about him. Sitting down at her desk, she opened her laptop's browser and typed the word cryptology into the search.

* * *

March 1943

Bad Tölz, Germany

Blood red banners fluttered in the spring breeze that wafted down the mountains. On Keck's orders, the Junkerschüle's cadets had spent three days hanging the swastikas from every building and lamp post in the town, and now, as Hitler's car prowled slowly down the road behind the school's drum corps, Keck watched the roaring citizens toss flowers and offer their *Hitlergrub* with a sense of pride. This was what Germany would be, now and forever.

"*Mein Herr,*" an aide called from behind him. "Regarding the orders you have issued, the *Sturmbannführer* you transferred requests an audience so that he may know why he and his command have been reassigned."

Keck turned from his vantage point above the school's gates and let out a heavy sigh. He had not anticipated dealing with this level of detail upon his return, and the logistical demand on him had become unrelenting, but this matter needed to be handled delicately.

"Tell the officer that his keen eye is needed to the west," Keck said. "He is the best man to help us ferret out any Allied spies that are looking into our highly secret operations. Also tell him that the *Reichsführer* himself will be watching his performance."

"*Jahwol,*" the *Schütze* said as he clicked his boot heels and jogged away.

"Will I?" Himmler asked from the shadows. Keck could not restrain his smile as the drum corps marched underneath the gate at his feet. He followed Himmler down the stone stairs to meet the man he'd come to save.

"But of course, *Mein Herr.* I promised to amaze you, did I not?"

20

Hitler smiled, rising from his half-eaten salad to greet the handsome Nazi who approached. The man had slicked his blond hair against his scalp and walked with the broad shoulders of a movie star. He wore a double-breasted suit with the Nazi armband tightening the fabric of his left arm, but when he stopped at the side of the table, he clicked his heels with long-practiced military precision and then saluted.

"*Heil* Hitler!" he said loudly, his bellow reaching the thick rafters of the school's dining hall.

Hitler waved his wrist, and the man's smile grew. Keck had spent the last two hours with his idol, growing more and more amazed at the man's ability to inspire and motivate those around him. Hitler was an incredible treasure, but one that had to be protected from the excesses and sycophants that Keck knew lurked at every turn.

"Speer, it's delightful that you could come," Hitler said.

"*Danke, Mein Herr.* Things are going well with the production effort."

"Thanks to your excellent work," Hitler replied.

"I will do my best to continue the effort. And with the help of the *wunderwaffe* that *Herr* Himmler informed me of ..." he said, nodding in Himmler's direction. Himmler stood and reached out to shake his hand.

"Albert, it is good to see you. May I introduce ..." he said as he turned to where Keck stood, frowning slightly as he remembered the one request that Keck had made. "For now, let's just say he's a personal friend. Due to the sensitive nature of what he has brought us, he wishes to remain anonymous for the moment, but I can assure you that he has been thoroughly vetted. He possesses the most sterling Aryan heritage and loyalty to our cause."

"A man able to keep his identity from the SS *and* his *Führer*," Speer said as he greeted Kristock. "This must be a man of true talent. What may I call you?"

"I am fortunate, and truly pleased to meet you," Keck said. "As for my name, simply call me a friend. To me, the success of National Socialism trumps any personal recognition."

"Well-spoken my friend," Speer said as he sat next to Keck on the side of the table facing Hitler. Waiters surrounded them, bringing wine, mineral water, and a rack of boar that was served alongside the *Führer*'s steamed vegetables. Noise filled the cavernous hall as the officers and school faculty all reengaged in their previous conversations.

"You know, I will be glad to call you my friend if you truly have the wonder weapons that you claim," Speer said as he leaned toward Keck.

"Tomorrow morning, it will be my pleasure to show you," Keck said.

"Albert," Hitler said as he patted his lips with a napkin, "this man may give you a run for your money if the *SS* has been truthful with us."

Keck glanced at Himmler, who returned his smile. The thrill of experiencing the highest level of power in the Reich filled him, and as he sipped wine better than any he'd ever tasted, chewed on the delicious boar, and listened to the conversation around him, he could not wait to begin his work.

"The *SS* is not, however, known for its truth telling," Speer said as his knife scraped his plate. "Is it, my friend?"

"No, *Herr* Speer," Keck said. "We are known for our lethality."

* * *

The next morning, Keck led Hitler, Himmler, and Speer through the dewed parade grounds south of the school, and all the way to the forest at the edge of the field. The sun was just crowning the mountains, and they were all wearing thick coats with mufflers to guard against the morning chill.

"Please tell me again why we're taking this nature walk?" Speer asked. The head of German manufacturing was obviously hung over and frowned at the mud that was clutching at his boots.

"I have found, *Herr* Speer, that demonstrations are much more powerful than any explanation I can provide," Keck replied. After a dozen more meters, he stopped at a thick tree trunk and peered up into the canopy. The branches shook as a young *Schütze* dropped out of the tree and brushed off his hands. When he realized who stood in front of him, his eyes widened, and he sprung immediately to rigid attention. Hitler waved his wrist, but the boy kept his palm in the air.

"At ease, *Schütze*," Keck called to him. The boy fell to parade rest, clasping his hands behind his back. "Please explain to *Herr* Speer why we are here."

"Because this tree is exactly four kilometers from *Junkerschüle's* parade grounds, *Mein Herr.*"

"Yes, how fascinating," Speer grumbled sarcastically.

"And what were you doing just now?" Keck asked.

"Placing a canister of petrol at the top of the tree so that we can confirm a hit."

"From four kilometers?" Hitler asked.

"Are you insane?" Himmler whispered at Keck's side.

"Yes, *Mein Führer*," Keck said. He winked at Himmler, and then turned to face the forest. "Come, let us begin the demonstration."

The private nodded and trotted into the trees. A moment later, the throaty sound of an engine roared to life and a clanking *Panzer* lurched from the shadows to stop in front of them. Keck seized the private's hand and lifted himself up onto the tank, then helped Hitler, Himmler, and Speer aboard. He cupped his hands around his mouth and yelled to the men as the tank trundled out of the forest toward the school.

"This is one of *Herr* Speer's new *Panzerkampfwagen* prototypes known as the Tiger II. It is the fastest, most powerful *Panzer* in our armed forces. 180-millimeter-thick armor, and an 8.8-centimeter gun capable of a kill at just over two and a half kilometers."

"How do you know this?" Speer demanded. "No one should know these specifications yet!"

Keck watched as Hitler patted the iron underneath him. The *Führer* pursed his lips and nodded as though he were satisfied with the machine's great strength. He also knew that Hitler was listening to their exchange, curious to see if they'd be able to operate together.

"I must ask you to accept that I know many things," Keck said. "Among them, the top speed of this *Panzer* across country is twenty kilometers per hour. Private!"

Gears ground below him, and the *Panzer* shifted into a bouncing roll across the meadow. The breeze was cold but pleasant, and Keck enjoyed the feeling of his closeness to the tank's power. It was a well-built machine, at least for its day. It was the best that Speer had been able to provide, and he smiled as the Minister of Armaments and War Production scrabbled for a handhold to avoid falling off the tank, while Hitler sat placidly next to the turret.

The Tiger II reached the school's distant walls in a few minutes, and one by one they disembarked from the tank. Rather than taking the hand that Keck offered him, Speer leaped down into the mud beside him, spattering his boots.

"Terribly sorry," he smirked.

The tank's engine dropped to idle, and it was finally possible to use a normal speaking voice once more.

"Private," Keck called. "The tree, if you please."

"You said the range was two and a half kilometers," Hitler said. "That tree is four."

"Yes, that's correct, *Mein Führer*, but I believe that this is necessary for the demonstration."

The *Panzer's* turret whined as its gun tracked toward the grove. An aide distributed binoculars, and Keck's group focused on the tree with the petrol can attached to it.

"You may want to cover—" Speer began, but just then the Tiger unleashed a massive thunderclap as it fired. Muzzle wash flooded out in front of them, and Keck led the group to the side so that they could study where the shell had impacted the parade ground two kilometers distant.

"So, you brought us out here to show us how to kill worms?" Speer asked.

Keck nodded to an aide, and the man raised a green flag above his head.

A new sound suddenly emerged from the distant forest, a throaty scream that none of the others had yet had the opportunity to hear. The trees shook as a massive shape took form within them. Himmler's, Speer's, and Hitler's mouths fell open in unison as they refocused their binoculars.

"You won't need those in a moment, gentlemen," Keck said.

A strange green machine burst from the trees, moving at a far different pace than the clanking crudity of the Panzer. Its turret and tracks showed it to be a tank, but to the eyes of the others, the boxy shapes jutting from its armor made no sense. A series of snorkels jutted out next to the tank's main gun, while strange, chunked rectangles topped with a football-shaped white sphere cluttered the turret.

The machine covered ground at an impossible speed. So much so that everyone but Keck took a startled step back as it neared. When it came to within twenty meters in front of them, the tank shifted into an expert turn without slowing, and then came to a purring rest just beside the *Panzer*.

"*Mein Gott,*" Hitler said.

"Where did you get this?" Speer asked.

"All will be explained in due time, I assure you. Captain!" Keck called.

The strange machine's hatch burst open, and a tanker wearing the crushed cap of the *Panzer* grenadiers and the bars of a captain rose from its heart.

"*Ja, Herr Sturmbannführer?*"

"The demonstration, if you please."

The man nodded and dropped back into his compartment. In the blink of an eye, the new tank's gun rose and fired. Its roar echoed throughout the valley like the launch of a rocket, and Keck held back a smile as Speer and Himmler ducked involuntarily. His respect for the *Führer* grew as Hitler's attention remained solidly on the range. Four kilometers distant, a fireball erupted at the top of the tree line.

"I bring you the weaponry of the future," Keck said. "Machines so advanced and powerful, that none can stand in their way. Private!" he called.

The cadet nodded and dropped back into his *Panzer*. The suddenly antiquated machine lurched forward at a speed that had once been the fastest among any tank in the world.

"With these weapons, our total victory will be assured," Keck said.

"But how is this possible?" Speer asked. "Who has made this?"

The strange tank allowed the *Panzer* a kilometer head start, then roared in pursuit. In less than a minute, it caught the sluggish *Panzer*, circled it twice, and then stopped as the *Panzer* rolled toward to the tree line.

"I offer these and many other great gifts freely, on one condition."

"Albert," Hitler said. "You will give this man everything he needs. If it takes the entire production machinery of our government, we *will* have these machines."

"*Ja, Mein Führer*, but what is his condition?" Speer asked.

"My condition is that we maintain the project's utmost secrecy," Keck said. He felt like he'd made his point, but he really wanted to drive it home, so he motioned to his aide once again. The aide raised a black flag, and something was signaled back in the distance. The occupants of the Tiger II tank leapt from the vehicle, not even pausing to stop its engine.

Speer looked at Keck with contempt, and as he opened his mouth to speak, the new tank's turret tracked the *Panzer* and fired. The Tiger II prototype seemed to melt away under the crushing firepower, and a few seconds later its magazine exploded, showering the surrounding area with the shrapnel of the past.

"Terribly sorry about your tank," Keck said, throwing a cocky glance at Speer before he turned his attention back to Hitler. "I can win the war for you, *Mein Führer*, but it must be done as I say. If anyone else learns of our secret, it could spell the end of the Reich."

"Anything you need will be at your disposal," Hitler said.

"*Danke, Mein Führer*," Keck said with a polite nod.

21

July 1943

Southampton, England

"Wolcott!" his section head bellowed down the hallway. "Get in here!"

David hurried toward the open door, clutching the folder he'd only started compiling the day before as he wracked his brain trying to catch any little detail he might have missed about the strange case.

Outside, the sun was shining. It wasn't even half-past eleven on a hot summer day, but the black-painted windows of the Special Information Services headquarters let in only a tense, oppressive grayness. The Blitz had largely ended, but no one in the section honestly believed that Hitler would not come again.

Knocking into the doorjamb with his shoulder, David nearly dropped the folder. Staunton's irritated jowls were already flushed an unhealthy pink, and his superior's eyes burned at the new indignity of working with someone as clearly incompetent as David Wolcott.

"Still learning my way around, aren't I?" Wolcott said with an awkward grin as he closed the door behind him and joined Staunton's interrogation. The intelligence chief was legendary for his foul humor, and today's coming explosion felt as if it would turn epic.

"Free medical service courtesy of His Majesty, but this addled git still makes no sense to me," Staunton grumbled. "See if you can ring anything out of him."

David licked his thumb, opened his folder, and scanned all that they knew about the mysterious man who sat under guard across the table from him. Heavy bandages ringed the man's head, and he was grimacing with the effort of sitting for so long after his surgery. Wolcott dropped the folder to the desk and tented his fingers.

"Pulled from the channel, were you? A wrecked skiff it says here," he read from the page. The man nodded. "And the boy who was with you, the one you say has your bag and can prove your story. Where'd he go?"

"I don't know. He was scared," the man said. He was speaking through clenched teeth; his jaw had been wired shut after the doctor removed the bullet and cleared the resulting infection. It was strange to see a man speak with no movement other than his lips. Almost as strange as the man's story.

"Where are you from?" David asked. "Egypt? Syria?"

"Israel."

"I didn't catch that." Staunton said. David opened his folder and checked the third page.

"ISRAEL," the man repeated as loudly as he could through his clenched teeth.

"Yes, Israel," David said. "A Jewish state that is to be created after, what did you call it, Mr. Miller? The Holocaust?"

"Yes," Miller said. Their subject's eyes sparkled with an intensity David had rarely seen in his interrogations, and he found himself leaning forward, surprised at how drawn he'd become to the man's story.

"So how does it all end?" David asked.

"I've already told you," Miller said. "Germany lost. Operation Overlord was a success. Hitler killed himself a year later and Germany surrendered."

"A wonderful fairy tale, isn't it, Wolcott?" Staunton said dryly.

Across the desk the man's eyes flared, not with anger, but with desperation. The subject's lucidity was what drew David to him. His story was complete bollocks, and though it was obvious that he believed it with every fiber of his being, nothing else in the report pointed to insanity.

"What would you do if you were me, Mr. Miller?" David asked. His SIS instructor had taught him to use questions like these to gauge a suspect's capacity for empathy, and this Miller person showed a clear understanding of what his captors were trying to do.

"If I were you, I'd ask to see the evidence. Which you already know I haven't got."

"Yes, the boy that ran off. We have a witness who says he was carrying ..." David said as he flipped through his folder. "Yes, here it is. He was carrying a small rucksack. And that's the bag you say has the machines from the future, like a computer that fits in your hand, and the evidence of alien technology."

"You're mocking me," Miller said.

"No sir, I'm most certainly not!" Staunton said sarcastically.

"We're simply trying to understand what's happened. That's all," Wolcott said. "You've given us information that sounds credible, but it's impossible to verify. If you could be more specific about troop deployments, commanding generals, that sort of thing, it would be easier to establish the veracity of your story. As it is, we're left with—"

"Eccentricities," Staunton finished for him.

"You have to believe me," Miller pleaded, his face mottled with the effort of conveying his point. "Hundreds of thousands of people are going to die if you don't. Your soldiers, my people. There won't be any stopping them."

"Because of the alien time travel device," Staunton said. "The one they used to take the weapons from ... when did he say, Wolcott?"

David was watching Miller's face, and somehow the decision Staunton had already made about what would happen to Miller didn't feel right. Rationally, David understood that he was experiencing the simple desire to help a fellow man in need, and that he couldn't stop the procedure without any credible evidence, but there were so many hints of truth in what the man said. That, plus the fact that the doctor had removed a *German* bullet from the man's jaw, all left him feeling that this man was, in fact, telling the truth.

"Wolcott?"

"The year 2014, sir," David said.

"The Nazis killed six million of my people!" Miller seethed. "They have modern weaponry… things you've never even seen. You won't be able to stop them. They'll know what you're planning. Please, you have to understand!"

"Glasses that let you see in the dark," Staunton said. "Tanks that drive fifty miles an hour. I understand just fine, Mr. Miller," Staunton said as he leaned back in his chair and nodded to the guards on either side of the wounded man. "Take him to Bethlem Royal."

"The asylum, sir?" Wolcott asked. "I'd thought—"

"I saw Dachau," Professor Miller crowed from behind his clenched teeth. As the soldiers lifted him by the armpits, the prisoner kicked the table and knocked it back into Wolcott's stunned chest. "You have to believe me!"

David sat in the dim light, listening to the man's strangely muffled scream recede down the corridor until the stairwell door banged and silence filled the hall. Beside him, Staunton stood, sighing under the effort of heaving his own bulk.

"War isn't good for the public's psyche," the section chief said as he reached for the door. "Fancy a spot of tea, Wolcott?"

"Uh, yes, sir. Yes, of course."

"You can't let that man's stories get to you. If we believed everything the loonies told us, we'd have allied ourselves with Hitler and fought the Russians!"

* * *

November 2014

The Zitternberg

Martin Steiger pushed his foot to the floor, urging his Maserati forward up the winding road that led toward *Der Dom*. Unexpectedly delayed by his associates' continued failure to locate Yanis Miller, he needed to make up ground as the sun set among the Alps. The *King Under the Mountain* was many things, most of which would be revealed to the others tonight, but patient was not one of them.

The mountains burned orange, then violet, and then faded to nothingness as the sun disappeared beneath the horizon, leaving him with only the glow of his headlights to guide him.

He flew past the occasional van topped with skis, the tourists and climbers who flocked to Bavaria, oblivious of its secrets. What incredible wonders had Keck opened to him these past few months? And after so much hard work, so many days without sleep, the mystery of an alien race and the resurrection of the Third Reich lay within their grasp.

The other traffic fell away as he turned onto the little-used spur that would bring him close to the *Zitternberg*. An orange and white gate appeared in the distance, and he reached it in the space of a breath. The guard stepped half out of his station as he approached, just enough to show Martin that he was armed. Then, recognizing the professor's face in the lowered window, the man nodded, and the gate rose.

The official explanation for the activity at the *Zitternberg* was that the Steigers had begun development of a resort on property that had been in his family for generations. As Martin whisked through the night, his face lit by the unearthly green dashboard light, he smiled at how close to true the lie was.

His headlamps splashed across the chrome and fascia of the sleek luxury cars from all over Europe that filled the facility's parking lot. He parked at the rear, nodding to the hulking security guards who doubled as drivers. A few of the guests stood outside their cars, clutching pale hands to smoldering cigarettes. Steiger nodded to these men as he passed, turning up his collar against the cool wind pouring down the mountain. Car doors opened and slammed like gun shots behind him, and the Fourth Reich's footfalls followed him up the lot's dry gravel.

Stopping underneath the boom of one of the earth-moving machines, Martin turned to face the glares of his assembled membership. They rubbed their hands together, flicked ash into the darkness, and glanced at each other to take a headcount so they could establish who was missing. Martin held them there for a few moments, feeling his own excited trembling flush away the cold.

"You have been summoned," Martin said. "You will follow me."

"Why should we do that?" a voice called from the darkness.

Martin glared at Baldwin. The man had proven adept at spiriting away anti-aircraft weapons from the crumbling Russian military but had yet to learn respect.

"You were comfortable before, Baldwin, *ja?* I see you here today with a new driver and a new car, the cost of which would buy some in Munich a house," he said, pausing to listen to the wind crackle in the dry branches around him. Behind him, the boom groaned as though it were eager to return to work. "Remember who gave you this good fortune. You are to meet him once more tonight, and if he asks more of you, you shall give it."

"And if I'm fat and happy enough already?" Baldwin asked.

"Then everything will end," Martin said. "In much the same way it did for those others in Bad Reichenhall."

22

Maria waited for Martin just inside the tunnel. Her fur jacket fluttered as she ran toward him and threw her arms around his neck. He kissed her for a long moment, feeling her cheek grow cold against his, then released her and drew in a breath scented with the lilac of her perfume.

"All is ready?" he asked.

"Yes. It's time," she answered.

Behind her, the tunnel glowed with a soft blue light. It had been greatly expanded in the past several months, and the grade that led to it had been strengthened. The tunnel mouth was cut wide and tall, smoothed with concrete to allow entrance to the hundreds of deliveries that had entered the mountain.

"Excellent," he said, smiling approvingly. "Then I believe it's time to begin."

He stepped aside, waving the members of the Fourth Reich into the tunnel. He smiled at their cautious footsteps over the newly poured cement, their surprise at the warmth that greeted them, and the murmuring light that danced like neon in the distance. Every few feet, black swastikas whispered from the blood red flags of Nazi Germany. Several of the group reached out to touch the banners, as though they were trying to convince themselves that it was all real.

Maria separated from Martin's grasp and pressed a control mounted to the salt stone. The great tunnel doors swung shut behind them, sealing with a booming clang that echoed through the tunnel.

"Steiger, what do you think you're doing?" one of the art sisters asked in a shrill pitch.

"Martin is keeping a secret," came an answer from an unseen source. It was the same voice they'd heard in Bad Reichenhall, calling from the far end of the tunnel. "A secret that you will now witness with your own eyes."

Music suddenly filled the tunnel. At first, Martin couldn't place the thundering horns and martial beat, but as the lyrics came, he recognized the *Horst-Wessel-Lied*. It was the Nazi national anthem that had been banned for so long in the Vaterland. Now it was resurrected, just as so many other things long-buried soon would be.

In front of them, a man stepped out from behind a group of banners. He wore a black SS uniform with glittering silver death's heads on each collar. A swastika shone from the top of his cap, and he came to an easy parade rest next to a pool that had been carved in the concrete floor. Behind him, the strange scrawl of *Der Dom* rose and fell in its alien rhythm.

The portal had been closed for the occasion, but Martin still held his breath. Even after so many nights spent inside its workings, studying the time travel stasis device, the alien construction had never ceased to awe him. Exploratory shafts dug from other sections of the mountain had not yet begun to reveal the full scale of the craft.

"Ladies and gentlemen, you have carried out my instructions well, and it is because of this that I have called you here to celebrate," The King said as he gestured toward a robed table filled with wine. "Now we'll begin the final phase of our plan. But first, an initiation."

The man drew a small box from his pocket, struck a match, and then dropped the flame into the pool at his feet. Flames erupted in a violent roar before quickly dying down to a glimmer at the concrete edges.

"My name is *Sturmbannführer* Kristock Keck. I have used the machine behind me to travel forward in time from 1945, the period of history when our great Reich last trod the Earth. You have been helping me to change that despicable history, and as a symbol of my gratitude, I invite you to join my *Schutzstaffel*."

Maria was the first to step forward, and while the others around her shouted questions and expressed their disbelief, she simply joined Keck in silence. The *Sturmbannführer* offered Martin's wife his hand as she slipped off her heels and laid her coat to the side. She then followed him to a table near the pool. Keck raised a silver chalice to her lips as the members of the Fourth Reich fell quiet once again, and Martin could just see the dark liquid within.

"Drink ... in remembrance of what will come again," Keck said. Maria's throat worked as the wine passed her lips, and then Keck replaced the chalice and led her to the head of the pool with his outstretched hand. Blue flame still curled at the pool's edges, but when Maria's foot touched the water she did not cry out.

"Face your comrades as you lie back," Keck ordered. Martin watched his wife tilt backward until she floated in the pool. Keck knelt and pressed Maria's forehead under the water, whispering an invocation too softly for Martin to hear. The professor held his breath, not fully trusting Keck despite everything the man had done for him.

Maria's hands clenched, and her feet thrashed out of the pool. She tried to rise, but Keck's hand held her face underwater as he continued his ritual. Martin pushed the others out of the way, running toward his wife, but just as he reached the pool Keck released Maria and she emerged, gasping for breath as the blue light of *Der Dom* sparkled off her glistening skin.

"Be still, Martin. This is simply so we may remember how close we came to our dreams flickering out," Keck said. Maria stepped out of the pool and stood steaming beside him. A puddle of blackness the same color as the wine spread at her feet.

"Now ... if you please," Keck said. After meeting his wife's triumphant gaze, Martin stepped forward and entered the pool.

23

One by one the other members of the Fourth Reich endured the ritual. They all remained strangely quiet until right near the end, when Baldwin muttered something just before his lips fell under the water.

Keck's hand froze in the air for a moment, and then the *Sturmbannführer* slapped his hand down on Baldwin's forehead and held him firmly under the water. Martin did not hear what was said, but it didn't sound German. Baldwin thrashed hard as bubbles rose violently to the surface above where his mouth was. One of his hands shot glistening from the pool to grasp at Keck's wrist, but the *Sturmbannführer* held the bigger man down with ease as he chanted his incantation.

After nearly a minute, Keck had still not released the man. The others whispered among themselves, until finally Maria stepped forward.

"We will need him for what you have planned, *Herr* Keck," Maria said.

The Nazi's jaw tightened as the tendons in his wrist stretched against the skin.

"*Mein Herr* ..." Martin said.

Finally, Keck released Baldwin. The arms dealer came bursting to the surface, drew a heaving breath, and then spewed out numerous curses in the guttural slur of Romani. Quickly he crawled out of the pool and then stood heaving next to Martin.

"He tried to kill me!" Baldwin shouted breathlessly in German.

"He may very well have, and I suggest you think long and hard about how you may recapture his loyalty if you want to live beyond this evening," Martin said coldly.

* * *

Even filled with wine, the members of the Fourth Reich passed quietly into the darkness after the tunnel doors opened.

"Tanks?" one of them said to Baldwin as the pair passed Martin. "He expects us now to steal tanks from the Americans?"

"Stuttgart is a difficult target, but the ammunition travels separately under much heavier guard. The tanks they simply ship by commercial rail," Baldwin explained.

"If we do this, it will mean war," the other said as he passed from Martin's sight.

"Yes," a voice behind Martin whispered. "Yes, it will."

Keck joined him at the tunnel threshold. The Nazi clasped his hands behind him and studied the cold stars overhead.

"It was a powerful evening, *Sturmbannführer*," Martin said.

"Will they do as I ask?"

"It will be difficult. Governments have more surveillance tools available to them now than they did in your time, but I think so, yes."

"There is weakness among them," Keck said. "There is pollution."

"Their grandfathers guarded these very tunnels," Martin said.

"And what if their grandfathers lied to me of their heritage?" Keck asked. "Shall I let their offense go?"

Maria reached Martin's side, still clutching a glass of wine in her hand. She'd drifted too close to *Der Dom* during the celebration, and the usual red lines of sunburn slashed her face as a result. She nuzzled next to Martin, resting her head in the hollow of his throat, and spoke to him softly.

"May we have at least one night to celebrate?" she asked in a voice slurred with wine and drowsiness. "One night away from work?"

Keck's head drew back, his eyes wide.

"I think perhaps you should both stay here tonight. Your work on the device's calibration is not yet complete, and my patience is not inexhaustible. Remember that when you'd offer leniency to those whose value will end. And remember your failure to secure Professor Miller before you grow too comfortable in your position. If I'd not had the foresight to falsify the coordinates I supplied to my dear *Reichsführer* before I left 1945, our efforts would already be lost," Keck said, and then he strode into the darkness, leaving Martin and Maria alone. Martin reached around his wife's shoulders, holding her close so that the winter air would not numb her still-damp skin. She let out a heavy sigh, and then took one last sip of her wine.

"Come … let's finish our work," she said as she turned and headed toward the alien ship, her husband following her.

* * *

June 1944

Normandy, France

The second platoon's landing craft dropped its ramp and opened a gateway straight into Hell. Cold surf clutched at Jim's legs as he struggled forward into the chest-deep water. He bellowed orders as the shocking cold numbed him but couldn't hear his own voice above the bombardment that struck from the sea to the shore and back again. The German guns on Pointe du Hoc were proving to be incredibly deadly and were possessed of an extraordinary range and accuracy that was absolutely ravaging the invasion fleet.

Waves slopped over his face, and Jim ended up swallowing a mouthful of briny water before he was able to regain his bearings and push ahead toward the cliffs to lead his men. All around him, boats were sinking and men were screaming, but his job was to get his men up onto the gray beach.

He looked behind him to check their progress and saw that their landing craft was listing badly. The British pilot who'd successfully landed them there now hung limply over the controls with a bullet hole that went straight through his helmet. Bodies floated all around him, and a hissing line of what could have been raindrops chewed up the left side of his platoon. Four men fell, floated, and screamed.

Beside him a private slipped and quickly disappeared beneath the waves. Jim fumbled for the man's collar, grabbed hold of it, and then pulled him upright out of the surf.

"Keep your weapon dry!" he screamed at the Ranger, then he pushed the man on ahead of him.

Haze obscured the cliffs as the big guns traded punches. Hulking metal hedgehogs lined the beaches, their rust bleeding into the sand. Men were falling. Dying. Screaming. The sheer scale of the landing awed Jim. His worst fight back in Brooklyn, where he'd been pushed against the ropes and pummeled nearly unconscious, had never been like this. Part of him wanted to turn back, to hide somewhere in the water, but raw determination drove him on.

There was a moment like this in every match he'd ever been in. It was a moment when the animal in him took over, and all thoughts of himself ceased. He had a job to do, and as he rose from the water and ran across the heaving sand, he was more determined than ever that nothing would get in the way of him and his men.

* * *

Jim sprinted through the deadly sheet of lead that swept the beach. A few Rangers from other platoons had beaten him to the rally point at the base of the cliff, then crouched frozen in the sand.

"Where are your ropes?" Jim called over the din of the battle.

"Sarge, our boat was hit!" one of them screamed back. "Where are yours?"

Jim stared back toward the water. Thousands of men were churning their way up the beach, working through the wire and obstacles, burrowing for cover behind the dunes. He saw an engineer run forward with two heavy Bangalores in either hand. The man shuddered and then stumbled as fountains of blood erupted from his face and shoulders. He pitched forward, twitching, while a medic scrambled for him. They were dying by the hundreds on the beach, and out on the churning waters, the fleet was suffering appalling losses.

Two more waves of reinforcements were supposed to follow the vanguard, but every DUKW and landing craft he could see seemed to be foundering or listing with a smoking hole in its hull. He felt the cliff behind him shudder as the German guns lashed out. A strange projectile like a rocket slammed into a DUKW that had been nearing the shoreline.

The amphibious vehicle erupted, its metal melting into a steaming pile as the pilot's charred corpse sagged into the water. All the other soldiers on the craft had been vaporized.

"What the hell have they got up there?" one of the Rangers called.

"It doesn't matter," Jim answered. "It's our job to take it out!"

Thirty or so Rangers had gathered at the foot of the cliffs, with more churning through the sand every minute. He found Mitchell and Ellis beside him and grabbed Ellis's shoulder.

"Did you see any grapples?" he yelled into the private's ear.

Ellis pointed twenty feet back down the beach to a mound of bodies clustered in the wire line. Jim could see two mortar tubes sticking out of the corpses. The fallen platoon had brought the backup plan, grapples that could be launched by hand if needed.

"All right," he screamed above the thunder of the battle. "Meeks," he called to a private laden with rope and pinions. "You get that rope ladder going. Find as much rope as you need. You!" he shouted as he pulled aside a weaponless corporal who'd been staring at the ridgeline. "Corporal, get yourself a weapon, and get the men organized. I want them to be prepared to keep the Germans from firing down on us."

The non-com nodded, his eyes seeming to refocus as he set about the task that was given to him.

"What about the grapples, Sarge?" Mitchell yelled.

"That's my job," Jim said as he moved away from the cliff.

* * *

Sand gripped Jim's boots, trying to trip him and pull him down so the Germans could fill him with lead. He knew he should zig and zag as he ran, but he'd always been a straight-ahead puncher. If the Germans were good enough shots to take him down, they were welcome to try.

The hedgehog obstacle was twenty feet away, then ten. As he ran, Jim passed incredulous men clinging to the sand for their lives, while others were screaming in pain with their guts in their hands. He even passed a chaplain who was giving what was left of some poor soul his last rites. The spatter of shrapnel and the chunky thud of bullets tearing metal and flesh were everywhere.

Something suddenly yanked his leg out from under him, and he fell chin first in the sand. Rolling over, he found a coil of barbed wire wrapped around his ankle. Bullets chewed the sand around him, and then hissed overhead. He laid perfectly still in the sand, hoping that if he played dead the Germans would move to another target. Before they did however, another GI skidded into the dirt with a wire cutter and clipped Jim free.

"Where the hell did you come from?"

"Seabees, at your service!" the man shouted, and then he got back to his feet and was about to run when Jim reached out and stopped him.

"Wait," Jim said as he clutched the naval engineer's shoulder and pointed at the man's pack. "What do you have in there?"

"Bangalores and grenades."

"Come with me. I could use a hand"

The Seabee nodded, joining Jim as he charged toward the obstacle.

The Ranger platoon had been devastated by machine gun fire, but a few of them were still operating, flattening themselves on the sand as best they could so they could return fire. Behind the safety of the rusting scrap iron, a medic worked on a screaming soldier who'd lost half his leg.

"The grapples," Jim called as he hefted one of the launchers. "Follow me."

The remaining Rangers clutched their helmets and rose with him. They were shouting at the top of their lungs, though whether it was out of courage or terror, Jim couldn't tell. Not that it mattered. They were one and the same now anyway.

Jim kept his head up as he ran, watching the edge of the cliff face as he drew closer. As soon as he determined that he was at the appropriate distance, he dropped down onto one knee, raised the launcher to his shoulder, tapped it once for luck, and then squeezed the trigger.

24

On board the *HMS Resilient*, Captain Tunnicliffe watched the Germans cut the Allied invasion to shreds while the fleet's ships foundered and sank all around him. Two kilometers offshore from Pointe du Hoc, he'd anchored his destroyer with its port broadside, facing the distant cliffs so that they could provide fire support. Just as he raised his glasses to scan the effectiveness of his ship' guns, something blurred from the cliffs, and a gout of oily smoke and flame rose from the vessel in front of them.

"What the hell are they hitting us with?" his XO called out. "That rate of fire at this range ... it's just not possible!"

"Well, it seems as if it's bloody well is possible, doesn't it, Alan?" the captain said.

Tunnicliffe scanned the mounds of corpses clogging the beaches, the landing craft peeled open by shells and mines, the DUKWs foundering against shore obstacles. The *Resilient's* guns boomed and shook the bridge as the captain searched the cliff face for any secondary explosions. Unfortunately, all he saw were whiffs of smoke rising from mounds of beaten dirt. A sudden chill overtook him as he watched a new streak of deadly flame erupt from the cliff.

"Incoming!" he screamed as he ducked behind the con station with the rest of his officers. By now, they all recognized the terrible whooshing roar of the projectiles that seemed to fly faster than rockets with the precision of a sniper rifle. Three seconds passed, then four. His heart throbbing, Tunnicliffe stood and eyed the *Resilient's* bow, not willing to believe his ship hadn't fallen victim to the Germans' incredible fire-power.

"Christ, it's the hospital ship," Alan said.

Captain Tunnicliffe turned to starboard and found that the *Land's End's* stern had been ripped away from its keel. Men and women in white bandages and coats screamed and tumbled from the shredded metal as the gray ocean rushed into the lower decks.

"Get our lifeboats out," the captain said.

"Yes, Captain."

"Sir, it's the admiral," the radioman called out. Tunnicliffe grabbed the phone from him and pressed it to his ear.

"Admiral Ramsay, sir," he said.

"All right, Fred. What do you see?"

"They're slaughtering us, sir. I don't know what Jerry's got on the cliffs, but I've lost a dozen ships to the damned things."

"You're faring better than most, I'm afraid. All right, we're going home. Turn your fleet around."

The deck shuddered once more as the *Resilient* returned fire.

"And the men on the shore?" Tunnicliffe asked.

"I'm afraid there's not much hope for them now," the admiral replied.

* * *

The ground shook, lifting Jim high into the air. He landed hard, then had to remove the sand from his mouth and eyes before he could get his bearings. His helmet was lost, and when he sat up amidst the sprawling men, he noticed a giant crater a few feet to his right. *What the hell could make a hole that big?*

"Sarge, look!"

The Ranger was pointing back in the channel. Jim shook his head, trying to make sense of what was happening. So many of the ships were sinking, battered by whatever the Germans had on those cliffs, but they should have been at least two miles out, well beyond range of anything the Germans could throw at them. As he watched, one of the invasion fleet's transports broke apart and sank to the bottom. How on earth was any of this happening?

"What are they doing?" Jim asked. "Those ships are moving!"

The Seabee squinted, then paled.

"The fleet's turning around!" he shouted.

"Oh my God, they're leaving us!"

"What do we do, Sarge?" someone asked.

Jim gazed up at the murderous cliffs, then back to sea. The channel was a mass of smoke and metal and flame. He met the panicked faces of those around him, men tangled in the grapple cables, and barbed wire, and the blood of so many others. How did he tell them they were all going to die ... that they'd failed?

"Sarge, what do we do now?" another Ranger shouted.

"Wait!" the Seabee cried. "Wait, I see something!"

* * *

"Lieutenant, visual astern if you please," Captain Tunnicliffe ordered. "Let's find a free course."

While Alan jogged to the rear of the bridge, the captain focused his binoculars on the thousands of men on the beach. The Germans and the tide would erase them all soon enough. Men he'd dined with, hoisted ales with in the pub, Yanks, Canadians, Brits, and even the poor French, all thinking that they had a chance, and now their only lifeline was running away.

"Captain, I've got a wake!" Alan screamed.

Tunnicliffe spun, finding his XO pointing at what looked like a long lipstick tube curling through the slate waters. The torpedo rose into a white froth as it met the hull of the Yank destroyer, *Vigilance*. It erupted in a massive bloom of shredded metal as the desperate nature of their situation suddenly became even more desperate.

"Jesus, they've got U-boats behind us," someone said.

"Get me the bloody radio," Captain Tunnicliffe ordered.

"Signal the engine room, full ahead if you please, Alan," he called with his eyes on the cliffs. "Helm, come to port 90 degrees."

"Sir?" his XO asked.

"I said full ahead, Mr. Pendleton!"

"Ah, yes, sir. Full ahead. Helm come 90 degrees to port."

As Alan repeated the order, the captain keyed his microphone. He had only one choice. If there was no retreat for the men on the beach, then there'd be no retreat for him.

"Destroyer Group B," he said. "This is Captain Tunnicliffe. We have U-boats behind us. Our orders are to withdraw to port, but I find myself unable to do so while the fight remains in doubt on the beach. Therefore, I am ordering the *Resilient* to improve our fire support for those boys, and I ask that you join me. I understand that this is in violation of the admiral's orders, but I intend to beach my vessel and do what we can rather than let the bloody Germans drown us. It's my sincerest hope to see you on shore for our court martial. Tunnicliffe out."

The destroyer's screws churned the sea underneath him. He felt the *Resilient* throb and surge as it came about and cut through the waves toward the swelling cliffs.

"Captain," his lieutenant called.

"If you're going to relieve me, Mr. Pendleton, at least have the decency to do it before I wreck the bloody ship."

"Not at all, sir. I just thought you may need this."

Captain Tunnicliffe turned to see the pistol in his XO's hand. A grim smile played at the corners of his mouth as he tucked the weapon into his jacket pocket.

"Right then," he said. "Bloody right. Let's go help our boys."

* * *

Jim watched the navy destroyers grow larger and larger. Their guns blasted shells overhead in a near continuous stream that chewed the

German blockhouses on the cliffs to pieces. For the first time since Jim had reached shore, the German barrage slackened.

"Jesus, they're gonna beach themselves," the Seabee said.

Turning, Jim found the Seabee still holding the thick rope from the launcher. High above them, both their grapples had miraculously cleared the summit and dug in. Jim drew his knife, slashed the rope clear of the launcher, and started forward.

"With me!" he called, "With me, before those boats run us down!"

His ragtag group of Rangers, infantrymen, and engineers sprinted toward the relative safety of the cliff base. Bullets combed the beach around them, jerking men backward, shredding their limbs, and sending them stumbling to lie still against their companions. Jim ran, screaming curses and wordless pleas while his boots chewed the sand until he was at a full-on sprint in front of his survivors.

* * *

Jim was hauling himself up the line when a horrific screeching tore the sky behind him and all of Pointe du Hoc shuddered as if an earthquake had struck. Dangling from the cliff, he saw that a hedgehog had torn a massive gash into the first destroyer's hull as it had plowed onto the beach. The ships had reached shore, and the Germans high on the cliffs couldn't depress their artillery enough to fire on them.

The destroyers' guns elevated and began peppering the ridgeline with heavy shelling. It was a desperate measure, a haymaker he never thought would land, but by God it was working.

A ragged second wave of men hit the ground from behind the beached ships. As he climbed toward the top of Pointe du Hoc, Jim could see many of the GIs making it through the obstacles and onto the beaches thanks to the naval cover. The Germans were damn good, but the Allied navy was no slouch either. He dug in his boots and hauled the rope through burning hands, now more determined than ever to even the score.

* * *

Ellis's legs slithered over the cliff face above him. The constant battering of the big guns shook dirt free every time they fired, sending Jim twisting into space before slamming him back against the cliff. It was like no weapon he'd heard before, but regardless of what it was, it was his job to destroy it. He pulled himself up and over the cliff side, fumbling for his rifle with his sore arms.

"Stay down! Stay down!" Ellis hissed as he gripped his sergeant's harness and hauled him forward. Jim crawled to a nearby cluster of rocks that hid them from the German position, then he peeked through a crack to assess the situation. Fifty feet ahead of their position, a strange muzzle stabbed out of an earthenware berm. The barrel swiveled with incredible speed, then erupted in an enormous jet of smoke and flame.

"Jesus, what the hell is that?" Ellis said next to him.

"It doesn't matter what it is," Jim said. "We've got a job to do."

He waited until twenty men had climbed the rope behind him, then cleared a space in the dirt so he could use his knife to sketch out a plan.

"Third Platoon, you run along the ridge to those trees there. Take cover, and then lay down fire on those Germans. Fourth, you're with me. We wait for Third to draw their attention, then head straight over the berm. Understood?"

The Rangers all nodded, crossed their hearts, and worked the bolts of their Garands.

"Good," Jim growled. "Now, let's make 'em pay for what they did to us on the beach!"

25

Third Platoon sprinted along a rise in the terrain, heading for the remains of the orchard Jim had outlined. The Germans' gray helmets dotted the far side of the berm, and Jim could see them pointing and yelling at the Rangers that had slipped past them, but it was too late. Third Platoon hit the dirt and fired, drawing the full attention of the German soldiers.

"Let 'em loose," Jim bellowed to the Fourth. Each man pulled his grenade pin and tossed the explosives into the German position. They waited a beat for the concussion, and then started sprinting toward their objective. Simultaneously, Jim heard a German screaming, the strange whine of the gun turret in front of him, and the battle roar of Private Ellis beside him.

A bleeding German popped up at the front of the berm. The man's eyes widened, and he started to yell something. Jim fired, hitting the Nazi in the throat.

As they closed on the position, he saw that the gun wasn't an artillery piece at all, but rather some kind of tank hidden behind the berm. It was a monster like nothing he'd ever seen before. He just hoped the thermite would work its magic, because if it didn't, he wasn't sure what else they could do to stop it.

More Germans appeared in front of the tank. The Rangers fired, mowing them down one by one while Jim heaved another grenade into the German position.

"Hit the deck!" he screamed. Rangers ducked for cover all around him, and a split second later the earth shook. Jim found his thermite grenade and rose to toss it into the tank's gun barrel. As he did, the ground shuddered once more and threw him sideways. The tank's engine had started, and its barrel was receding at incredible speed.

"No!" Jim called out. He started to climb up the berm, but his feet kept slipping on the soft earth.

"Sarge!" a voice shouted. Ellis held out his hand as he raced past. Jim tossed him the grenade and the private topped the berm.

"Cover him!" Jim called. He crawled to the top of the berm and saw the full battlefield in front of him for the first time. Bunkers and earthworks ran everywhere, and he saw hundreds of Germans sprinting between their positions. The true size and power of the tank was incredible; its slabbed armor and strange glimmering attachments seemed like something years beyond a Sherman, and the *Panzer* dwarfed Ellis as he ran toward it.

Ellis pulled the grenade's pin and lofted the explosive into the tank's muzzle. The *Panzer's* hatch unsealed, and a tanker rose to man the turret's machine gun. Bullets churned the earth around the Ranger as he spun and sprinted back toward the safety of the berm.

"Take that tanker out!" Jim screamed. "Take him out!"

Ellis ran, firing wildly behind him while the rest of Fourth Platoon peppered the German tanker just a few seconds before the strange tank erupted in flames.

"Ellis!" someone cried. "Ellis!"

As the smoke cleared, Jim watched the Ranger that should have been him writhe on the ground while the strange tank's ruptured barrel swung useless above him.

"Sarge!" someone yelled.

"Forward!" Jim cried, lifting himself over the berm. They'd finally put one gun out of commission. Now it was time to find the others.

* * *

June 1944

Berlin, Germany

Those who worked in the *Reichskanzlei* did not know his name, but they looked upon him in awe as *Sturmbannführer* Keck strode the Chancellery's marbled corridors. He'd predicted the Allied assault. He'd known its exact target despite all indications that it would fall elsewhere. With a man such as this on their side, the Thousand-Year Reich was within reach.

"*Herr* Speer has done a remarkable job with this building," Himmler remarked.

"If only he could do the same with metallurgy," Keck said.

They passed a squad of guards and entered the ground floor of the *Führerwohnung*. After an aide led them past a thicket of radio men and telephone operators, they entered the room that Hitler used as his military nerve center. A group of generals was already there, carefully studying a wall map of the force distribution in Normandy.

"They are contained, *Mein Führer*," Field Marshall von Rundstedt said. "The intelligence and weaponry we received has allowed us to anticipate and counter their every movement."

"If they are so contained, how then are they still on the beaches?" Hitler asked.

"*Mein Herr*, we are facing a force of significant size. It's comparable to the forces along the Italian front. The *Luftwaffe* has observed the American and British navies reinforcing their position, despite our heavy U-boat presence—"

"Were the weapons with which you were supplied insufficient, *Herr* General?" Himmler asked.

Von Rundstedt and the others turned to greet their visitors.

"Ah, Heinrich! And our *friend*. Many of my men owe their lives to you and your mysterious *Sturmbannführer*. I give you my thanks," von Rundstedt said as he shook hands with both of the SS men. "The limiting factor now is not weaponry *Herr Reichsführer*, it is men and material. Even the crudest rifle can kill, and the Allies have many."

"And the tanks?" Hitler asked.

"I am sorry to say they are not invulnerable," von Rundstedt said. "The Americans have taken to throwing grenades down their barrels, and we have suffered damage to five of the ten allotted. They are en route to Paris for repair. I do not believe we yet have the capability to create replacement parts, but this is a small matter compared to our great victory.

"Your advice on the Allies' tactics and landing points was impeccable, *Sturmbannführer*. We are prepared to hold for as long as necessary and to counterattack in force wherever they may add reinforcements."

"Excellent," Keck said. "Then we may begin the discussion of the invasion."

Von Rundstedt's eyes slid to Hitler, who studied the large map of Western Europe on the table before them. The sound of typewriters and telephones drifted from the antechamber. Keck did not know how the *Führer* would respond to his gamble with Himmler. In the past he'd come from, Hitler had always been reluctant to cross the channel by sea, but now, armed with new confidence, how would he react?

"When will we be able to produce the weapons you have brought us?" Hitler asked.

"*Mein Führer, Herr* Speer is working around the clock to—"

"I spoke with Speer this morning," Hitler said, quickly interrupting him. "He is as loyal as any of my best, but his efforts with the *Wunderwaffe* proceed slowly. An invasion of Britain is a possibility, but in light of our current defensive advantage, this …" he said as his finger tapped a second map where red and blue arrows faced each other along the Eastern front, "this is what concerns me, *Sturmbannführer*."

"We can conscript the Czechs, or the Greeks," Himmler suggested. "Perhaps even the Poles."

"Yes," von Rundstedt answered. "And how many will the Russians conscript? How many will the Chinese, or the Americans? In the East, only one in three Russian soldiers even has a rifle, and yet they attack. They suffer appalling losses, but so do we, and they are gaining ground."

"I have given you a means to close one of our fronts forever!" Keck said, his voice rising along with his irritation.

"What you have given me are a few toys that—"

"Enough!" Hitler shouted. Instantly the men in the room sprang to attention, but Hitler's voice quickly softened. "I agree with our SS friends. If we are to take advantage of our victory, we must eliminate the British Isles quickly and decisively. This is why I have summoned one of my best and most daring. Erwin ... come."

Keck's eyes widened at the man who entered the planning room. General Erwin Rommel had the clear blue eyes and close-cropped hair of a true Prussian and carried himself with the same nobility that Keck felt within his own veins. From his research in 2014, Keck knew that the man had reservations about Nazism and Hitler, but the general would do his best for Germany, and his best might just be enough to win.

"It is a pleasure to meet you, General," Keck said. Rommel offered him a reserved smile.

"The pleasure will be mine, *if* our partnership proves fruitful."

"I ask you both to be mindful of our material realities," Hitler said. "We must rebuild our invasion fleet, and it will take the *Luftwaffe* time to recover. We have that time now, but our secrets are revealed. I want you to return to *Der Dom, Sturmbannführer*. Bring us more of your *Wunderwaffe*. Bring me planes and ships that may carry us to England. Bring me petrol, soldiers, anything that may help us. And then," Hitler said as he raised his finger into the air, "when we have shown our Anglo-Saxon brothers the light of National Socialism and closed the Western front, then we will grind the Communists' bones into dust, and set ourselves to the task of building our new Reich!"

26

"You appear pensive," Himmler said. As the *Reichsführer* slid their rail compartment's door closed, Keck watched the countryside south of Berlin flash past them. Among the green fields and towns stood many bombed out buildings, but fewer than he'd witnessed previously in what now felt like another life. The anti-aircraft guns and their night vision scopes that he'd brought with him through *Der Dom* had caused stunning losses among the Allied bombers, and Speer was rebuilding the lost factory capacity at a fevered pitch.

Crops waved along the rolling hills, while citizens everywhere stood in line for their shifts to help support the Reich. This was the beginning of the future.

"I was just remembering a different time, *Mein Herr*, and wondering how we will sustain our progress."

"Don't be concerned, Kristock. *Der Führer* always talks this way before a campaign."

"But Hitler makes a wise point. Every tank and plane I bring is useless without fuel. The tanks alone require five men each, but what if the Russians soak up those men like a sponge? Even with *Der Dom*, resupply is not infinite," Keck said.

The *Reichsführer* leaned forward to pat him on the leg. "Do you know what today is?" he asked.

"No."

"On this day, many years ago, I joined the *Nationalsozialismus*. It's my Nazi anniversary."

"It was a wise decision, *Mein Herr.*"

"Yes, and one that I have never regretted, in spite of the many sacrifices that were required and all the mistakes I've made."

"*Herr Reichsführer,* I do not think you should sell yourself so short. You are the architect of the *Führer's* revolution!" Keck said, but Himmler brushed away his praise with a gloved hand.

"Kristock, no man ever fully becomes the *Übermensch.* We can eliminate the *Untermenschen,* as you have so skillfully done, but we will all make mistakes. Even Hitler."

Keck scanned his superior's face for any sign of treason but found only a fatherly kindness staring back at him.

"My point is that you, and you alone, can do what men have always dreamed of. You can change history to resolve any fault, to pre-empt any mistake. If we are short on fuel, bring Hitler a chemical engineer from the future and send him to the factory. If we need men, bring them. You will come and go in the blink of an eye, able to summon vengeance with a simple thought, just like the gods of old."

As Himmler spoke these last words, Keck found himself realizing how little he'd truly understood of *Der Dom's* power. He would live in the alien machine and shuttle back and forth in time as much as was needed. He'd ravage the future to build the new engine of Nazism that would bend the world to his will.

27

December 2014

Zilina, Slovakia

Jillian Qualmes crouched behind Harry's riot shield, flattening herself against the warehouse wall. The teenagers she'd paid to spray paint the building's security cameras sprinted away as Slovak's Soviet-era armored personnel carrier turned down the street. She worried that the rumbling machine would tip the raid's hand, but as the carrier gathered speed and the Slovak *kuklaci* special forces took position in front of her, she knew there was no turning back.

The carrier crashed into the warehouse doors, and as metal squealed and tore from the cinderblock, Jillian clutched Harry's shoulder to keep from losing her balance. The *kuklaci* vehicle backed away in a spray of sparks, clearing a space for the first squad of Slovak special forces to charge inside. Jillian counted to ten, then gave the signal and charged inside at the head of Interpol's second wave.

Inside, the *kuklaci* charged after men in track suits and jeans who sprinted away from the workstations where they'd been assembling 120 mm shells for the tanks stolen from Stuttgart. Each workstation was filled with precision measuring equipment, brass shell bases, combustible cellulose fiber casings, and alarmingly huge containers of granulated explosive propellant. One errant shot or a spark in the wrong place could vaporize them all.

Jillian and her team fanned out, combing the warehouse for any criminals who'd hidden from the special forces. Automatic fire rang out in a far corner of the building, and Jillian quickly took cover behind one of the crates the smugglers had been using as a table. The heavy thud of Slovak shotguns filled the air, followed by screams and shouting. Her radio burst with the methodical progress of the commando teams.

"Clear," they called in heavily accented English.

"Two more down. Northwest exit."

Her attention turned back to the half-assembled shells in front of her. She could see hundreds of rounds of shells in many different configurations. Some looked to be armor-piercing sabot rounds, while others were high explosive rounds. There were also dozens of crates that were spray painted with NATO markings that she'd need to be opened and catalogued, but the data gathering would come later. Right now, she needed suspects. The theft of a train full of tanks was unprecedented, and the Home Office had tasked her with recovering them. The loss of all the overhead satellites due to EMP was stunning. The German EMP technology was something they'd borrowed from the U.S. and weren't really supposed to have. The precision of the theft was incredibly disturbing. Shocking in its brazen nature. The crashed train ran off the tracks almost 120 kilometers from the first report of trouble. A runaway, it slammed into an embankment when it took a curve too fast. It derailed in a devastating mangle of cars near a small village. But there were no tanks on the cars, as if they'd vanished somewhere along the way and been offloaded. Some bodies were recovered, but this was a brutal way to cover their tracks. It would be weeks in sorting it out.

"Vazni," she called into her radio as she ran from the crate. "Remember, we need prisoners!"

Small pockets of men stood with their hands up. They'd been disarmed by the *kuklaci* and were waiting for Jillian's team to arrest them. Others were still running, desperately trying to escape. Just then, another burst of gunfire chattered against the warehouse's far wall.

"Two more dead," her radio said.

"Inspector, it's Harry. The south section is clear."

"Copy that, Harry," she said as a satisfied smile spread across her face. The raid had been an incredible success. The phone tip they'd received after the train's disappearance had been dead on the money, and after so many months of frustration, all she could feel was relief. She was just about to shove her pistol back into its holster when she heard a shuffling from inside an open shipping container. Reaching up, she whacked her pistol against the black space between two slabs of metal.

"If you're in there, you're surrounded," she called. "Give yourself up!"

No voice answered. Creeping toward the container's doors, she reached for the handle just as the metal hatch burst open and knocked her to the ground.

A man with a shaved head and in a trim suit sprinted away from her toward the assembly tables.

"Halt!" she cried as she struggled back to her feet.

The man twisted a pistol back over his shoulder and fired. Jillian rolled behind the container door as his wild shots pinged off the metal. She peeked around the door just in time to see the suspect shove a crate aside to reveal a trap door.

"Freeze!" Jillian cried as she charged the smuggler. The man snarled and aimed at Jillian with military precision. Just before he fired however, two Slovaks barreled into him and knocked the gun from his hands.

Jillian jogged to the man as the *kuklaci* zip-tied the suspect's tattooed hands behind his back. Harry came puffing over to join her.

"We're almost all clear, Inspector," he panted. "That was quite the chase. Look at this place. It's like they're gearing up for—"

"For war," Jillian finished as she returned the suspect's glare. A Rolex glittered from his wrist, and his suit would have easily cost her a month's salary. She nodded to the *kuklaci*, and the Slovak soldiers immediately forced the prisoner upright.

"Where are the tanks?" she asked. "What did you do with them?"

The man's defiant eyes chilled her. The plates of his skull shone under his shaved scalp, and he seemed comfortable with his hands pulled awkwardly behind him. This was a man who knew pain.

"What's the Fourth Reich's target?" she asked. "What are you planning?"

The smuggler stayed silent. Jillian knelt in front of him and seized his collar as her voice suddenly turned hard and bitter.

"I know you're not alone in this. If you give me the answers I need, maybe you won't rot in jail for the rest of your life. Now, where are the tanks going? Who are you working for?"

The man only smiled. If anything, Jillian thought she saw sadness in his eyes.

"It seems I'm no longer useful to The King," Baldwin said. "But we can't change who we are, now can we?"

"Come on, ya bloody bastard!" Harry practically shouted. "Just tell us what you know and maybe we won't let the CIA waterboard you."

"He already has what he needs," Baldwin said as he looked over at an empty portion of the warehouse. Something had recently been there but was now gone.

While Jillian and Harry glanced over to where he'd been looking, Baldwin's jaw suddenly started working, as though he were biting something. A few moments later his eyelids fluttered, and he began a tortured panting.

"What's he doing?" Harry asked.

"I don't ..."

Foam bubbled from the man's lips. It was a white paste that seemed to chew through his skin.

"Is poison!" one of the Slovaks called. With a gloved hand, he seized the smuggler's jaw and tried to force it open, but the chemical had already done its job. Baldwin's eyes rolled back into his head, and his throat convulsed in rapid spasms. The smuggler made a last retching sound, then toppled over on his side, adopting the perfect stillness that comes with death.

"I knew the lead was too good," Jillian said. "Nothing for months after our raid, and suddenly our phone rings with an anonymous tip."

"I don't understand," Harry said. "What just happened?"

"The King Under the Mountain used us," Jillian said in disgust. "He's done whatever he came to do, and now he's tying up his loose ends."

* * *

Alone in her apartment, Jillian was restless. She knew the definition by heart.

"Cryptology: the study of mathematical, linguistic, and other coding patterns and histories. Modern cryptology exists at the intersection of the disciplines of mathematics, computer science, and electrical engineering."

Yanis could be useful, she told herself. His story was becoming more believable as the sight of the dying man replayed itself over and over in her mind. She would have to apologize to him, but it would be worth it to discuss the case with someone who really cared.

She scrolled through Yanis' unreturned messages, and held the phone for a long time, as if she were waiting for the call to make itself.

It rang four times before he finally answered.

"Professor Miller," he said distantly.

She wanted to hang up, but she knew there was no point thanks to the Caller ID.

"Hello, Professor," she responded, feeling suddenly out of place, like a teenager trying to act like an adult. There was an awkward silence before she finally continued. "Mr. Miller, this call is in reference to the *Der Dom* investigation. There have been some developments and I'd like to discuss them with you."

Her higher-pitched voice told Yanis that she was nervous, which caused him to feel both relief and excitement. It wasn't just that she thought he was useful to her investigation. He wanted back in the game, and she was his ticket. What was even more encouraging was that for the first time since they'd met, she was the uncomfortable one.

"What did you have in mind?"

She briefly described the status of the investigation, and they set up a time for a phone meeting. Jillian paused before saying goodbye, so that she could ask him a question that had been nagging at her since the investigation started.

"If you don't mind my asking, how did a devout Jewish boy grow up in Montana, and then end up as a math professor in Jerusalem who dabbles in cryptology?"

He chuckled. He didn't like talking about himself, but he didn't want to get off the phone, either. "Well, it's a pretty short story, really. My mom is Jewish. Her parents died in the war, and she had some problems that my dad thought would be helped by living a more rural lifestyle. He was a psychology professor, and he loved the outdoors, so we headed for Montana State University. My first love is still the Bobcats."

"So, you're the son of a Jewish mom and a nature-loving psychologist, you grew up in Montana, and you were really good at … whatever you have to be good at to be a cryptologist?"

"That pretty much sums it up," he said, excited about the seemingly personal slant their conversation had taken. "So, what about you?"

"Tell you what. You help me solve this case, and I'll give you my whole life story. Every last boring second of it," she said.

"You know, that's about the best offer I've had all day. I think I'll take you up on that," he said, smiling as he leaned back in his chair.

28

June 1944

Near Portsmouth, Hampshire, United Kingdom

The unrelenting weather shrouded the Supreme Headquarters Allied Expeditionary Force's encampment in a thick haze. Mist dampened each set of orders before they left the typewriter's spindle. Even the voices coming through the radio, reporting the progress from Normandy's beaches, seemed to be deadened by it. General Eisenhower's staff shuffled about in near disbelief, tightening their jackets against the inclement British weather.

They processed report after report of the strange weapons that the Germans had used against them in the assault. There were sniper rifles made from some feather-light material with telescopic sights that could see in the dark. Anti-air batteries capable of knocking bombers from the skies with pinpoint accuracy were decimating their bomber squadrons, and shoulder-mounted missile launchers wreaked havoc on the few Sherman tanks that had reached the beaches. The worst, however, were the strange tanks that had somehow managed to ravage the naval invasion fleet.

"Hold for the general," a signalman said into his radio. He held the earpiece up to the man standing beside him in a damp khaki dress shirt and mud-caked boots. General Eisenhower had left his cap somewhere, and small droplets of mist ran down his pale face as he took the receiver. He hadn't slept for three days, but the voice that he used on the radio was calm, almost gentle.

"Hello, son," Eisenhower said.

"Good afternoon, sir," the sergeant replied.

"What's your name?"

"Sergeant Jim Thompson, sir. Fourth Platoon, D Company, Second Rangers."

The deep booms of a bigger gun burst through the radio, followed by the cracks of M1s and captured German weapons.

"How are you holding up, Sergeant?"

"We've occupied a series of bunkers just beyond Pointe du Hoc sir, but we're running short on just about everything. We could use more ammunition, medical supplies, and another combat division or two over here."

The signalman froze, watching the general from the corner of his eye to gauge Eisenhower's reaction to what sounded like the Ranger's insolence. Instead, the first smile he'd seen in days spread across the general's face.

"We'll get them to you as soon as it's safe for our boys to make another crossing. Now, tell me about the tanks."

"They're, uhhh ... I'm not really sure how to say this, sir. I don't think you'll believe me, but if you could see one of these things, then you'd understand."

"I'll believe you, son. Go ahead and tell me."

"Sir, we got inside one. It's got glass that you can touch to control the tank. It's also got some kind of electrical optics that let the gunner see at night. It can see heat, too. There's also an ... *Eniac,* I think one of the Seabees called it. It's a computer that targets the gun automatically. That's what the Germans were doing to the fleet. It was like they couldn't miss. General, these things are ... well, I mean ... the only way I can say it is that if they don't have 'em in Brooklyn, then they don't have 'em anywhere. They're so much beyond anything we've got, or anything the Germans should have. It's like they're from the future or somethin', and I mean that in the literal sense, sir."

Eisenhower's frown returned.

"We'll get our intelligence boys on it as soon as it's safe enough to get over there, but Sergeant, I have to ask, are you sure you aren't exaggerating, even just a little?"

The sound of shouted orders came through the line, followed by a hissing rattle. The radio muffled for a moment before the sergeant returned.

"Sorry, General, that was one of the snipers," the Sergeant said. "I think we got him though. We captured a few of those rifles ourselves, so we've been usin' whatever ammo we could get with 'em to shoot back. General, there's somethin' else about those tanks you should know."

"Go ahead, Sergeant."

"The markings on the inside of 'em, the instructions and what not. It's all in English, sir. Our Seabee here looked under the hood, too. The parts are stamped *Made in Detroit.*"

Eisenhower stared at the rain drizzling off the encampment's tarpaulin and into the mud as if he were trying to make sense of something far deeper than the weather. Heavy booms rattled once again through the receiver so loudly that the general had to pull it away from his ear for a moment, lest he be deafened by all the squeals and static.

"Jim, are you there?" he shouted as he brought the receiver back to his ear. He could hear heavy rifle fire in the background. "Sergeant, report!"

"Sorry, sir," Jim said. "They got a little close that time."

"Can you hold, son?"

"Yeah, we can hold, sir. We can advance, too. I think we got all the tanks they had with the thermite. The Krauts are fightin' like hell but it's more of a fair fight now than it was before. We just need supplies and ammo."

An aide tapped a watch in front of the general. It was time to leave for London so they could update the politicians.

"Thank you, Sergeant," Eisenhower said. "What'd you do in Brooklyn before you joined up?"

"I was a fighter, sir."

"That's good, son," the general said with a smile. "You take the fight to those bastards while we figure out just what the hell it is you're up against."

***

David Wolcott fanned himself with his sheaf of folders. The packed briefing room was sweltering, and he couldn't tell if he felt faint from the bunker's poor ventilation, the Prime Minister's cigars, or the fact that he'd been summoned to a room with the most powerful men of the Allied war effort to help explain just what had gone wrong.

"The only one missing is King George himself," Staunton whispered to him.

Montgomery and Eisenhower sat on either side of the Prime Minister, who looked like a grumpy old toad as he gnawed on his cigar. Nearly thirty other generals crowded the table in order of descending rank. All were listening attentively as Sir Stewart Menzies delivered the Intelligence Service report that Staunton's section had prepared for them.

"As you can see in these photographs, the weapons and reinforcements our forces encountered did not arrive onto the beaches until late in the night of June the 5th," Sir Stewart said as the slide carousel clicked and whirred beside him. "All other German activity had appeared normal up until that point. This leads us to the inevitable conclusion that—"

"Someone spilled the bloody beans!" Churchill spat. His beaded eyes swept the room as if daring anyone to argue with him, while his cigar's smoke rose to cloud the projector.

"I can accept an intelligence issue," Eisenhower said. "That's a solvable problem, but what I cannot accept is what those tanks are."

"Yes, General, about those," Sir Stewart said. "Captain, the next set, if you please."

An aide lifted the carousel, momentarily pinning Sir Stewart against the white screen. Eisenhower's was the question every man in the room had come to have answered. How had none of them, not even their most closely placed spies, been aware of such advanced weaponry coming on the horizon? Not only that, but just *where* had it come from?

The projector clunked, and then a blurred image of a massive gray machine appeared on the screen. The captain at the slide controls twisted the lens, and the machine snapped into focus. Gasps rose from around the room as many saw the disabled tank for the first time. The next slide showed an interior view. A third displayed the strange, sleek controls made of what looked like glass and light.

"U.S. Army Rangers captured this example after its commander opened the hatch to use the machine gun," Sir Stewart explained. "Both the weaponry and the controls appear to be incredibly advanced."

"And my men on the beaches say it's stamped *Made in Detroit*," General Eisenhower said. "They also said it looks like it came from the future."

Sir Stewart offered a thin smile.

"Yes, well, we all understand what combat can do to the nerves."

"Are you implying that the men fighting these things don't know what they're talking about?" Eisenhower demanded as he rose from his seat. "What exactly is *your* explanation for that thing?"

"I must admit that we simply don't know, General," Sir Stewart said.

David stared at the controls, trying to seize the intuition that was flickering at the back of his mind.

"For God's sake, Stewart," Churchill roared, "that's the whole point of this bloody briefing! You're supposed to tell us what we're up against. After all, that's what intelligence *is*, isn't it? Right now, you and your boys look a damn sight short of it."

"I—" Sir Stewart said awkwardly. "My apologies, Mr. Prime Minister. We simply haven't got the slightest—"

"General Eisenhower is right," David called. All eyes turned toward the source of the voice, trying to locate it in the deep shadows of the room.

"Wolcott!" Staunton hissed. "Sit down!"

"The tanks, they're from the future," David said.

"What in God's name?" Sir Stewart asked.

"Let's have the lights," the Prime Minister called. The overheads blurred on suddenly, and David had to blink his eyes a few times to clear his vision.

"May I present intelligence analyst David Wolcott," Sir Stewart grumbled.

David nodded to the room, twisting his cap's brim in his fingers. He could only hope they'd believe what he was about to tell them.

"Well, go on, Wolcott," the Prime Minister said. "Let's hear what you have to say."

"We were told of these types of electronics before, by a man who washed up on shore and claimed to be from a Jewish country called Israel in the year 2014. He'd been shot and was desperately trying to warn us that Operation Overlord, D-Day, would happen on June 6th, and that the Germans would be ready for it. He said they had weapons from the future, and another man like him working for the Nazis."

"And when did you first hear about all of this, Wolcott?" Sir Xavier asked.

"A year ago, sir. Right before we put the man in a mental hospital."

29

February 2015

Berlin, Germany

"Do you mean to tell me that your listening network has gone cold?" Deputy Director St. Pierre asked.

"There aren't any more emails, and we haven't processed last week's SMSs yet, but …" Harry said, but then he trailed off.

"But it's been weeks since we've picked up any sort of a reference to *Der Dom*, or to The King Under the Mountain," Jillian finished for him. "Given our most recent suspect's final words, it appears that this so-called *King* is covering his tracks."

"I find this new development distressing, Inspectors. Quite distressing," St. Pierre said, his expression suddenly turning sour.

"Director, we've never come across anything that had this level of sophistication. It's an unprecedented threat, and we need to—"

"Yes, Ms. Qualmes, I'm perfectly aware of what we're up against, which is exactly why I'm speaking to you now. You've proven to be incapable of stopping the massive weapon shipments that are flooding the continent, and now we've had two dozen tanks stolen as well. The EU governments are demanding to know where these weapons are going, and who is funding this private army. I tell them that after nearly a year we finally have a suspect, and that my best inspectors have broken the case, and yet your last suspect—"

"He'd never been fingerprinted, sir. His DNA isn't on file."

"I'm well aware of that, Junior Inspector," St. Pierre said harshly. "There's no doubt that you've sniffed out what's been happening, Jillian. The doubt lies in your ability to see this case through and finish it. Effective immediately, I am reassigning you to administrative duties."

"But sir, if I could just—" Jillian pleaded.

"Goodbye, Ms. Qualmes. I'll speak with you in London on Monday about your future," he said just before he abruptly closed the call.

* * *

Jillian didn't even bother to change before sinking into her bed that night. She laid there with her eyes closed for what felt like hours staring at the ceiling as she listened to the clunk of hotel room doors and muted voices from the hallway. There was a whole world going on around her, a world that had no idea of what was happening. The entire trail had gone cold, and it was all her fault. She just hadn't been good enough to stop it.

After she laid there tossing and turning for a while, she eventually gave up on sleep and picked up her phone. Scrolling through the weeks and months of calls and texts and emails, she looked for something she might have missed, but the review got her nowhere. The clarity she'd always found in her work had fled, and in a passing moment of frustration she tossed her phone down onto the sheets. It had all been for nothing, but she'd have to find a way to move forward. There was no other alternative for her.

Picking up her phone once more, she scrolled back down through her history. There wasn't a single personal call or message during the entire time she'd been on the case, except for the messages from Yanis.

Maybe it was finally time for a different approach. Even if she wasn't long for Interpol, she couldn't let *Der Dom* slip away so easily.

Discussing the case on the phone was helpful, but she and Yanis might be able to accomplish more if they worked together directly. Yes, that was the best way to move forward, she decided as she dialed his number. He answered a few moments later.

"Hey, Jillian," Yanis said awkwardly.

"Yanis, I have an idea, but I need your help," she said.

* * *

February 2015

Bad Tölz, Germany

An older woman opened the door shortly after Jillian's first knock. The innkeeper's hair was curled and gray, though it still bore hints of the rich chestnut color it'd held in her youth. She smiled kindly as she stepped aside and allowed Jillian to enter the foyer.

"I wasn't expecting any guests, what with the skiing being as bad as it is," Miriam said. "We just haven't had the weather for it this year."

"I'm afraid I'm not a guest. A few months ago, I came here to ask about someone who had been staying with you. Do you remember?"

The woman's eyes widened.

"This is about Yanis again, isn't it?" Miriam asked. "Oh, I told him not to go sneaking around. I knew someone would find out."

"Is Yanis in?" Jillian asked. They weren't supposed to meet until tomorrow, but she had hoped she would find him here. *Had he not told Miriam she was coming?* Her anticipation surprised her. She'd never felt this kind of emotion on a case before. "Would you mind telling me his room number?"

"I'm sorry, Inspector. I'm happy to show you to his room, but he hasn't been back for days. In fact, I'm glad you're here. I was starting to get concerned."

* * *

January 2015

Bad Tölz, Germany

Martin Steiger's Maserati was easy to spot from where Yanis had hidden himself within the mountain underbrush. After the car passed,

Yanis stood to work the cold from his legs, and then began hiking through the night. The days he'd spent following the Steigers, after their goon attacked him, had finally paid off. There was no doubt he'd found *Der Dom* here at the base of the *Zitternberg*.

The strange "ski resort" where all the equipment was trundled underground through steel doors so thick they looked as if they'd survive a nuclear blast, and the cloak of secrecy with armed men that constantly patrolled the area … this had been what Jillian was after.

He felt his phone in his pocket and thought of calling her, but let the idea go. Thinking about what might happen if he led her astray again made his stomach churn. He needed real evidence this time, and the anticipation of finally finding it only served to strengthen his resolve.

Through a break in the trees, he could see the Steigers parked in the turnaround that had been filled with dozens of other vehicles just hours earlier. Each driver had known their way to the steel doors, which meant they'd been here before, and they certainly weren't dressed as miners. If Jillian was right; these were Neo-Nazis, and all the weapons they'd been gathering were being stored behind those doors. All he needed was a picture or two with his phone, and then the authorities would have to believe him.

Yanis jogged ahead, trying to catch up with Martin and Maria without making too much noise in the forest. He knelt at the edge of the clearing in front of the tunnel mouth and watched Martin tap a keypad mounted into the rock. The doors hissed open, the couple entered, and then the tunnel sealed itself again. After waiting for ten minutes, Yanis crept out of the pines. His feet crunched across the clearing's gravel, and his heart pounded in his chest.

This was the moment of truth. He knew the Steigers had tried to kill him, but he had no proof. He knew what was happening beyond those doors, but it would be his word against theirs until he had solid evidence. He paused at the tunnel entrance, looking over his shoulder to make sure he was unobserved, but no one else had come. As soon as he was satisfied that he was alone, he rested his fingertips on the keypad.

Before he could enter the first part of the code that he'd seen the Steigers enter, a sound came from the other side of the door. Yanis pressed his ear to the cold metal, every inch of him fighting the urge to run. He heard a sharp snapping, and then the sound of cries and screams. And then, much closer, as if the sound came from right on the other side of the door, a final thump that shook the earth at his feet.

Yanis sprinted back into the woods and took cover behind a downed tree. He waited for well over five minutes, but no one emerged. Everything had been silent while he'd been waiting. Finally, he got to his feet and snuck back toward the keypad.

He'd watched Martin's fingers and knew that the first two numbers had been one and nine. He pressed those digits, and then dropped down to the middle row. That had been the third. He tried five, but the keypad flashed red. He tried one-nine-six, but the controls denied him a second time.

After he pressed one-nine-four, the keypad stayed green. Yanis' fingers stayed on the second row, and playing a hunch, he tapped six. Rewarding him for his successful guess, the keypad flashed green, and a dim blue light spilled through the opening doors.

30

Yanis skidded on a soft material just inside the tunnel entrance, and then pressed his hand to his mouth to stifle his shocked gasp. The frozen eyes of Maria Steiger gaped at him from the bloodstained floor. Her lower limbs had somehow been torn off, and a look of horrified betrayal was slowly slackening from her face. He'd stepped on the remains of one of her legs and struggled not to vomit as he passed her. What had happened here?

Everywhere he looked, mangled bodies filled the tunnel. Many had been shot, their blood just beginning to clot and dry on the white stone. The dead faces of those he'd watched enter the tunnel one by one just an hour before glowed an unearthly green in the blue light. Squinting ahead, he saw the light source illuminating a strange wall at the far end of the tunnel, and a lone figure walking toward it.

Yanis dropped to the ground as quietly as he could, trying to blend in with the bodies as the figure at the end of the corridor raised a hand and touched one of the glowing lights. A blackness appeared, and the man stepped through a portal that had not existed just a second ago. The man stopped, glanced back at the tunnel, and then the strange doorway closed to leave Yanis alone with the dead.

He knew he should run and tell the authorities what he'd seen, but something about the strange blue swirls at the end of the tunnel drew him forward. With each step he felt the warmth emanating from it continue to intensify, just as the light continued to brighten. The undulating script seemed to be just on the verge of speaking some sort of a memory as he approached the glowing wall and wriggled around as though it were alive. Yanis shook his head, trying to focus on his task, but pacing back and forth in front of the barrier, he could find no door.

The man had disappeared simply by waving his hand. Yanis raised his own hand, but nothing happened. He tried again, positioning himself where he thought he remembered the figure standing, and again, nothing. He stepped closer to the wall's uncomfortable heat, then inched forward another foot. He could just make out what appeared to be indistinct borders in the wall before him when a sharp pain seized his palm, causing him to jerk his hand back.

As he shook his scorched fingers, a portal opened in front of him. After a last glance back at the dead strewn about the tunnel, he turned and followed the strange man right into the heart of *Der Dom.*

* * *

The air was eerily still beyond the wall where Yanis had entered the portal. He crept along, his breath clutched tightly in his throat, desperate to remain undiscovered. The man he'd been following was several hundred yards ahead of him by now, dimly lit in the bluish light. Yanis looked around, searching for a place to conceal himself should it be necessary. The walls were covered with smooth glass panels, much like computer screens, filled with continuously scrolling data. He raised his hand, still sore from where it had been scorched, and tried to touch one. But as soon as his fingers approached the moving text, it blipped and buzzed. Like a momentary power surge, barely lasting long enough to restart a temperamental clock radio, the data quickly resumed its scroll.

"Hor auf!" came the man's voice as he spun around. *"Raus hier!"*

Yanis froze, his eyes fixed on the swastika centered on the man's red armband. His stomach clenched, sickened by the thought of what the Reich had done, as well as the metallic scent that permeated the space. He debated whether to raise his hands or to rush the man.

A blistering flash made his decision for him. The bullet ripped into Yanis' jaw, dropping him to the marble-white ground.

"Schmutzinger Jude," the man muttered as he returned his pistol to its holster and proceeded forward. A smirk of satisfaction lifted his lips.

Yanis was still, blood flowing steadily from his jaw. He heard a door opening, much like the portal he'd just entered, and then it closed. At that point, he began to waver in and out of consciousness. Thoughts drifted together, intermeshing in nonsensical order. The warm stream of blood began to pool beneath his face, pressed onto the spongy white floor.

Desperate to keep his eyes open, he tried to focus on Inspector Qualmes. What was it she had said? That she was sorry for involving someone like him in all this? Someone who played with history instead of facts? If this were playing with history, then how could she dispute the fact that he'd been shot and left to die?

But his strength, like his blood, was draining quickly. Shock was setting in. He was dizzy, his skin cool, his limbs starting to shake. As his breath accelerated in short, rapid bursts, he wondered if he'd ever get a chance to persuade Inspector Qualmes to reconsider her impression of him.

With that thought, he slipped from consciousness. When he did, the lights within the space dimmed and then surged. Sensors and ethereal blue displays emerged from the walls, all showing Yanis' life slipping away. From the shimmering lights near the ceiling, a broad red beam shone down on him, heating his body as shock took over. Still, he was slipping away, organs shutting down as the blood continued to flow from his face.

A spindly metal arm extended from the ship's walls, a syringe of eerie blue fluid poised within its grasp. As Yanis laid on the floor, oblivious to his surroundings, the ship's robotic device injected the syringe's contents into his neck. At once, his blood began to clot. The gleaming white floor absorbed it, erasing it from sight. His body temperature slowly began to climb again, and his pulse normalized.

When he came to, Yanis couldn't tell how long he'd been unconscious. His memory was clouded. And his jaw screamed in pain. Something inside his mouth felt like it didn't belong there. He spit, expelling two teeth and a fleshy glob of cheek matter. They bounced on the floor, splattering blood, but again, the floor absorbed it. Yanis stared in amazement as the floor cleaned itself before his eyes. He ran his tongue gingerly over the space where his teeth had been, feeling fresh nubs already in place on his gums. He raised his hand to touch it, then drew back as his fingers brushed against the hole that was beginning to close. His clothes and hands were soaked in his own blood, but somewhere deep inside him he could hear a voice, or a murmur of a voice just outside his hearing. He needed to get out, and he found himself stumbling toward the light.

All around him, the blue lights continued to scroll, an endless exhibit of refreshing data. As Yanis began to feel stronger, the lights dimmed to their previous setting.

PART THREE:

DAGGER

31

July 1944

Normandy, France

Baker Company had been wiped out. George was gone as well. Platoons One, Two, and Six of Dog Company were down to ribbons. Jim stood watch in the early morning, peeking out from the hedgerow a mile from Pointe du Hoc. It was the farthest progress the Rangers, or what was left of them, had made in an entire month of fighting. He took the watch himself during the quiet times so that he could give his men some much-needed rest.

"Sarge," Mitchell breathed next to him. The Ranger had darkened his face with charcoal and stuffed the netting of his helmet with twigs and leaves. "You think they're gonna come again?"

"They want us off this coast," Jim whispered.

"But why fight? They know we're gonna be going anyway."

Jim thought back to all the times he'd had an opponent on the ropes, battering him until the poor bastard was staggering like a drunk around the ring. The fight was never over until your opponent couldn't fight back, and the Germans knew Dog Company still had some fight left in them.

"They're still trying to kill us so we don't survive to fight 'em somewhere else."

"Jesus, Sarge, we really lost this war, didn't we?" Mitchell asked. Jim studied the twisted knots of the hedgerow in front of him. The vines had grown for centuries on the same land that had seen so much killing, and just as it'd done so many times before, the blood of the slain was fertilizing their roots once more.

"You know, I think we're saving our best punch for the end of the fight," he said just as the quick rattle of the German MG-42 stuttered through the hedgerow. "Here they come! Everybody get on the line!"

Veteran combat instincts that had been honed with just a few intense weeks of training snapped the Rangers instantly awake. They flew to their firing positions and began peppering the Germans. Mitchell suddenly let out a pained grunt, and Jim looked over to see the private wincing at a slug that had just torn into his shoulder.

"Medic!" he cried.

"No, it's OK. I can still shoot," Mitchell said bravely.

"Well pour it into 'em, Mitch! Let's show those bastards what Hell looks like!"

Jim turned back to the hole he'd bored through the hedgerow and fired at the dim figures that were sprinting toward them through the early morning light. Germans fell to the ground screaming, while all around him the shots of his men rang out in a pattern so random that it was almost rhythmic. All down the line, a third of his Rangers were firing captured German weapons due to scarcity of the ammunition for their own weapons.

"Pick your shots!" Jim called out to them. "Conserve your ammo!"

Peeling away from his cover, Jim ran down the line behind his men to check their status. Dog Company had finally secured a good position, but they wouldn't be holding it for much longer. Soon they'd be leaving. They just had to hold out a little bit longer.

"Who needs ammo?" he yelled, tossing his few remaining bandoliers to the Rangers who waved their hands.

Someone suddenly grabbed Jim's shoulder. Reflexively, he spun around with a half-raised fist, only to find a stubble-faced runner from headquarters standing there cringing away from a blow he fully expected to come.

"The boats?" Jim asked as he shook out his hand and looked at the kid apologetically.

"They're ready!" the messenger shouted.

Jim nodded, and then ran down the line once more, tapping each man's leg in the signal to begin their withdrawal.

"Let's go, let's go, let's go!" he shouted.

"Grenade!" someone screamed. Jim hit the deck. The ground shook, spouting dirt and pieces of hedge up like fountaining fireworks that fell back down on his back. He lurched back to his feet, saw that his platoon was peeling back off the line, and then turned to join them. After a few steps, he found the runner down with his chest torn open from the blast.

The boy twitched as he reached out his hand to grasp at Jim's leg. The big man knelt and held the runner's hand for last few moments of the young man's life, and then he slowly closed the poor soldier's eyes. It was just one more to add to the list he carried in his head of all the men who wouldn't be coming back home. The list made him angry enough to fight the whole German army by himself. Whenever he needed to find the strength to carry on, he'd think about that list and use the rage it created within him to push himself onward.

His revenge would have to come later, though. Right now, his only concern was getting his men to safety.

"Get to the beach! I know you're all tired but run like your lives depend on it!" he shouted, slapping Rangers on the back as they sprinted toward the bunkers.

32

January 1943

The Zitternberg

Yanis laid on the boiling ground, gasping for breath and trying to understand what had just happened. The pieces of his life suddenly seemed jumbled. He was sliding down a glacier, sitting in the lonely light of a desk lamp with index cards in a strange language, a woman shook her head at him in disappointment, and mummified eye sockets watched him over his shoulder. He tried to scream, but his jaw felt like it was on fire, and all he could manage to get out was a choking gurgle.

As the afterimage of a blinding flash slowly faded from his vision, he finally started making sense of his surroundings. He could see at least a dozen tanks stretching into the distance, and crate after crate stenciled with the old Soviet hammer and sickle design. When he finally found the strength to flop to his side, he noticed that he was lying at the base of a shimmering pillar that rose to meet the strange ceiling.

Reaching up, he gently pressed his palm against the sticky blood on his jaw, and the searing pain erupted once again. It was then that he realized the truth of his situation, or at least part of it.

The man he'd followed into the tunnel under the *Zitternberg* was here. It was the same man who'd shot him just before the strange machine reached its fever pitch.

Yanis slapped his palms against the strange floor and pushed himself upright. He could hear a familiar sound somewhere near him and crawled toward it. Droplets of blood dribbled onto the spongy white surface beneath him and disappeared as though they were being consumed. What on earth had the Steigers found here?

He rounded the glass tube and froze. The man who'd shot him squatted with his back to him as he rummaged through a footlocker. From it he pulled out a black cap that glimmered with a silver death's head and placed it on his head before he slammed the trunk shut once again. Yanis could just make out the man's harsh profile, the black uniform jacket, and the blood-red Nazi armband. He knew exactly what that uniform was, and what it represented, and it horrified him.

The man tightened his belt, adjusted one of his lapels, and then jogged out of the strange room.

Yanis' momentary burst of strength faded after he was gone, and he quickly crumpled back down onto his chest. Blood trickled on his neck as he coughed. He pressed his hand against the wound, applying just enough direct pressure to stop the bleeding. He had no idea where he was, or what the man had done after he'd murdered the Steigers and the others under the *Zitternberg*, but what he did know was that if he didn't want to die here in this strange place, he'd have to get himself out and then find some help.

* * *

July 1944

The Zitternberg

"I must be honest with you, *Sturmbannführer*," Himmler said as he admired the view of Bad Tölz and the Isar Valley from the *Zitternberg's* edge. "I have been very much looking forward to this day."

Keck smiled as he stood with the new squad of *Totenkopfverbände* he'd assigned to guard *Der Dom* after the workers from Dachau had improved the tunnel.

"Well, *mein Herr*, considering what you are about to see, you may get to experience this day again and again."

Himmler rubbed his hands together as the *Schütze* cranked open the doors to reveal the familiar blue light. As Keck's eyes adjusted from the bright summer sun, the illumination seemed more faint than usual, as if nearly exhausted. The tunnel's warmth returned as they walked, however, so he paid the change no mind at all.

"Jews did all this?" Himmler asked as he marveled at the tunnel.

"Yes. They performed quite admirably before their services were no longer required."

"I must stop by Dachau and congratulate their commander."

"He will appreciate the compliment, I'm sure. Now, *mein Herr*, if you please," Keck said with a flourish, ushering Himmler into the alien craft.

Each new chamber they passed through brought a fresh exclamation from the *Reichsführer*, until at last they reached bridge. His eyes widened at the alien bodies that had reappeared after Keck's journey through time and had not yet been removed. Cautiously, he reached out a gloved hand toward one of the gray mummies that was laying exposed at its station and pressed his finger to its flesh.

"I can assure you that they are all quite real," Keck said. "They are also deceased, though they do not decompose as our bodies would."

Himmler's glasses reflected in the clouded black rings of one of the alien's eyes.

"What do you think they wanted in coming here?"

Keck tilted his head as he looked down at the shimmering creature.

"To bring us a gift worthy of the Reich, *mein Herr*. What other reason could they have possibly had?" Keck asked with a haughty smile.

* * *

"It's everything you said and more," Himmler said from the center of the artifact chamber. "It will be the culmination of our dream."

"And this is where we will continue until our task is done," Keck said as he turned to the controls that two generations of Steigers had worked with him to understand.

"You're sure that only one may travel at a time?" Himmler asked. "I'd very much like to join this second expedition."

"My experiments in another time proved that it would not work," Keck reassured his superior. In truth, the Steigers had not even tried, but Keck wanted to reserve both the pleasure *and* the power of time travel for himself. The authorities of 2014 had proven all too capable and sending too many to the future would likely draw some very unwanted attention. Not only that, but the *Reichsführer* was a very well-known historical figure, and they couldn't take the risk that he might be recognized.

"But how can one craft hold so much?" Himmler asked.

"As you can see, *Herr Reichsführer,* the craft's measurements are … indistinct. I have come to believe that the craft exists in multiple dimensions that we are not able to observe. This may well be how it makes possible the miracle of time travel. What it does to our eyes, is that it—"

"Opens a window into the infinite," Himmler finished.

"Yes, *mein Herr,* I believe that to be the case," Keck said as he waved his hands over the controls. Their familiar heat felt different to the nerves of his palm, almost as though they had an edge of winter to them. The portal, however, opened in the tube, just as it had done in the past, with the same glistening blue interior.

Suddenly, another icy blast shot at his hands. Inside the tube, the blue drained to a muddy brown. The glowing control disks pulsed orange, and then the glass portal swiveled shut.

Turning, Keck studied the room, counting the flicking blue rings in the chamber. There seemed to be ten, although he could not be sure he had an accurate count. Yet when he counted the tube's control rings, he found only eight. He tried to adjust them again as his anger rose but was stymied by the same brown light of failure.

"Keck, is this normal?" Himmler asked.

The *Sturmbannführer* drew his Luger and marched to the other side of the chamber. There was no blood, no evidence of the man he'd thought to be dead some seventy years in the future. There was nobody.

"Someone has been here," he said in a low hiss.

* * *

January 1943

Bad Tölz

Shivering and growing numb from the subzero air, Yanis hunched on the ice frozen at the bottom of the sewer culvert that hid him. He tried to quiet his breathing, listening to the boot falls of the German patrol fade from the stone bridge above him as they crossed over it and continued on their way. They looked as though they'd marched right off a movie set, but he knew what he was seeing was real.

He'd stumbled down the base of the *Zitternberg* in the direction of Bad Tölz. The forest had been much thicker than he'd remembered, and came closer to the town, but the village itself was still there, though it was different than what he'd seen before. The roads were made of cobblestone or dirt, and most of the buildings had been replaced by old stone and wood houses with thatched roofs. The lights had been off in the first few houses he'd reached, and no amount of banging on the doors had brought a resident to help.

Until he'd seen the German soldiers emerge like ghosts from the night, he'd been trying to convince himself that what seemed to have happened really hadn't happened at all. Now after seeing the things he'd seen, there was no way of doubting it. The man Jillian had been chasing had discovered time travel, and he himself was now a Jew in Nazi Germany, growing more desperate with each unsteady step.

He counted to one hundred, and then scrambled out of the culvert. His numb hands grasped clumsily at the rocks and straw along the riverbank as he tried to scramble his way back up to the road. He knew he wouldn't last much longer, but he had one final hope. As he turned down a street he remembered from a much different time, he said a prayer that he would live to see 2014 again.

* * *

The woman who answered the door tried to slam it in his face as soon as she saw Yanis' condition. Her chestnut brown hair fell out of her nightcap as they struggled, and her mouth opened as if she would scream but she made no sound. With the last of his strength, Yanis wedged his shoulders in between the door and the jamb.

"*Bitte*," he pleaded in the little German he knew. "*Bitte*."

The woman's eyes met his for just a moment, then she stepped away from the door. Yanis stumbled inside, crashing to the floor as his legs gave out. He rolled over just in time to see the woman lift a fireplace poker over her shoulder, ready to swing it at his head.

The room was dimly lit. A candle burned on a ledge near the door, its flame flickering wildly as his consciousness faded.

"*Jude*," he whispered with the last of his strength. "*Ich bin ein Jude*."

* * *

He woke in the dark, at first unable to tell if his eyes were open or closed. His body felt constricted, but as his mind started to focus, he realized that he was lying in a bed with the coverlet tucked tightly around him. Streaks of dusty light filtered down from the ceiling, revealing his surroundings. He was in an earthen cellar, along with a few clay jugs that had been sealed with wax, and naked white roots that reached out to him through the walls.

A dirty hand slapped against his mouth and lips pressed against his ear, whispering a string of German to him that he couldn't understand. He blinked a few times and strained to see the boy that was next to him. He was wearing a dirty white smock that hung down over his bare feet. The child raised a finger to his lips, his eyes pleading for silence. Yanis nodded at him, and suddenly a massive amount of pain exploded from the wound in his jaw, running both down his neck and up into his eye socket. Reaching for the wound, Yanis tapped a bulge of puckered skin with his fingers. Someone had stitched him up and hidden him down there.

Above them, a deep, angry voice barked questions at a woman whose answering voice was airy and polite. The conversation continued until finally a door slammed, and then Yanis waited with the boy in the tense silence while the minutes crawled past.

After what must have been an hour, two taps sounded on the floorboard above them, followed by a string of German. The boy stood fully upright and pushed his shoulders against the wood so that the trap door lifted. Light flooded down into the small cellar, and Yanis found himself looking up into the eyes of Miriam's grandmother, who was reaching out a hand to him so that she could help him stand.

"Welcome my home. I'm Jew as well. This safe house," she said, using her limited English skills as she pulled him to his feet.

* * *

Her name was Hanna, and for two days she fed him nothing but a delicious soup full of hearty onions, parsnips, carrots, and potatoes. The warm broth renewed his strength until he felt back to his old mountain climbing self again. That is, all except for the pain in his jaw, which hadn't lessened at all.

She brought him down another bowl, and he nodded his thanks to her from the small bed in the cellar.

"*Danke*," he said as he wiped his lips. It pained him to talk, but he found that if he kept his jaw tight and opened his mouth as little as possible, he could eat and speak with minimal pain.

Hanna spoke in German, but when she saw the confused look he was giving her, she switched over to rudimentary English.

"Must go. Nazis."

"I know there are Nazis. What do I do?"

Hanna shook her head in frustration and then let out a string of German. The boy nodded, then positioned himself so that he was sitting across from Yanis. Their knees were touching in the cramped space, and he could smell the sweat that greased the boy's smock.

"I speak English better," the boy said. "My governess English. My name Gregor."

"Thanks, Gregor. Now, what's she saying?"

"She says doctor, you need. Uh, thing from gun is still in mouth. Need out. You go doctor soon, or bad things happen," he explained.

Yanis nodded, wincing at the pain once again. "And before that?"

The boy cocked his head, asked Hanna a question in German, and then turned back to Yanis.

"She says you not stay. Nazis search here. It not safe. You go Austria, then make way Greece."

"I need to get back to *Zitternberg*," Yanis said, hoping that they'd be able to sense the urgency of his statement, despite his inability to speak properly. The boy translated what he said, and Hanna's face suddenly grew angry when she spoke to the boy.

"She says Jews not stay Germany. Not safe here."

"And it's about to get much worse," Yanis said. "That's why I need to go to the mountain. I have to stop the Nazis."

The boy translated. The woman said a few more words, and then stood and went back up into the house.

"What did she say?" Yanis asked.

"She seen too many her people for last time. You do what you want," Gregor said. Yanis planted his feet firmly on the dirt floor and grasped the edge of the boards so he could stand.

"Please thank her for me. I'll never be able to repay her kindness, or yours, for that matter. I'll be on my way now. Best of luck to you both."

"No! You stay! Teach me English!" the boy pleaded.

"I can't stay, Gregor. There's no time. Please tell Hanna what I said," Yanis said as he prepared for his departure. The boy stopped him just as he was about to climb out of the hideaway.

"I tell, then I come. I want help fight Nazis," the boy said firmly.

33

August 1944

Berlin, Germany

"I want whoever is responsible for this to be found and executed, and I want you to handle it personally, Keck," Himmler said.

"I have already given the order, *mein Herr*," Keck said.

"This failure cannot be tolerated! It will look bad, infinitely bad, if we cannot deliver on our promise."

"With your permission, *Herr Reichsführer*, I will dispatch our scientists to *Der Dom*. Some of the greatest minds of our time exist within Germany. They will resolve the situation, and then we'll—"

As the train entered the tunnels that led under Berlin to the Anhalter Bahnhof, the *Reichsführer* reached over and seized Keck's lapel, pulling him close until Keck could smell the wurst on his breath from their sullen lunch.

"Someone must be held accountable for this, Keck. We are to report to Hitler immediately upon our arrival. Would you rather his anger fell upon you, or me?"

Keck stayed silent, his mind churning over the problem of *Der Dom's* sabotaged controls. Looking back on what happened, it was a simple mistake, but it'd had devastating results. The man from 2014 had been gone when he'd returned to the chamber, and so he'd assumed that the body had never made the trip. In hindsight, the man had undoubtedly traveled with him, and what was even worse was that he'd somehow managed to sabotage *Der Dom*.

"So, is that it then, Keck?" Himmler asked. "Would you see me deposed so you can take my position for yourself?" the *Reichsführer* demanded as he pushed his subordinate back against the compartment's upholstery. The train's brakes squealed, and the carriage jerked to a halt. The china before them rattled, and Keck stood bolt upright, eager to reassure the man whom, he suddenly realized, had just gained a great deal of power over him.

"*Nein, mein Herr,*" Keck said. "I only wish to ensure the future of the Reich, and to fulfill my oath."

He'd already altered history so much that he'd lost the advantages that his hours of historical study in 2014 had given him, and now he couldn't even travel back there to stay ahead of what was happening, nor could he go back to retrieve the weaponry he needed to see his plans come to fruition. He had no choice now but to face the war as *Sturmbannführer* in Bavaria with an impeccable lineage and a shining service record, just as he'd been before.

"Fine, you will have your scientists, Keck," Himmler said. "But in exchange I will take *Der Dom's* pilots to Dr. Rascher in Dachau."

"But, *mein Herr,* will this not risk revealing our secret?"

"Not if you remain loyal. This is my decision, and you will follow my orders. Do I make myself clear?"

"Of course, *Reichsführer.* I will remain your faithful servant until the end."

"See that you do so, Keck, because if I am to be hung for any of this, it will be you who precedes me to the gallows," Himmler promised.

* * *

"It remains our best option," Keck said as he faced the map Himmler's staff had prepared. It had arrows that swept from Antwerp and Narvik, all the way toward England's eastern shores. "The British war production must be eliminated, and until the *Luftwaffe* returns to full strength—"

"So, you'd send our soldiers and fleet ahead without adequate air cover?" Rommel asked.

The generals and officials in the room sat with rolled sleeves and shining foreheads. Several were pacing nervously, as they were under orders from Hitler not to leave the room until they produced a workable invasion plan.

"Enough of our invasion force will survive to be a serious threat to the British," Keck said. "If we move quickly enough, we can take the ports and deny the Americans the ability to resupply the islands."

"And then what?" von Rundstedt asked. "What of the Russians, and the Southern Front? Our oil fields must be held at all costs."

"The Americans would not be able to stomach the loss of England. They will fear a second great defeat much more now after the losses they took during the Normandy invasion. We must force them to ask for peace."

"And how would we do that?" Rommel asked.

"We still have the *Wunderwaffe* tanks. *Herr* Speer has been able to retrofit their guns—"

"How will you hold an entire country with two dozen tanks?" Rommel asked. "It's nothing but smoke and mirrors."

"But our opponents have no way of knowing the true extent of our capabilities. They are in chaos right now, and their leadership will be operating from a place of fear rather than strength."

"And you would know this because you saw it in the future?" Hitler asked from the doorway. Keck slammed his heels together, stiffening to attention with everyone else as they threw up their arms in the *Hitlergrub*.

"*Nein, mein Führer*," Keck said as Hitler waved his acknowledgment. "We are past the point where our history corresponds with the timeline I studied."

"*Der Dom* is real," Himmler said. "Of that I can assure you, *mein Führer*. The setback is minor. Think on what Keck has said. As all of us in this room well know, fear of what *might* happen can be very power-ful."

The doors to the room suddenly cracked open, letting in the first cool air that Keck had felt in hours. A runner stepped between Keck and Himmler and slipped a message into the *Reichsführer's* hand.

"As long as we hold the threat of *Der Dom* over the Allies, they will be forced to plan for our superior weaponry, even where it is not present. We will be unstoppable in their eyes, and they will misuse their resources to counter us."

Beside him, Himmler tore open the envelope and pulled out the note. He read it in silence for a moment, and then balled the paper and threw it on the desk.

"More good news?" Rommel asked.

"The Gestapo has just informed me that the Allies have become aware of *Der Dom*. Our intelligence believes that they're redistributing their forces to assault it as soon as possible."

"And how would they know this?" Rommel asked. "Beyond your hand-picked guards, there are only two that know of its location, are there not?"

"I'm afraid there was one other—" Keck said in a somewhat subdued tone to the angry faces that surrounded him.

* * *

May 1943

Augsburg, Germany

Yanis pounded along the rail cutaway, his pack beating against his back as he struggled to match pace with the final rail car. The locomotive's engine screamed as it hauled its supplies for the Vichy government, but he was gaining. If he could just reach this train, it would carry him west over the German border and away from the Nazis. Gravel flew from his feet as he ran. He reached for the iron handle and barely brushed it with his fingertips when suddenly Gregor cried out from behind him.

"Yanis!" he called. Looking back, Yanis saw that the boy had fallen too far behind. So much so that there was no way that they could both make it.

The rail car's metal slipped from his fingers as the train lurched away from him. When Gregor finally caught up, they sprinted across the tracks.

"What do we do now?" the boy gasped.

"We'll hide here for a while and wait for the next one. There's not much else we can do," Yanis said as they ran. As they reached the top of the far embankment, he tried to halt his momentum. Unfortunately, Gregor wasn't watching what was happening ahead of him, which resulted in him charging right into Yanis. The pair tumbled down the hillside, and Yanis' aching jaw skidded along the earth, nearly paralyzing him with pain. He howled and screamed until he reached a drainage ditch at the bottom of the earthworks.

When the pain had finally subsided enough for him to open his eyes, the first thing he saw was a pair of meticulously shined jackboots right there in front of his face. The leather flexed as the man in front of him squatted down and cocked his head.

"My name is *Sturmbannführer* Keck, and I'm afraid I must inform you that stowaways are not tolerated here in western Bavaria," the man said.

34

"The boy should not cry," Keck said in English. He rode with Yanis and Gregor in the back of a troop transport and was just tugging his glove back on. He'd removed it to slap Gregor for not answering a question about his ethnicity. "You see, it's only through struggle and pain that we can truly become men."

"You didn't need to hit him," Yanis said coldly.

"You didn't need to run when we asked to see your papers, and yet here we both are. Life is indeed strange sometimes, isn't it?" Keck asked with the cocky grin of someone who knew he was in a superior position.

Yanis had been in this helpless place before, as a young kid who'd been so different in so many ways from the other boys in Montana. They'd used taunts and punches to dampen his enthusiasm for the way he looked at life, and the way he lived it. It occurred to him that evil often found its roots in the small acts of violence that were allowed to take place every day without retribution. *Would the world never be rid of bullies?*

He stayed silent, feeling the truck's rattle in the inflamed bone of his jaw. This was the man that had shot him in the alien craft, but for some reason he didn't seem to recognize him. *Could it be that there were two Kecks loose in Germany, and the one before him had not yet discovered* Der Dom *or traveled to the future?*

"I would like to know who you both are. You're not related in any way. I can tell that simply from looking at your faces. You have no papers to speak of. In fact, the only possessions you seem to have are these strange items here," he said as he held up Yanis' bag. "You don't even speak German. Tell me, why I should not execute you both for spying?"

"Where are you taking us?" Yanis asked. Keck stared at him in silence for a tense moment before he answered.

"That's dependent upon your cooperation. As of right now we're on our way to the prison at Dachau. There you will work at serving the great German people for as long as is required."

The concentration camp's name curdled Yanis' stomach. He was the only one who could stop what the other Keck had unleashed but eyeing the SS guards on either side of this Keck, he felt his hopes quickly fading. The soldiers watched his every movement and were possessed of an incredible discipline. If he were to escape with Gregor, it would not be through force.

"What do you want to know?" Yanis asked.

"Let's start out with something simple. Tell me your name, your occupation," Keck said.

"My name is Yanis Miller. I'm a professor of mathematics."

"And how did you come to be in Bavaria?"

"I have worked on the Enigma Encryption, among many other projects for our government."

Keck tilted his head for a moment, and then the *Sturmbannführer's* gloved hand shot out and seized Yanis' jaw. He twisted his head to the side as he dug his thumb firmly into the healing wound. Yanis screamed out in agony through his clenched teeth.

"You have no papers, and you ran when you saw my men approach, so I'm forced to conclude that you're lying," Keck hissed as his hard eyes flicked to the boy for a second. "You are Jews? Both of you?"

Yanis shuddered in the Nazi's grip, but his only hope was to press forward.

"As you're very well aware, my people are no longer welcome in the Reich. Imagine you were someone such as myself. Someone who'd traveled willingly from America to help the Vaterland of my ancestors but was then declared an undesirable. Would you not have run?"

"No, I would have kept my papers," Keck said as he released Yanis and held out his hand. One of the SS handed over Yanis' rucksack, and Keck hefted the bag's weight as the truck bounced over a series of potholes. "There are those of your kind who are useful, but I think you are both thieves, and most likely spies as well. Tell me what this is that you've been carrying."

Gregor wiped a hand under his nose while one of the soldiers sneered at him. Yanis studied the rucksack for a moment, trying to think of a way to use it to his advantage.

"I'll have to show you," he said finally. "You'll have to stop the truck though. I can't show you in here."

Keck squinted at him suspiciously for a moment, and then barked some orders in German. A soldier then stood and banged on the pass-through to get the driver's attention.

"Stop the truck!" he called.

They climbed out of the vehicle, and then Yanis and Gregor were pushed over to the roadside by the barrels of the German rifles. They'd stopped next to a river heavily flowing thanks to the hard spring rains. On the other side, a field of sullen cattle stared at them passively. Keck handed Yanis the bag, and then drew his Luger and pressed it against Gregor's temple.

"The boy will die if you try anything," he said coldly.

Yanis took a deep breath and nodded. It was the only plan he could think of, but he had to believe it would work. Slowly, he lifted one of the warm rings he'd taken from *Der Dom* out of the bag.

The Nazis' eyes widened as he pulled it out for them to see. The white glow given off by the mysterious component dimmed even the daylight around them. He held the disk in the palm of his hand for a moment, wincing as the heat it was giving off intensified. He then spun his finger around its edge, just as he'd seen the other Keck do under the mountain. The burning on his palm grew intolerable, but he forced himself to walk calmly to the truck, where he set the disc down on the swell of the truck's petrol tank. He then stepped back and joined Gregor.

"What is this thing that you've found?" Keck asked as he drifted away from the boy and walked toward the gathering light.

"Just watch," Yanis said.

Yanis rested his burned hand on Gregor's shoulder and very subtly pulled the boy a step backward while the guards' attention was entirely focused on the strange disc that had heated the metal of the truck until it first glowed red, and then white hot.

One of the guards yelled out in German when he realized what was about to happen.

Yanis seized the bag from Keck's hand, and then both he and Gregor sprinted toward the riverbank. Keck bellowed in anger just as the alien disk's heat reached the truck's petrol tank. The explosion flung Yanis and Gregor out into the river's swollen waters.

Yanis closed his eyes, giving himself to the powerful current. He kicked closer to Gregor, seized the boy's hand, and then the pair swam deep down under the water in the hopes that they could find a place where the Nazi bullets couldn't reach them.

A sizzling white cut through the murky waters around them, burst into their faces, and molded onto their bodies like clay. It was the alien disk, boiling through the water to return to its companion in the bag. Despite himself, Yanis smiled under the water. There might just be some hope of stopping Keck after all.

* * *

September 1944

The Skies above Rome, Italy

"I don't like this, Sarge, not one bit!" Mitchell shouted so that he could be heard over the noise of the engines. "I've never been higher than the ass end of a horse before."

Jim Thompson stood next to the jump captain with his hand locked onto a rail next to the C-47's open hatch as he fought the wind that buffeted his big frame.

"What about Pointe du Hoc?" Thompson shouted back. Mitchell stared at him for a moment, and then offered a pale smile.

"Yeah, but that was on land!" he shouted as he stepped forward and flung himself through the open door. His carabiner stretched taut, and Jim saw a sliver of gray fabric as Mitchell's parachute opened below the plane. The other Rangers followed one after the other until it was Jim's turn to hook in and make his own jump.

He stepped to the edge of the doorway, struggling to breathe in the 160 mile per hour wind that pulled the tears from his eyes, and then his stomach lurched as he hung his toes over the edge.

"It's all right, soldier. In the dark, you'll never see the ground when it hits you," the jump captain shouted from behind him as he raised his foot and pressed it firmly against Jim's rump to push him out of the plane.

* * *

Jim tried to form himself into the box position that the overtaxed airborne instructor had demonstrated to his company just a few hours earlier. Before he could manage it, however, a tremendous force suddenly seized him, hauled him upward on his shoulders and crotch, and nearly made him soil himself. His chute had deployed, and as his panicked breathing slowed, he realized he was now swinging around under it.

Craning his neck, he could just make out the dark shape of the C-47 flying into the distance. He found the toggles that controlled his canopy and gave them each an experimental tug that jerked him first left, and then right as he sailed down gracefully.

Slowly his heart rate started to return to normal. It was quiet up here, almost peaceful. He could see what had drawn men to the Airborne and hoped that at least some of them had survived their tragic defeat at Normandy. The destruction of the 101st and 82nd was why the Army was retraining its Rangers to jump out of planes. He wished desperately that they could have completed their mission at Normandy, but they did their damage and got out alive, so at least they'd accomplished something, even if it wasn't what they'd set out to do.

He knew that Dog Company could have broken through and reached some of the desperate paratroopers whose radioed pleas for aid had grown fainter and fainter as the invasion bogged down. Rather than sending them in on a rescue mission, however, the Army had sent them to get their wings, and to learn how to stab a knife deep into the Nazis' hearts.

Peering down below his feet, he saw a distant square of red light that the pathfinders had marked for his target. He pulled his toggles and drifted toward the landing zone. This was his first jump, and he'd do as many more as he had to to complete his training. He had a score to settle, and he'd do whatever it took to succeed.

* * *

September 2010

London, England

Jillian tossed the folder of resumes onto her desk. Was the economy really so poor that she'd gotten three hundred applications just to be her Junior Inspector? Her eyes ached from reading line after line of qualifications, but the job needed to be done. Financial criminals were getting more and more sophisticated, and her workload was already intolerable. Sighing, she flipped to the next candidate. Harry Donners, a graduate of the London police academy.

"Jilly," a voice called from her doorway. "Got a parcel here."

"Please refer to me as Inspector Qualmes," she answered.

"My apologies, Inspector," the section assistant said as his smile suddenly faltered.

"Will that be all?" she asked.

"Um, yes, ma'am," Matt said as he turned to leave. "That's all."

"It's not ma'am, it's *Inspector Qualmes*," Jillian sighed, but he was already gone. She put the package aside and tried to focus on Donners' resume, but she couldn't seem to keep her mind from wandering. She'd been short with Matt, but that was just her way. The only thing worse than having too much work was having someone get too close to her. Matt had tried at the pub a few nights earlier, and it had not gone well.

Her attention suddenly turned to the package on her desk. It looked ancient. It was covered in water stains and posted with a fistful of antique stamps printed with busts of Queen Victoria and King George. When she gripped the wrapping to pull it open, its surface powdered and crumbled against her fingers.

"What on earth?" she asked no one in particular as she eyed the odd package. A small bundle wrapped in cloth had fallen out in a cloud of dust. She unwound the brittle fabric and found herself staring at a scarred and scratched cell phone.

She tried to turn it on, but nothing happened. Opening her drawer, she pulled out her charger and plugged in the phone, but it was most certainly dead. Finally, she took it with her as she went to pour herself a cup of coffee.

She found Matt in the break room, took in a deep breath, and then went to see him, trying to redeem herself.

"I'm sorry about earlier, Matt," she said apologetically.

"No, Inspector, you were right. It wasn't proper of me—"

"You were fine. I was just concentrating, that's all," she said. His smile quickly returned as he handed her the cream. "What can you tell me about that parcel?"

"Not much. It arrived via legal courier this morning."

"Legal courier? The ones that deliver last wills and testaments?"

"Yeah, now that you mention it, it was the same guy who delivers that stuff. He said something about how long he'd been holding on to that one, but that's about it. What was in it?"

"This," she said as she held up the phone. "It's dead, though. I tried plugging it into the charger, but no dice. It won't even start charging."

"Oh, well that's no problem. The surveillance guys can fix that," Matt said.

"Surveillance? How do you know?" she asked. He smiled as he walked past and led her toward the elevator.

"You know, you really should talk to more people around here. You'd be surprised at what some of 'em know how to do."

* * *

"I'm sure it's nothing, but I can't shake the feeling that for some reason this is important," Jillian said. "The stamps, the way it arrived—everything."

"Of course it's important," the surveillance tech said from behind his magnifier. "You hate to see a beautiful thing like this go to waste."

Jillian could see every pore and line in the man's fleshy nose through the glass, and she turned to find a smiling Matt sipping his coffee.

"Think about it, Inspector," the office manager said. "A perfectly good piece of equipment gone to waste."

"How long do you think this will take?" she asked.

"Not long," the tech said. "Just got to get under the hood and have a look at the battery."

The tech unfastened two tiny screws next to the phone's speakers, then used a suction cup to lift the screen.

"Well, there's your problem," the man said as he tapped his screwdriver on the warped, cracked metal of the battery. He rolled his chair to a filing cabinet and began rummaging through the contents.

"Is that because it hasn't been used?" Matt asked.

"Not exactly," the tech said. "It's more like age. Batteries store chemicals, but they can't do it forever. Eventually they'll break down and start leaking."

"How old would you say this battery is?" Jillian asked.

The tech found a replacement battery, rolled back over, and popped the old one loose.

"I don't know," he said. "In all my years, I've never seen one this bad." After laying the new battery into the device, he reset the screen, twisted the screws, and then handed it back to Jillian once he'd pressed the button to boot it up. "And Bob's your uncle, Inspector. It was a pleasure to assist you."

She thanked him, ignoring Matt's smirk as she spun and left the room. He followed her into the elevator, unable to take the hint.

"So, it's working now?" he asked.

Holding up the phone with its loading screen, she pursed her lips.

"Now why do you have to be like that, Jilly? I was just asking you a question."

"Matthew, I told you before that my name is—"

"JILLIAN!" the phone blared, crackling with static and booming with air hitting the speakers.

"What was that?" Matt asked.

"JILLIAN, I HOPE THIS GETS TO YOU!"

35

A handsome man with dark curly hair and a scar on his jaw was facing her in the video playing on the phone's scratched screen.

"This is the last of my battery," the man said. "I hope this works. I guess all I can do is tell you what I can and pray that you believe me. It's 1944 here, and I'm in England during World War Two. You won't believe that, or anything else really, but just please, I'm begging you, do just two things for me. My name is Yanis Miller. I'm … I *was* a Professor of Mathematics at Jerusalem Polytechnic. In the future … well, I don't really know when you'll get this, but you and I will work on a case together, and it took me a while, but I finally found out who was responsible for it all. Wait, you won't know what I mean. Please investigate Martin and Maria Steiger in Munich. They've been using Nazi gold hidden under *Zitternberg* Mountain in Bavaria to smuggle weapons. They're Nazis, and they're both killers, so *please* be careful. You and all of Interpol need to see what's in that mountain. Please, please believe me. When you get in there and see what's inside the mountain, you just need to put back the two rings I sent you. You'll be able to tell where they go. There are two packages. The people I'm with want to hold on to the rings for a while before I send them, but I couldn't wait with this. Anyway, put the rings back in place, and then move the biggest one toward the floor by two centimeters. It'll take you to … well … to now. At least, *my* now here in 1944, I guess I should say. Once you get here, you'll need to—"

The video ended there where the phone's battery must have died. The elevator doors opened when they arrived at her floor, and the pair stepped out into the hall together.

"What a loon," Matt said from behind her. "Do you know that man?"

"No, I don't believe I do," she said, but on a hunch, she opened the phone's photo library.

"What the hell?" Matt asked as he stood next to her and looked at the screen.

Jillian was staring at a picture of the man from the video standing between a jubilant Winston Churchill, and a sour-faced Sir Stewart Menzies. He was holding a glowing orb in his hand.

"That's the Prime Minister," Matt said. "Where did this phone come from, Jilly?"

She brushed the screen with her finger and gasped at the next picture. It had been shot from the back seat of a car. It showed a snow-covered mountain, and what looked like a ski resort through the wind screen. Her hand began to tremble, but even so she could recognize her own profile in the passenger's seat. In the photo, she had a radio pressed to her ear and was staring straight ahead toward a destination that she'd never seen in her life.

"And you're sure you don't know that man?" Matt asked again.

"We need to get this to forensics," Jillian said as she tried to push past Matt to get back into the elevator.

"Miss?" a voice called suddenly. "I have a delivery for you."

She turned, still dazed by what she'd seen, and accepted a small metal case from the courier without even thinking.

"You need to sign here, and here," the man said, but she only stood there, staring blankly at the same antique stamps that had been plastered all over the other package, and below them, the faded paint that flaked as she ran her thumb over it.

"From Yanis Miller," she muttered.

* * *

July 1944

London, England

Bethlam Sanitarium squatted under a lead sky, its crumbling brick mercifully hidden behind great swaths of ivy that could not quite hide the bars that secured its windows. Walking up the drive, David Wolcott saw blurred shapes behind several of the portals. Faces that were there and then gone again just as quickly, like the breath of a ghost.

"Officer Wolcott," a spectacled doctor in a white lab coat said as he stood in the doorway to greet him. A gray ring of remaining hair receded from the man's temples and faded into a cream-colored baldness on the top of his head.

"Yes, and you must be Dr. Pierce."

"We spoke on the phone. It is good of you to come, but I should warn you before we go in that one's first visit to a sanitarium is never a pleasant experience. In fact, it can be quite traumatic."

"I can think of worse," Wolcott said as he recalled the corpses he'd stuffed with false orders and floated into the Channel in an effort to protect the secrecy of Operation Overlord. Then there were the sallow faces of the children at the orphanages he'd gone to when trying find the boy that had escaped the skiff with Professor Miller a full year prior.

The doctor led him through a double set of doors, and then through a gate that was opened by a white-shirted orderly who had dozens of keys swinging from his belt. A strange moaning filled the halls, as if despair itself stalked along with them. The sound continued to grow louder as Pierce led him through the halls.

"How has the patient been?" David asked.

"He's been quite frustrated, and constantly angry. He's had bouts of violence and has attempted to escape multiple times. We have him scheduled for a lobotomy within the month."

"Lobotomy?" Wolcott said.

"That's correct. It is the only way we know of to pacify these extreme cases."

Dr. Pierce stopped at a cell marked 74 and nodded for the orderly to open the door. The thick man stepped forward and snapped a key into the lock. When the bolt clanked open, the orderly first stuck his head in to locate the patient. Once he was satisfied that they could enter safely, he relaxed and allowed them entry.

"He's asleep," the man grunted.

"Well enough," Pierce said as he led Wolcott into the cramped, white cell filled with a bed and a small desk that was wedged under the room's narrow window. Yanis lay motionless on the mattress with his eyes half-shut, oblivious to everything that transpired around him. A string of drool ran from his mouth and was pooling on the pillow.

Wolcott squatted down next to him so they could speak.

"Professor Miller?" he asked.

The man's eyelids fluttered, and he swallowed hard, causing his beard to scrape against the linens. That was the extent of his response, though, before he quickly drifted off again.

"Yanis Miller," Pierce called in a loud voice behind him.

Yanis' lids slogged open, showing dulled pupils amidst bloodshot eyes. The professor groaned, trying to roll over, but Wolcott reached out and stopped him.

"I wouldn't do that, officer," Pierce said.

"Professor?" Wolcott asked Yanis.

Miller's jaw opened silently, and then closed again. He blinked a few times, knuckling his eyes tightly, but he still seemed groggy.

"Christ, what do you have him on?" Wolcott asked.

"Paraldehyde. It works to reduce violence quite well. I'm not sure he'll be able to help you, officer. What do you think he knows?"

"Something of interest to the section."

"I can assure you that he's not lucid. Anything he may have told you before you brought him to us would be—"

"Are you here to take me back?" Yanis mumbled. He strained himself to sit up, but he couldn't seem to manage it and quickly fell back against the pillow.

"I need to ask you more questions, Professor," Wolcott said.

"Does that mean you believe me?" he mumbled as more drool slipped from the side of his mouth and sank into the mattress.

"I do, but I need you to help me prove it. Can you do that for me?"

"I'll do anything it takes to stop those bastards," Yanis groaned as he struggled to sit up once again.

* * *

Yanis blinked, trying to clear his head. His lips were cracked and dry, and it felt as if the water running down his throat was the first he'd ever tasted. They'd given him loose-fitting trousers and a plain shirt to replace his hospital gown. Someone had come to shave him, and now the hairdresser was finishing her last touch-ups.

"What's all this for?" Yanis asked, though it was a struggle to speak without slurring his words. His tongue still felt heavy in his mouth from the months of drugs that had been forced into him, and he found that he had to squint to focus on the man sitting to his side.

"I can't tell you that," Wolcott said.

The hairdresser brushed away the last of her cuttings, and then swept the sheet aside and snapped it into the air. David helped Yanis back to his feet. His muscles still felt incredibly weak from the confinement that had been forced upon him over the past year.

"There you go, that's the way," Wolcott said encouragingly.

"Thanks, I mean, for believing me," Yanis said.

The intelligence agent nodded at him, and then led him through the narrow hallways that allowed the military officers to navigate the bunkers that existed below London. Bulbs overhead illuminated the concrete, and as Yanis walked he felt the haze that had covered him for so long finally begin to recede. As it did, however, his bitterness quickly returned.

"How many died?" he asked.

"I beg your pardon?" David said as he held open the door to a larger room.

"I asked how many died at Normandy."

"We lost more than thirty thousand men," a voice said.

Yanis sagged into a chair that Wolcott had pushed under him just in time. His head lolled forward, and then with great effort he lifted it to face the men he'd joined at the table.

"I know you," he blurted out.

"Well, you've certainly seen our faces in the newspapers once or twice, haven't you?" Prime Minister Churchill asked.

"And you're Eisenhower!" It was difficult to even put together the jumbled words in his head, let alone to get them out in a coherent fashion, but he was doing his best.

"*General* Eisenhower," Staunton said from across the table.

"We don't need any formality here," the general said. "We just need to understand what you know."

"I know that Nazis have been murdering my people, and that rather than believing me when I tried to warn you about Operation Overlord, that man there put me in a mental institution," he said bitterly as he pointed directly at Staunton, who cringed as all eyes were suddenly upon him.

"Would any of you have believed the wild stories he was telling?" he asked. A few heads around the table shook, while others stayed still.

"I think Wolcott here is on a wild goose chase," Staunton said. "The pressure's getting to him."

"Well, David?" the Prime Minister asked. "Where's your proof?"

David set the bag he carried in front of him on the table, and then turned it over to dump out the strange devices that Gregor had been carrying when David found him at the orphanage in Kent. A small white metal and glass rectangle slid across the table, followed by two disks that glowed with an alien heat.

The Prime Minister's chair groaned as he leaned forward to get a closer look.

"Staunton, you're sacked. Sir Stewart, see to it immediately," Churchill said firmly.

Staunton sat still in his chair for a moment, frozen in disbelief. Then he lifted himself from the table, pushed his chair back, and walked stiffly from the room. On the way out, he gave Wolcott a murderous glance which Wolcott and Yanis returned in kind.

"Now, son, we need to know what the Germans have, and we need to know how to stop them. Will you tell us?" General Eisenhower asked.

Yanis' head was getting clearer, and as he continued to return to his former self, he felt echoes of the old pain in his jaw. He owed Keck some payback, and he was going to do whatever it took to make sure he got the chance to even the score.

"Yes, I can," Yanis said. "The first thing you need to do though, before you do anything else, is to figure out how to get under a mountain in the middle of Bavaria."

36

September 1944

Rome, Italy

"We should have jumped already," the U.S. Army Air Forces lieutenant slurred. "I don't know what the hell they're waitin' for."

Smoke filled the bar, and their table rattled with empty bottles of beer and glasses of wine. Jim and the other ranger NCOs had come in to relieve some of the tension that came with the endless waiting, and the lieutenant had joined them when he realized these were the same men that he'd been taking up for their training jumps.

"You know more than we do," Jim said. "We haven't even been briefed."

The lieutenant downed his wine quickly, then pushed the glass to an empty space on the table. Behind them, voices rose as a group of Italians started pushing back against some MPs who were just trying to maintain some order in the place.

"They're being real cagey about this one. They're currently in the process of retrofitting my plane, but I don't even know what they're doin' to it. They won't let me see her," the lieutenant said just as a glass shattered somewhere behind Jim.

"I never really liked wine until we got to Italy," Corporal Mitchell said after things calmed down again.

"Heh. What do you know about wine, Mitch? You don't know the difference between wine and piss," someone else from their group called out so that he could be heard over the noise.

"Now that's just a lie! Hey!" Mitch shouted as bodies surged against their group, knocking the table into Jim's stomach, while the other Rangers were thrown off balance. Jim raised himself to his full height, balled his fists, and then pushed his way through the crowd like a mad bull. Someone needed to be taught a lesson, and he was just in the mood. Instead of a brawl, however, he found a group of MPs shining flashlights at the nametags of every soldier in the bar.

"What's this all about?" Jim asked as one of them approached and shined his light right into Jim's eyes for just a moment before he turned it away again.

"Oh, sorry about that. We're looking for Sergeant Thompson!" another MP bellowed. "Does anyone know where—"

"I'm right here," Jim said. "No need to shout."

The MP nodded, then stepped aside. The MPs were escorting another man dressed in a Ranger uniform with no unit or rank designation. A wicked scar slashed his jaw, and his eyes held an intensity that drew Jim's attention. It was the same look he'd seen in dozens of cracked mirrors in Brooklyn basements before a big fight.

"This man is assigned to your regiment effective immediately," the MP said. "You are to come with us and report back to base ASAP for an immediate briefing."

"Does that mean we finally get to get outta here?" Mitchell asked as he regained his feet. The new man stepped forward and shook hands with Jim.

"My name is Yanis Miller," the man said. "Listen, I already know you're going to be asking me this a lot in the next few days, so I'll just tell you right now. No, I'm not crazy."

* * *

September 1944

Bad Tölz, Germany

The work was hot, and the late summer sun on his black-jacketed shoulders made it even hotter, but Keck would not remove his cap, nor the coat that showed his rank. He presented himself as the true Aryan example the cadets from the *Junkerschüle*, the Dachau guards, and the lower races needed to see so they could gain a full understanding of Nazi supremacy. He strode among them while they shoveled earth, poured concrete, and dug the trenches they would use to defend the road that led to *Der Dom.* He could hear their whispers, and he knew they were watching him. He also knew why. It was because he looked so much like another SS officer that many of them knew. One who they thought had been reassigned to western Bavaria as a punishment, and yet here he was … or so they thought.

The preparations were hasty, but they were taking shape. Three divisions had just departed France for the long trip south. As soon as they arrived, Keck would have nearly fifty thousand men at his command. The generals fighting at the Eastern Front had howled, but in truth, Keck himself had been shocked at the size of the command. It was a strong indication of the importance that Hitler had placed on both him and his project, and he was determined that he wouldn't fail a second time.

"What do the reports say about the Americans? What are we facing?" Keck asked his new adjutant. He was a man named Reinhold, and next to him stood Horst Vogle, now returned from the dead thanks to Keck's time manipulations. They'd been watching the pale specters of Dachau's workers as they performed the heaviest work of breaking stone and clearing trees.

"They are raising two, possibly three more airborne brigades," Reinhold said. "Their units have been in training since July. Our evidence indicates they may strike just as our first brigade arrives."

"Damn Rommel and his foot dragging," Keck said irritably. "Reinhold, order our brigades to move more quickly."

"Yes sir," the aide said, snapping him a hasty salute before he turned and ran off toward the radio tent.

"Horst, how many planes do they have?" Keck asked. "How many paratroopers could they possibly bring?"

"Thanks to the Italian capitulation, we have not been able to challenge their airfields on the Southern Front. Every plane in Africa and the Mediterranean has been called to Rome. It could be nearly twenty thousand men, *Sturmbannführer,* but that may prove our advantage. The Americans lost their entire airborne command in Normandy, so we can assume they won't be sending seasoned troops against us," Horst said.

Keck smiled as he climbed the grade amid the steady clatter of work going on all around him. Finally, some good news after so much frustration. The *Zitternberg* would be the hammer with which he'd break the Allies, and then he'd head up north with his command to join Rommel for the counterattack into Britain.

"Let them come," Keck said as he looked around at his men. "Let them bleed themselves upon our Reich until they have no strength left for the fight. It'll only help to speed along the inevitable."

* * *

In the last of the day's light, Keck climbed the road to *Der Dom* with a look of tight determination on his face. Three *Radschlepper Osts* barreled past him up the trail, belching black smoke into the sunset while their drivers pounded their horns to clear the tired workers from their path. Keck fell into a scowling jog after them. The trucks were filled with SS men he did not recognize, which meant that the *Reichsführer* had come to claim his insurance.

When he reached the clearing in front of the tunnel entrance, he found the SS men from the trucks facing off with his *Totenkopfverbände,* who'd long obeyed Keck's orders to allow only him into the tunnel once its excavations had been complete.

"*Herr Sturmbannführer,*" Reinhold called. "Thank you for coming so quickly. These men—"

"Are here at the pleasure of *Reichsführer* Heinrich Himmler," their leader called. The man outranked Keck and wore a *Standartenführer's* silver oak leaves at his throat. The dust of the road coated his face in a ring where he'd worn his goggles for the trip, and when he smiled, a scum of dirt and saliva coated his teeth. "I believe you know the *Reichsführer* personally, do you not, *Sturmbannführer?*"

Keck watched as the SS from the trucks unloaded three long and bulky metal canisters that could have been iron lungs.

"Yes, we're good friends," Keck replied. "*Mein Herr*, may I ask where the scientists are that I was promised?"

"They will be delivered when your *deposit* has been received."

Keck felt Reinhold's eyes on him. The humiliation that Himmler was forcing him to endure in front of his own men was burning him up, but there was nothing he could do about it.

"Yes, of course," Keck said. "Please, follow me and do exactly as I say. The bodies are remarkably preserved, and we do not yet understand everything about what you are about to see."

"Reports are that your little toy here is broken, *Sturmbannführer*. How dangerous could it be?"

Keck's blood boiled as he entered the tunnel in front of the colonel, but he forced himself to remain calm, for the insults mattered little in the long run. As Himmler himself had said, he alone had an infinite amount of time to make things right once *Der Dom* had been repaired. It also meant that he had all the time in the world to get his revenge, so for now he'd simply hold his tongue until that moment finally presented itself.

"It is not *Der Dom* you need be concerned with, *mein Herr*," Keck said. "It's the consequences of using it."

In only a few minutes, the alien bodies were sealed into the containers the SS men had brought to transport them. Then they were removed from the ship and taken back to the trucks.

With false respect, Reinhold excused himself to use the latrine before his special detachment headed out. Keck took this moment as an opportunity. While the men were focused on loading the containers, he walked with purpose to one of the drivers, and demanded to see his paperwork for the shipment.

He flipped through the Top Secret orders and noted that the containers were to proceed immediately to Kiel, where they would be loaded on a submarine and then taken to a coded base in South America called Knochenhaus. Keck handed the papers back to the driver with no emotion whatsoever, then returned to bid farewell to the adjutant.

* * *

October 1944

Airspace above the Swiss Alps

Yanis fought his rising nausea as the transport bucked through heavy turbulence. Somewhere below them, dark mountains rose to pierce the thick clouds. The assault had lifted off on a clear evening, but the weather had been deteriorating rapidly. However, the big sergeant sitting across from him didn't seem to notice. In fact, he seemed to be sleeping quite peacefully. Every so often, he'd let out a snore as the plane jerked this way and that, but other than that, he seemed totally oblivious to their situation. Yanis, however, was deathly afraid that the wings were going to be ripped from the fuselage at any moment.

Loaded with enough gear for a week's worth of fighting, most of the Rangers had painted their faces black and rode in determined silence. If anything, they seemed eager, as was Yanis. It was time for some long-delayed payback. He replayed the malice and disgust in Keck's words over and over in his mind. The man was evil incarnate, and whatever happened in the coming days, he swore to himself that he'd destroy Keck's precious cathedral.

A violent jolt threw him against his straps, tearing him from his thoughts. He swallowed hard, trying to force his stomach back down where it belonged. He noticed that Sergeant Thompson's eyes had opened, and the big man was smiling.

"They don't have turbulence in the future?" he shouted so that he could be heard over the roar of the engines.

Yanis shook his head, as he adjusted himself in his seat a bit. The constant vibration of the plane had been wearing on him, and the muscles in his back and rear end were starting to get a bit sore.

"In the future, we'd know better than to try something like this!" Yanis shouted back. Thompson laughed at his response, and while the men around them heard little of the exchange, they smiled anyway in response.

Yanis watched them all quietly as they nervously checked their restraints, tapped their pockets to make sure they'd remembered everything, and attempted to write letters, even though the turbulence was making it difficult for them to write legibly.

He had no one to write to, but it didn't matter. Gone was the tentative man of the past. It hadn't taken long for this war-torn world to change him, and at this point, he'd mentally adapted himself to the situation. Ironically, even though he'd never really felt like he'd found his place in the world back home, here in this place, in this time, he finally felt like he belonged. This was where he was supposed to be. This was what fate had planned for him all along, and he was determined to see it through, even if it cost him his life.

He closed his eyes, and while the sergeant watched him passively through half closed eyelids, he prayed that he and the men around him would be able to stop Keck's evil, once and for all.

* * *

The cabin lights flashed red. The jump captain next to Jim Thompson pressed his headset against his ear, trying to drown out the engine noise. The man nodded to himself, and then held up a fist with one finger raised. The pathfinders had left the lead planes, jumping thirty minutes ahead of the main force to mark the landing zones.

Jim tapped the man to his left, showed him one finger, and the signal passed down the line until everyone acknowledged.

"Thirty minutes!" Jim yelled across to the intelligence officer. The poor man swallowed hard and mumbled something in return. Yanis was praying, and Jim didn't blame him. He'd found himself backed into a corner so many times that he knew what it was like to be down to your last Hail Mary.

Jim had seen nothing but clouds outside the windows, and now rain and ice were mixing on the glass. Leave it to the Rangers to do things the hard way. Starting an airborne assault on the edge of a rainstorm was a tenuous proposition at best.

After another few minutes of bouncing through the turbulence, the jump captain released his restraints and swayed upright. As soon as he'd stabilized his footing, he cupped his hands around his mouth and pressed them against Jim's ear.

"THE PILOT THINKS WE'RE OFF COURSE," he shouted, though the sound of his voice was nearly lost beneath the drone of the engines and the crash of the rain. "THE WEATHER—" he said, but Jim missed the next part. "YOU'LL BE SCATTERED. DON'T KNOW IF WE CAN CORRECT."

The captain pulled away and Jim nodded. He'd caught enough to understand that they were jumping even though they probably wouldn't be near the designated jump targets.

The transport rocked and swayed, sounding like a machine that wanted to tear itself apart. Jim leaned to the man next to him and screamed into his ear.

"GET READY TO JUMP. IF YOU'RE SEPARATED, USE YOUR FLASHLIGHTS AND YOUR CLICKERS. NOW GROUP UP AND GET TO YOUR RALLY POINTS. PASS IT DOWN!"

The Ranger nodded and twisted to yell at the next soldier. As he did, the plane lurched into a momentary free fall that threw the jump captain into the ceiling. The man's head smashed into the plane's aluminum framing, and he fell limp against the deck as the pilot regained altitude.

Looking down the stick, Jim saw his Rangers screaming, their eyes screwed shut and their hands clutching at anything they could grab a hold of. The engines were still running, and Jim still saw the steady red light, but his hand drifted to his harness anyway. He'd be damned if he was going to die in a plane crash while he had a parachute strapped to his back.

Releasing his harness, he worked his way down the line toward the jump captain. Their medic, a man named Doc Bradford, was reaching for his release, but the sergeant held up his hand. He couldn't have his medic knocked silly trying to help someone else. He'd do the deed himself.

Just as he reached the moaning jump captain, the cabin light flashed yellow. Thirty minutes couldn't have passed so quickly, but the pilot was telling them it was jump time. Jim squatted and pulled the semiconscious man back up into his seat and strapped him in securely. Then he turned to face the eighteen men that were staring at him, wondering what to do.

Jim raised his hand into a C, drew his lead, and clipped onto the security rail. Then he waddled back to the door, wrapped his arm around the hand hold at the air captain's station, and leaned his weight against the plane's hatch release. The door cracked open, flying outward in the strength of the wind. A slurry of rain beat at his legs. It would be a tough jump, but there was really no choice. If they didn't reach that mountain, the Nazis would be unstoppable.

"EQUIPMENT CHECK!" Jim bellowed.

The Rangers repeated his order, then one by one called out OK until the man standing closest to Jim did the same.

When the cabin light flashed green, the first Ranger barely paused at the door before fixing his eyes shut and leaping. The rest of the Rangers followed in turn. Mitchell, Doc Bradford, and everyone else down the line made their jumps until only Jim and Yanis remained on the plane. The intelligence officer was white as a sheet, his hand locked on the railing next to his chute clip. Below them, the roiling clouds seethed with a bitter blackness that was swallowing up Dog Company's tumbling parachutes.

"DON'T WORRY. I'LL FIND YOU!" he screamed to Yanis, and then he seized the man's shoulder and tossed him out of the plane. As soon as he saw that Yanis was clear, Jim jumped out of the plane and into the darkness.

37

October 2010

München, Germany

"And you've not seen this man before?" Jillian asked Martin Steiger. The professor squinted at the glossy photograph she'd handed him and gave it a peculiar look of disdain. A few moments later, he handed it back to her.

"*Nein.* Should I have?"

"May we know what this is about, Inspector?" Steiger's wife asked from his side. They sat in the couple's drawing room while the maid stood at the edge of the room preparing tea for the Steigers' latest guest.

"It's a missing persons case," she answered. "The man in that photograph is a Professor of Math at Jerusalem Polytechnic, and the last information we have on him is that he traveled to Munich. I'm asking every professor here if they had any meetings with him, or possibly saw him at a recent conference or something."

"From Jerusalem?" Maria asked. Jillian saw the corners of the woman's mouth tighten. Her husband reached into her lap and covered her hands with his. "We've never traveled to that part of the world."

"I understand," Jillian said. "In case he does pay you a visit, I've left you my card. Please call if you hear anything."

"Of course," Martin said as he stood to shake her hand. "Elsa will see you out."

Maria shook her hand next, smiling in a way that seemed to draw the tight skin of her face against her forehead. As soon as they'd said their goodbyes, Jillian and Harry followed the maid's tentative footsteps as she led them toward the front door.

"It's a lovely house," Jillian said.

"Thank you, ma'am," the maid replied.

"The Steigers must do quite well. I'm sure they've made a lot of investments."

"I would not know of their finances," Elsa said tightly.

When they reached the front door, Elsa stood to the side respectfully as she held it open for them. After a quick word of thanks, the pair made their way to the rental car they had parked in the driveway.

"Was there something there?" Harry asked as he climbed into the car and pulled his door shut. Jillian smiled from the driver's seat as she turned and eased the car onto Munich's streets.

"Harry, you may just work out as an inspector after all. Tell me what you observed."

"Well, they were very stiff, and not just German stiff either. There was something else. It took them a long time once the maid announced us. They said they'd just been having tea, but when the maid brought the service into the room, she brought four cups."

"Correct."

"And the woman, Maria, seemed almost insulted by the insinuation that they might know Yanis."

"I noticed the same."

"But what does it prove to us about their finances? Why ask the maid?"

"I've found that those with legitimate wealth are often very clear about where it comes from. Those who come into their money by other means are much less so, and the university dean provided me with the Steigers' salaries just this afternoon. Something other than their tenure is paying for that house and those antiques," Jillian said as Harry watched the afternoon traffic pull around them.

"So, what do we do now?" he asked. "We don't exactly have a case."

"Have you ever known a household with a domestic to not ask that person their opinions of company? What they said, how they were received?"

"No, come to think of it, I haven't."

"Elsa will tell them what I asked. So now, we wait to see what the Steigers do," Jillian said with a confident smile.

* * *

Harry's chin slid from his cupped hand, startling him awake.

"What time is it?" he mumbled.

"Half past three," Jillian answered. Her eyes were painfully dry, thanks to a lack of sleep, and the caffeine she'd finally decided to down by the cupful was filling her bladder until it felt like it'd overflow any minute. But the strange feeling she'd had ever since the phone had arrived in her office kept her at the stakeout. Somehow, she knew there was something happening here, and that Yanis' message hadn't been just a hoax.

She'd verified Professor Miller's position with his school and understood that he had taught a lecture just that morning. The phone company had confirmed the serial number on the phone she'd received, and she remembered the tingle of excitement that had followed as she'd listened to their legal officer's surprise at discovering that there were two phones with that serial number currently on the grid. One was in Jerusalem, while the other was in Munich with her. That fact alone had been enough for Director St. Pierre to approve her travel to Jerusalem by way of Munich. She only hoped there would be something to this mysterious tip she'd received.

A car engine's throaty roar floated through her lowered windows. Headlights poured into the street, and the Steigers' Maserati soon emerged with Martin at the wheel.

"He's headed out of town," Harry said as Jillian keyed the ignition.

"I figured as much. We've rattled them, Harry. Now let's see where he's headed," she said as she quickly started the car and sped after him.

* * *

October 1944

Bad Tölz

Rain battered the side of Keck's face. His boots squelched in the mud, and his uniform felt tight and heavy. Still, he'd wanted to be present as the Fifth SS Panzer Division Wiking entered the village. If these were to be his men, they deserved to see him first as he should be, spotlit in the rain as he offered them the *Hitlergrub*.

Exhausted from covering hundreds of kilometers south in a handful of days, the division's weary soldiers tightened their straggling march as they recognized their commander and passed at attention.

"*Heil* Hitler!" Keck cried as lightning danced far off in the mountains.

"*Mein Herr*," a voice called from behind him. Keck turned to find Reinhold splashing through the puddles.

"What is it?" Keck asked.

"*Sturmbannführer*, we have reports of paratroopers to the west," Reinhold said. Cool rain dribbled down Keck's collar, and for just a moment he stayed silent. "*Mein Herr?* What are your orders?"

A group of men approached from the Wiking Division, and one of them stepped in front of the others before he spoke.

"*Sturmbannführer*," their senior officer saluted. "Colonel Liebner of the Wiking Division, reporting for duty."

"Colonel, you have come not a moment too soon," Keck replied. "Allied paratroopers have somehow landed in this weather. Your orders are to hunt them down. We do not need them alive. Just bring me their heads."

* * *

October 1944

Isar Valley, Bavaria

Jim Thompson sawed at his parachute's control toggles, fighting the buffeting winds that threatened to twist his lines. His altimeter showed barely eight hundred feet, but he couldn't see beyond the clouds. Soaked and freezing, he'd lost track of Yanis and the rest of his men. He didn't know how low the clouds hung or where he'd be when they finally broke, but he knew he'd have to land somewhere.

"Lord, I don't know if You're up there listening, I could sure use some help right about now," he muttered, though his voice was silenced by the buffeting winds.

The gray mist absorbed all sense of direction and sound. He thought he saw parachutes below his feet and sawed on his toggles to angle in the stick's direction. Gradually, the gray faded to black beneath him until he was descending through the calm of the night sky.

He'd finally come free of the rain clouds but saw no sign of the pathfinders' red strobe lights that were to mark his landing zone. The dim mushrooms of a half dozen parachutes glimmered far to his left, and he did his best to veer in their direction. The Alpine peaks were on his right, which meant that he was heading east. The valley below him was the Isar, near the town of Bad Tölz, but where were the landing zones?

He feathered his toggles even more, trying to maintain his altitude so he could identify any of the other visible landmarks within his range of vision. Four hundred feet remained, and then three. He coasted over fields, small hamlets, and a herd of cattle that became quite spooked as he sailed overhead. Finally, he saw a glint of what he thought was red light to the north, and quickly pulled on his lines to make the turn.

More details emerged as he grew ever closer to the ground. Darkened buildings, thick woodlands, and a stream trickling gently through a thicket. Here and there he saw canopies trapped in the tree line and did his best to mentally note their locations.

The ground rushed up toward him, seeming to gain speed as it closed. One hundred feet, and then fifty. Somewhere ahead of him a church bell rang, and rifle fire shattered the quiet of the night.

He lost focus as he was about to land, and he hit the ground in a crumpled mess. Dazed from the impact, he flopped forward as his canopy dragged him along the ground. Hollering in surprise and pain, he beat at his harness until his numb fingers finally found the release. He snapped open the buckle and dropped into the mud. He was surprised that he'd even survived at all, what with the rushed training he'd received, and the terrible weather that seemed intent on keeping them from their goal.

For a brief moment, he watched the white silk of his parachute drift across the field, and then he shrugged off his pack and started checking his gear. Satisfied that his rifle had made the jump intact and that all he had in the line of injuries were a few bruises, he stood and swung his pack back onto his shoulders. Then he froze as a voice broke through darkness.

"*Was ist das?*" the voice called out in German.

38

Yanis had kept his eyes closed from the moment he'd left the plane until he felt the storm's violent gyrations leave him. His stomach had finally revolted, but he'd had the presence of mind at least to lean forward so he wouldn't get vomit all over his shirt. The slipstream's force had torn his rifle away from him, but now he found himself drifting calmly over a field two hundred feet below. He ran through everything he remembered from the single training session he'd logged, including flaring his parachute and lifting his feet at the last moment. The ground rose to meet him, and his boots splashed into the waterlogged soil of a wheat field.

His canopy floated over his head, pulling him forward in a jog until he found the release and broke free in front of a tree line. Then he sank down and squeezed the earth with his hands. He'd survived, despite everything, and now it was time to find Keck.

A branch snapped in the forest ahead of him as he made his way forward. He quickly fumbled at his vest pockets, trying to work the snaps with fingers still numb from the jump. Finally, he pulled out his cricket, pressed down the small metal tab, and then released it.

"Two clicks," a voice said in English.

"We knew you were with us," another paratrooper said as he stepped from the shadows. "After all, who the hell else would be parachuting down out here?"

* * *

October 1944

South of Bad Tölz

"You said three brigades at the most," Keck said to Horst as they rode in one of the newly arrived *SchützenPanzerwagen* troop carriers. "Explain to me how all of a sudden these Americans have appeared all over Bavaria?"

"I'm afraid I have no answers, *Sturmbannführer*. We'll need to capture some prisoners to interrogate to gather more information."

"We are close, *ja?*" the weary driver asked.

"Yes, you will see the church after these trees," Keck answered.

Above the sound of the engine, Keck thought he heard the crack of rifle fire, but couldn't be sure. Their half-track passed a spray of canopies in the trees, but the silks drifted without any men attached to them. The truck splashed through a puddle as it entered the grounds of the church. There, he found a group of farmers with pitchforks and torches surrounding a tall man smeared with mud.

Keck leapt from the half-track's cab before it stopped, drew his pistol, and parted the circle of frightened citizens. He found the American standing with his hands half-lifted in front of him defensively. His rifle had been confiscated by one of the farmers.

"You've done well," Keck said to the citizens in German. "There will be more. Be on your guard."

The villagers shifted uneasily, a few of them shrinking at the sight of his uniform. No matter. They didn't need to like him, only to fear him, and they'd soon learn the benefits of obedience.

"How many more of you are there?" Keck asked the prisoner in English. "What is your target?"

"Sergeant James Thompson," the man answered. "Service number 12-44-7-8. United States Army."

Keck clicked off his pistol's safety.

"What is your objective?" he asked again. "Answer me."

"Sergeant James Thomps—"

Keck drew back and swung his pistol at the big American's face. The blow sliced the man's cheek, but the Sergeant stood his ground.

"You're one of the Nazis that kills the Jews, aren't you?" the Ranger asked. "You're gonna regret doin' that."

"I think not, Sergeant," Keck said. "It has been a pleasure, but unfortunately, tonight I have no time for prisoners. Goodbye."

But as Keck raised his pistol, a soldier screamed behind him. Bullets peppered the church, and Keck dropped to the earth.

"Sir, we must get to cover!" Reinhold cried.

Keck saw the American sprinting away behind the church and tried to track him with his pistol, but the terrified villagers blocked his shot. The *Sturmbannführer* beat his fist into the mud before crawling after Reinhold. This night was not going as planned.

* * *

October 2010

The Zitternberg

Jillian's first sign that something was wrong came when the lead *Polizei* cruiser braked to a skidding stop in front of her. She twisted the wheel hard to the side, halting just in front of a hastily constructed roadblock of felled trees that had not been there when she and Harry had followed Martin Steiger up the hillside two days prior. She reached for her radio just as bullets shattered her windshield.

"Get down!" Harry cried.

Ducking as low as she could in her seat, Jillian shifted into reverse and mashed the accelerator. A dozen other cruisers were behind her, but she had to hope they would see what she was doing.

"Oh no!" Harry said.

A fireball burst from the car in front of them.

"They've got RPGs!" Harry yelled. "Oh God, we're dead!"

"Out of the car!" Jillian cried. Harry shoved open the door and spilled out onto the dirt road. Jillian didn't even bother to stop. She opened her door and dove out as fast as she could, rolling partway down the steep hill before she finally came to a stop and painfully regained her footing. Without hesitation, she crawled behind a thick pine, and then scanned the area to see if she could see Harry on the other side. She spotted him hiding behind a tree, just as she was doing, and felt a wave of relief wash through her that he'd made it out.

"This is Qualmes," she called into her radio. "Get everyone back. Get them down and off the road."

"Qualmes, what's happening up there?" a German voice asked. Another streak of smoke flashed from the tunnel entrance, and a tree canopy just behind the scrambling line of police cars splintered and caught fire.

"I think we're at war," she answered. "Just get everyone back! Now!"

* * *

October 1944

South of Bad Tölz

Yanis waved his flashlight high overhead. On the other side of the stone bridge, a red beam blinked three times in response. He answered the pattern, then ducked behind the wall and waited for the cautious boot falls to approach. His unit had learned by now to stay out of sight until they could see whether it was Americans or Germans on the other end of the lights, so he was doing just as he'd been instructed to do.

"Clear," a hoarse whisper sounded. The Americans rose, their party now grown to nearly sixty men and adding more all the time as they pushed west toward their first rally point.

"Are we glad to see you boys or what!" one of the new paratroopers called. "Anyone got a medic?"

Doc Bradford rose and tended to a man limping over the bridge that was being supported by two others.

"All right," Corporal Mitchell said under the dim light of another flashlight. "As near as I can figure, we've got two more miles until we get to the rally point ..."

Heavy weapons rumbled off to the north, and Yanis could see muzzle flashes through a distant tree line.

"All right, that's our next target. Let's go find our people. Move out!" the corporal said as he and his ragtag unit splashed off into the slackening rain.

Yanis ran with the M1 he'd taken from a dead Ranger at his thigh, but he raised it to his shoulder when he saw the others charging ahead, ready to shoot whoever was attacking their men.

The fighting around the tree line intensified, hundreds of men were screaming and firing and calling orders, while the heavier weapon shook the ground with every shot. Before he knew what was happening, Yanis suddenly noticed that he was still running while the rest of the Rangers had ducked into cover.

"Yanis!" someone called from behind him, but he'd realized his error too late. He'd run into the rear of the German position, where a crew were pointing what looked like an artillery piece with four barrels at a farmhouse surrounded by thick hay bales.

One of the artillerymen goggled in surprise, then fumbled for his sidearm. Yanis raised his rifle and squeezed the trigger. Nothing happened, and a wave of panic suddenly washed through him. Then he suddenly realized he'd forgotten to flip the safety off. Instantly he flicked it with his thumb just as a dozen Rangers swarmed around him. They fell on the Germans with pistols and bayonets, stabbing and shooting and clawing. One of the artillerymen slipped from the fighting and ran for his life, but Yanis sighted down his rifle barrel, exhaled, and squeezed the trigger. The man fell and lay still.

In a matter of seconds, the fighting was over. Corporal Mitchell shone his flashlight at the farmhouse. A few moments later, the paratroopers trapped inside ran out to join them, but Yanis stared at the German he'd killed. It was a man whom he hadn't even known. A man who may have survived the war in another time, but he was also a Nazi. Sentiment and regret were wasted on those who'd mercilessly killed so many innocent people. Besides, this was his reality now. He'd likely have to kill again, so he'd better start getting used to it.

All over the valley, sounds of battle picked up in intensity. The final fight for *Der Dom* had come. Now they just had to get there.

* * *

"Report!" Keck screamed as he stormed through his headquarters north of the *Zitternberg.* "I want a report!"

On one wall of his tent, aides were marking reports of fighting with an X on the map. The indicators spanned a swath of Bavaria kilometers long.

"Sir," Colonel Liebner said, "It appears that the Americans number in the many thousands. They are gathering into larger and larger groups. My men are—"

"Your men must find every last one of them!" Keck screamed. "Hunt them down!"

"They will, *mein Herr.*"

"Where are the second and fourth *Volksgrenadier* divisions?" Keck asked as he looked over at Reinhold.

"They'll be here by the morning. They have been advised of the situation and are doubling their pace."

"It won't be enough," Keck hissed as he watched the red X's multiply on the map. "It will never be enough!"

"Sir?"

"The cadets at the *Junkerschüle.* Arm them, and then order them to keep the population pacified."

"But, *mein Herr,* they're only children," Liebner said.

"Roust my *Totenkopfverbände,* as well Reinhold. Colonel, it's every German's blood duty to fend off this threat. We're fighting for the Reich's very existence. If we should fail ..." Keck said, but then he trailed off and watched as more red X marks were placed on the map.

* * *

Jim Thompson knelt behind a stump next to the church, catching his breath while the German half-track tore into the distance. This was the type of a night it would be, he thought to himself. An endless stream of chaos, but nothing would stop him from finding Yanis and getting to that mountain so they could complete their mission.

He thrust his flashlight overhead and flipped the switch three times. An answering light shone from the forest, and Jim jogged back toward the clearing. The circle of villagers who'd initially captured him knelt over two of their own in the clearing. One of the women grabbed his wrist, pulling him to a stop with a bloody hand. She'd been trying to stem the bleeding of an older man who'd been standing at the edge of the crowd.

"*Bitte*," she wailed. "*Bitte, mein Papa!*"

Pounding boots and rattling equipment met him. Two dozen Rangers from mixed companies surrounded him.

"Sarge, are these people giving you trouble?" a private called.

Jim looked down at the kneeling woman. Below her, the grandfather writhed.

"*Wir ... sind keine ... Nazis,*" the wounded man said. "*Keine!*" He roared as his granddaughter returned to his wound. Around the pair, the other civilians held up their hands and blinked. They were young boys, women, and old men. They didn't deserve this.

"Do we have a translator?" Jim called.

"The man's saying that they aren't Nazis," one of the Rangers said. "They hate the Nazis. The Nazis come and force their children into the army school, and they shoot people. He's saying the whole village surrenders."

Jim knelt next to the old man and lifted the flap of his shirt. A thin stream of blood trickled from his abdomen.

"Medic!" he cried. A Ranger with a red and white cross on his helmet jogged over. Jim stood, turning to the private that had translated.

"Tell them that we're here to help end the war. Tell them that we won't hurt civilians, but that they should stay inside where it's safe."

The translator repeated Jim's words as the sergeant turned to take stock of his unit. But a hand on his arm stopped him once more. The girl tending to her grandfather had pushed back her hair, smearing blood on her cheek and forehead.

"She says her name is Hanna," the Ranger translated. "And that they would like to fight, too."

Jim looked perplexed. Everything he had heard from his contacts in intelligence had indicated that the people were devoutly committed.

The translator could see his expression, and commented, "Apparently the commander up on the mountain is some kind of an exceptional bastard that even the Nazis don't like."

Jim nodded to the girl, and she gave him a tight nod in return. They could use all the help they could get, so if these people wanted to fight, he certainly wouldn't stand in their way.

* * *

October 2010

The Zitternberg

For two days, Martin Steiger listened to the voice of Inspector Jillian Qualmes over his radio as she plotted to ruin everything that he'd spent his life working for. He sat just inside the tunnel entrance with the other members of the Fourth Reich, whom he'd summoned with desperate messages when the inspector had first appeared. The men smoked, finished what liquor remained, and played cards as they waited for their end.

"Do you think The King would have come?" he asked Maria.

"Yes, and he still may," she said.

"But we won't be here to greet him."

"What if we used *Der Dom?*" Maria asked.

"We swore to protect it, and that we'd never venture inside," he said.

"We swore to our parents that we'd resurrect the Reich, Martin."

The radio crackled with German *Polizei* discussing the approaching NATO column from the American base at Stuttgart. They were mere hours away now.

"Were we weak?" he asked.

"*Nein,* my love, we were never weak," she said as she stroked his hair.

"Professors!" a muddy sniper called from the clearing. "They're coming again."

"What would you have me do?" Martin asked.

"I would have you deny Interpol the satisfaction. The King may yet come in another life, at another time, but they must not learn *Der Dom's* secrets from us," Maria said.

Martin stood and tossed the radio to the floor where it shattered at his feet. A sad smile spread over his face, and he reached for his wife's hand as they turned toward the glowing blue light.

"You are as right as ever, my darling," he said as he led her behind the door and sealed the tunnel. "Come, let us make our final sacrifice."

39

Jillian ducked as a stray bullet ricocheted off the rock in front of her. Despite the terrain and dozens of ambushes by solitary sympathizers, the NATO forces were making good progress up the hillside toward the base of the *Zitternberg*. The American tanks' machine guns roared through the forest as black-clad men screamed and fell. Jillian and Harry trotted to one of the Steigers' wounded fighters as a medic dragged him back down the mountain.

"Ma'am, you're too close to the front," one of the Americans called to her.

"Captain Leonard, that's very protective of you, but I need to understand what's happening here," Jillian said.

"With all due respect, ma'am, nothing is worth your life. I don't know what the hell's up there, but I think you want to be around long enough to see it, don't you?"

She looked down for a moment at the wounded man the medics were working on, and then nodded.

"You're right, Captain. Just get me into that hill and I'll do the rest."

The American nodded, and then returned to the personnel carrier in which he'd arrived and began issuing orders.

Offers of surrender in German and English rang up and down the hill, but no one came forward. A NATO squad flashed into the forest in pursuit of a shooter. Their rifles snapped, and the radio reported another one down. Tanks groaned up the road out of sight and platoons of soldiers jogged past her, but she did not hear any more gunfire.

"Do you think that's all of them?" Harry asked.

The captain jumped back out of his command vehicle and jogged toward them.

"Ma'am," he said. "I think we found what you were looking for. If you'll just come with me."

* * *

Twenty meters from the set of steel doors built flush into the mountain rock, Jillian picked up a megaphone, pressed the button, and then spoke to the mysterious people that Yanis Miller from the past and future had asked her to track down.

"Attention!" she called out. "This is Interpol Inspector Jillian Qualmes calling for Martin or Maria Steiger. Are you there?"

Birds chirped high in the trees, while a pleasant breeze wafted down the mountainside. No sound came from inside the tunnels, however.

"Martin and Maria, I am offering you your lives. If we enter the tunnel by force, we cannot guarantee your safety. Surrender now and you won't get hurt."

"Seems like they ain't in the mood for cooperating," Captain Leonard said.

"I don't care how tough they think they are—" Jillian began, but before she could finish, the ground rolled underneath her, and a tremendous crack appeared beside the entrance. Smoke plumed from the portal's doors as Jillian stared in horror.

"Who fired?" the captain demanded. "Who was that?"

Jillian knew it wasn't one of their tanks that had fired the shot. Whatever the Steigers had wanted to protect, they were willing to take it with them to the grave.

* * *

October 1944
Near the Zitternberg

"As near as we can figure it, sir, we've got two thousand effectives converging on the approaches to the *Zitternberg*. There are probably another fifteen thousand working their way here, but they're spread out all over the place," Jim reported to Captain Dickson.

"Thank you, Sergeant. You've done an excellent job as acting Company Commander until my arrival. I'm going to be recommending you for another promotion."

Jim nodded, too weary to offer much of a smile at the praise. He'd been fighting and moving all morning, gathering more and more men with him as they made a desperate push through disorganized German resistance.

"Down in the lower valley," a lieutenant called. "They're doing it, sirs. We've got reports of the townspeople resisting the Germans!"

"They said the Germans had been taking their children, and that they'd been carrying out executions," Jim explained.

"Well, I'm damn glad they're on our side now. Every little bit helps. Anyway, gentlemen," the captain said as he looked over the ragtag group of men that surrounded him, "many of you are filling in for your superiors, or leading composite forces. I know it hasn't been an ideal operation, but we gotta play the hand we're dealt, and I just need to know one thing from you. Are the Rangers able to execute this operation?"

Jim looked at the weary group of non-coms and officers that had survived the jump and found their way here. Each one of them knew what was at stake. Nearly all had seen their friends butchered in Normandy, and that memory pushed them forward as one.

"HOOAH!" they all shouted.

"That's what I thought," Dickson said. "Any questions? You had something, Sergeant?"

"We're missing our Intelligence Officer. Without him, we don't know much about the objective."

"No one's seen him?" the captain asked. "Anyone?"

"No, sir!" several of the men said all at once.

"All right then, let's get up this hill and hope that Professor Miller catches up with us. Move out, men. Let's hit these Nazis where it counts!"

* * *

October 1944

Western Bavaria, Germany

Sturmbannführer Kristock Keck roared down the narrow road at the head of his *Totenkopfverbände*. For nearly a year now, he'd obeyed the strange orders given him by Heinrich Himmler to avoid Bad Tölz and the *Junkerschüle*. He'd been patrolling the peaceful border near Switzerland, which afforded him no opportunity whatsoever to distinguish himself in such a way that he could advance within the ranks of the SS. When he received word of the invasion, however, he decided that he could no longer stand idly by while American paratroopers in the thousands landed next door to his assigned duty area.

He didn't know the exact tactical situation. All he knew was that the recently installed SS commander had ordered every available soldier to his defense, and Keck was only too happy to comply. He'd finally received an opportunity to distinguish himself, and he was going to take full advantage of it.

As his car jounced into the Isar Valley, he rose in his seat and seized the windshield with a furious grip.

"Halt!" he cried "Halt!"

Through his binoculars, Keck watched hundreds of people converging on a small hamlet where a Nazi flag flew from its largest house. The villagers carried shovels, pickaxes, pieces of brick, and lengths of pipe.

"*Mein Herr?*" his driver called.

"That's a Gestapo post," Keck said. Two men in black uniforms stepped out of the distant house with pistols in hand, but the threat only stopped the crowd for a moment before the secret police succumbed to the angry mob. "It appears we have a rebellion before us. We'll have to deal with these vermin before we continue."

His column sped across the fields, and as it did, Keck saw another column emerge from the east. He recognized the insignia of the *Junkerschüle* and raised a hand to halt his column.

"Get the men ready to fight, Taschner," he called to his aide as he stepped out of the car.

As the *Totenkopfverbände* readied their rifles, checked the bolts, and set up in their positions, Keck marched to where the newly armed cadets were emerging from their trucks. They seemed to have no leader and little organization, but that didn't matter. He'd whip them into shape soon enough.

"Where is your commanding officer?" he called to the cadets. A boy of maybe seventeen clicked his heels and saluted.

"Cadet Winklemoss, *Sturmbannführer*," the boy called.

"Organize your men into fire teams immediately. We are going to deal with this insurrection."

The boy's eyes drifted to the village forty meters distant. The villagers were leaving the hamlet and lining up to face them across the field.

"Well, Winklemoss?" Keck asked as he stormed toward the boy. "I gave you your orders. Obey them!"

"But *Mein Herr* ..." the boy said, trailing off uneasily for a moment before he continued. "*Mein Herr*, they're Germans."

"Cadet! Those people are traitors to the Reich!" He said as he gripped the boy's head and turned it to face the field.

The villagers' mouths split open in wails of fear and rage as they charged toward Keck's position.

"Remember who you are, and why you fight. Now, draw your weapon, Cadet, and be quick about it!"

The pale cadet's expression hardened as he reached a trembling hand for his Luger. The other cadets drew their Mausers and pointed them toward the oncoming mob.

"Cadets! You may fire when ready!" Keck shouted.

* * *

At the foot of the *Zitternberg*, Jim Thompson dove for cover behind a mound of turned earth. He crawled behind his line while his men fired, loaded, or screamed for a medic. The road that led up the hill had turned into a bloodbath, with the Germans' positions heavily dug in and reinforced with concrete bunkers. In addition, their snipers had more of those damned rifles that seemed to be able to hit a target from any distance.

Dog Company was pinned down, and they could only hope that the Rangers trying to work their way through the forest would have better luck.

"Keep it up, you guys! Keep it up!" Jim called to them. "We've got to keep 'em occupied so they don't notice their flanks."

The Rangers rained hell onto the Germans, but the Nazis fought just as tenaciously. Jim crawled into the cover of a low ridge, slipping his map out of his pocket to work on a new plan, but a sudden burst of movement in the valley caught his eye. He lifted his binoculars, staring through the one lens that hadn't been damaged by shrapnel, and saw heads bobbing through the wheat fields below him. There were hundreds of them coming from the north, and they were wearing U.S. Army Ranger helmets.

He couldn't make out the unit insignia at this distance, but he could tell from the way they were moving that they were running, and they were headed right for his position.

* * *

October 1944
Isar Valley, North of the Zitternberg

Yanis sprinted away from the burning *Panzer* with the other paratroopers. Now that it was daylight, they'd found the mountain range and had been making good progress toward their objective. Corporal Mitchell had led them south, parallel to the main road, which had helped them skirt most of the German forces that had been rushing through the valley.

"Where the hell did that thing come from?" a Ranger yelled as he pushed past Yanis. "I hope we don't run into any more of those. We need to conserve our ammo until we reach the target."

The field in front of them began to rise as it turned into the foothills that would lead to the *Zitternberg*. When Yanis saw the mountain that he'd fled from a year earlier off in the distance, he felt a hot determination burning within him, but they needed to outrun and outsmart the Germans if they were going to reach their destination.

Corporal Mitchell stopped suddenly and spun around so that he could scan the valley below with his binoculars.

"What is it?" one of the Rangers asked as they all came to a halt. Fighting raged along the base of the mountain, but that's not what Mitchell was looking at.

"There are two more German divisions coming into the valley behind us," he said.

"Jesus, what do we do?" another ranger asked.

"We head for the rally point at the mountain," Mitchell said. "Then once we get up there, we fight like hell so we can get to the high ground before those damn Krauts reach us. Come on, let's get movin'."

* * *

October 2010

The Zitternberg

The sound of the jackhammers finally stopped, leaving a sudden vacuum of sound that felt awkward to say the least. The Americans had cleared a person-sized hole in the rubble at the front of the tunnel, and the NATO counterterrorism unit was squeezing one by one through the new opening in the rock. Jillian pressed her radio to her ear, listening for any sound of progress or survivors.

"This is gonna be one hell of a story," Captain Leonard said from where he stood next to her.

"You wouldn't even believe how it started," Harry answered.

"Sir," the radio squawked. "Sir, I think you better get in here on the double. And bring the inspector."

"What do you see?" Jillian asked.

"I wish I knew, ma'am," the soldier called back.

40

Jillian barely noticed the concrete dust on her clothes, or the bitter smell of explosives in the air. Her attention was drawn to the strange glowing wall in front of her that seemed to be whispering something just beyond earshot.

"Well, this is above my pay grade," the captain said. "Ms. Qualmes, I need to step outside and contact my superiors. You keep an eye on things in here," Captain Leonard said.

"I know how it works," she said, a look of wonder taking over her features.

"Um, could you repeat that?" he asked as he turned back around to face her. Instead of answering him, she pulled out the small tin from her jacket pocket and walked toward the machine. "Inspector, just what do you think you're doing?"

"I didn't really believe him, but he's been right about everything. This is a spaceship, and apparently there's something in it that allows you to travel through time."

"Ma'am, please, step away from the wall. I don't know what we're dealing with here, but I don't want anything bad to happen to you."

Jillian ignored his request, and instead raised her hand to the wall. She felt an intense heat burn across her palm, and then a portal suddenly opened in front of her.

"Captain, I didn't tell you everything," she said. "Harry can explain, but right now I need to see what's on the other side."

"And why is that, ma'am?"

She opened the tin and stared down at two rings glowing with an intense light. It was a last, desperate plea for help from a man she'd known in another life.

"Because it's time I started thinking about others for a change," she said as she stepped through the portal.

* * *

October 1944

The Zitternberg

Dealing with the revolutionary citizens took less than thirty minutes, and then they were back on the road again with the cadets in tow. When Keck finally arrived at the farmhouse serving as the SS headquarters, he was surprised to see the chaos that had enveloped the valley. The outpost was less than a kilometer from the front lines, not far from a burning half-track where, just a few moments before, paratroopers had snuck through the grass to destroy it with a shot from a bazooka. The front was disorganized, but it appeared that as more of the SS arrived from the north, the dispersed groups of paratroopers were being driven toward the mountain.

Despite the fluid situation, the Germans had managed to maintain their tactical advantage. He'd have to congratulate the commander in charge.

Keck offered his salute to the *Schütze* standing guard at the door, registering the man's break in attention as an item that he'd also have to address with the superior. It was not polite to stare at one's officers.

Inside the house, he found an SS officer with his back to the entrance. He was monitoring radio reports, and closely examining a large map that was scattered with red Xs. When the officer turned to greet him, Keck's eyes went wide and he froze for a moment, mentally trying to process what he was seeing.

"I don't understand," he mumbled. His head seemed to ache, and a strange nausea crept through him. Part of him wanted to go back through the headquarters door so he could return to his car and flee Bavaria completely, but the other more rational part of him wanted answers.

"Ah, *Sturmbannführer,*" his mirror image said. "I'd hoped to avoid this unpleasantness, but it seems that knowing myself the way I do, I should have anticipated it. The situation on the mountain is coming under some semblance of control, so I suppose I have a few minutes for you."

In every way, the man in front of him was identical. He wore a different insignia, but his widening smile, the close gray stubble at his jaw, the hawk gaze of his eyes—they were all him, only it wasn't him.

"Who ... who are you?" he asked as he stared into his doppelganger's face.

"No doubt you have many questions," the man said. "Come, we have much to discuss, and soon all will be revealed."

In the few short hours that they spent together, all was in fact revealed. At least, everything that could be shared had been revealed, and now the world had not one, but two exceptional threats, both of the same mind, and with the same desire to bring glory to the Reich.

* * *

October 1944

The Lower Zitternberg

Sergeant Thompson's reinforcements, if they could be called that, flopped down wherever they could find cover from the Germans that were peppering their position with rifle fire. They chugged from their canteens and readied their weapons in preparation for the battle that was about to commence.

"It's damn good to see ya, Mitch," Jim said. "What'd you see down there?"

"A hell of a lot more Germans," he wheezed. "They're coming from the south. I saw two different corps' insignia on 'em."

"Two more divisions?" Jim asked. "My God, what are we gonna do?"

"We've gotta get up there before they reach us," a familiar voice said. Jim turned to find Yanis taking cover behind a rock, a half-smile playing at the corners of his mouth.

"I told you I'd find you," Jim said, smiling back at him.

"It looks like *I* found *you*."

"I could sure use some help gettin' up this mountain," Jim said. "Where do we go from here?"

Yanis looked up as bullets and mortars churned the earth around him. A group of Rangers surged a few yards up the hill, taking cover before the German machine guns could catch up with them. Grenades flew uphill, rattling and exploding, but the Germans countered, pouring withering fire down onto the American position.

"I don't know," Yanis said. "I never had to fight my way in before."

* * *

The battle surged up and down the steep approach to the *Zitternberg*. Jim's Rangers pressed their attack with a desperate ferocity that slowly carried them forward. The German positions had been hastily prepared, and there were blind spots their bunkers and machine gun nests couldn't reach. D Company fell into a steady pattern of creeping into the blind spots, launching a furious assault on a German position, then repeating the process.

Jim charged forward while the gunner inside the bunker in front of him focused on another Ranger at his flank. He pulled the pin of his last grenade, tossed it inside, and then threw himself into a gully for cover. The blast singed his hair as it washed over him, and after everything had settled down, he rose to make sure he'd gotten the last of them.

"Clear!" he called in a voice hoarse with exhaustion. As Rangers swarmed up and took cover beside him, he glanced over to see how the other runner had fared.

"Oh no. God, no!" he whispered as he scrambled his way over to where the medic was crouching over Corporal Mitchell.

"Sarge," the wounded man gasped. "I think I'm gonna have to sit the rest of this one out."

The medic was knotting a bandage around his thigh to hold the limb together, and another mound of gauze already hid one of his eyes. Shrapnel peppered his forearms, and he tried to reach for his rifle, but Jim stayed his hand.

"You just take a break now, buddy. We can take it from here," Jim said, trying to fight back a wave of emotion he couldn't afford to succumb to.

"Doesn't matter. I was out of ammo anyway," he said as he pulled his one good leg up, drew out his boot knife and clutched it to his chest. "Tell ya what. I'll hamstring any of them bastards that try to get past me."

"You do that, Mitch. You're a good man, and a great soldier," Jim said sincerely. He gave Mitchell's shoulder a squeeze, and then after flashing him a tight smile, Jim made his way down the line to take stock of his men. Nearly every one of them was wounded in one way or another, and the sun was starting to dip down into the mountains. His men had been in continuous combat for nearly twenty hours, and he had no idea of his effective strength, nor did he know how much farther they needed to go. There were just too many Germans and too few Rangers.

He slid down the hill toward his command platoon, grabbed the radio, and tried to raise the captain.

"Dog Company to Captain Dickson. Over," he said as bullets tore the underbrush around him. "Dog Company to Captain Dickson. Over. Sir, are you there?"

A voice finally erupted through the radio's static.

"Dog Company, this is Command. I'm afraid I don't know where the captain is, sir. It's pretty hectic down here."

"What's going on?" Jim asked.

"We've got a full division trying to crawl up our ass down here. We're trying to hold, but ..."

"Command?" Jim said. "Command, are you there?"

Yanis skidded into the leaves next to him as Jim threw down the radio in disgust.

"I don't know if you came to the right time," he said to Yanis. The Israeli was panting as sweat rolled down his face and blood dripped from his hands.

"I should have died up here sixty years in the future, but I didn't. You never know what might happen," Yanis said, smiling at him encouragingly. Oddly enough, of all the things that could have gotten Jim moving again, it was the smile of a professor who'd found himself trapped in a different time.

"Come on. Let's see what we can do to get you back where you came from," Jim said as he got up and ran toward the recently captured bunker. Just as he reached it, the thunderous roar of German artillery blotted out everything.

Jim hit the ground hard, inhaling dirt as he landed. When he finally looked up, a wave of gray uniforms was sprinting down the hill toward his position.

"They're comin', boys! Jesus, it looks like every damn one of 'em is comin' for us!" he shouted as he rose to meet their charge.

41

The German counterattack tore Dog Company in two. The Rangers with Jim gave ground until they found themselves defending a crescent ridge of rock above the roadside that the Germans couldn't penetrate. He'd lost dozens of men in the retreat and had no radio to contact the rest of his company. By the time the Germans finally halted their assault, he had maybe two hundred combat effectives remaining.

"How are we on ammo?" he called out.

"I'm out here," a Ranger shouted.

"Here, take two. I won't use 'em all," another soldier called as he tossed over a couple of magazines.

"Anyone hurt? Anyone need the doc?" Jim asked.

"My pride is hurt," one of the soldiers called back.

The jokes were forced just to keep their morale up, but the men soon fell silent once again. Sporadic fighting rang out from the other approaches to the mountain, but Jim had no idea if help would be coming or not.

"What are we gonna do, Sarge?" one of the privates asked.

"I need to put some runners together. Head down and find out what's goin' on below us. What I want you to do is ..."

"AMERICAN RANGERS," a voice blared in German-accented English. "AMERICAN RANGERS, YOU ARE ALL SURROUNDED. YOU ARE FACING THREE DIVISIONS, AND YOU HAVE NO PROSPECT OF AID OR REINFORCEMENT. IF YOU SURRENDER NOW, NO HARM WILL COME TO YOU."

From where he lay on the ridge, Jim could see movement on the road below. He shook out his binoculars and focused on the long line of men marching beneath a white flag.

The Germans had captured most of Able and Charlie companies, which had been trying to make their way through the forest. He saw Captain Dickson near the head of the column, a few Rangers he recognized from Echo who'd been in the rear guard, and then poor Yanis, the man who'd come back from the future just to get shot a second time. A brief moment of regret washed through him. He should have kept Yanis close instead of splitting off with the others.

"I think we're all that's left," he said to his men, and then he watched as a group of German officers under a white flag marched down the road to the beginning of the column of prisoners. An SS commandant raised a megaphone to his lips.

"ATTENTION! AMERICAN RANGERS, MY NAME IS STURM-BANNFÜHRER KECK, COMMANDER OF THE THREE WAFFEN SS DIVISIONS YOU ARE FACING. YOU CANNOT HOPE TO ACHIEVE VICTORY, AND WE'RE OFFERING YOU ONE FINAL CHANCE TO SURRENDER. IF YOU DO NOT, THEN THIS WILL BE THE FATE THAT AWAITS YOUR FRIENDS," he said as he motioned behind him. His men lifted the first prisoner and held him in place. Keck pulled his pistol from its holster and fired. The man gagged and fell, struggling in the leaves for a moment before death silenced him forever. Jim lowered his binoculars in horror.

"Sarge, what the hell are they doin' down there?" one of the Rangers asked.

"What do you want us to do, Sarge?" another one called out.

All his life it'd been the same answer. It was the only answer, because he knew the captured men were only a bargaining chip, and that if they surrendered to the Germans, none of them would be leaving that place alive.

"We, uh ..." he said with a heavy sigh as he looked around at his wounded and exhausted men.

Before he could finish, down on the road the Germans lifted another prisoner. He didn't need his glasses to know that it was Yanis—the man he'd promised to protect, but whom he'd let be captured instead.

"No!" Jim screamed as he stood and waved his hands, but the Germans had turned behind them. Then Jim realized that he'd heard someone else call the same thing. Someone behind Keck who'd emerged from the mouth of the tunnel.

* * *

When she heard the first gunshot, Jillian had drawn her pistol and sprinted from the tunnel. She saw the line of men under guard, and the Nazi soldiers forcing the man she recognized as Yanis to his knees. When the man in a black uniform had pressed a pistol to the back of Yanis' head, she'd screamed without thinking.

Now, as the soldiers turned their weapons on her and she faced them with her own, the full reality of what was happening sank in. These men were in the middle of executing American prisoners and dressed as if … as if they were from World War II. She realized then that she was in the past, and she was in deep, deep trouble.

"The King Under the Mountain, I presume," Jillian said.

The man in black drew his gun away from Yanis' head and smiled at her.

"It appears that *Der Dom* is functional once more, Professor Miller, despite your best efforts. Seize that woman!" he shouted to his men.

It was a confusing scene. Jillian backed toward the tunnel, trying to keep her pistol from shaking in her hand as hundreds of soldiers rushed her. What had she thought she could do? Everything Yanis had said was true, but none of it seemed to matter now. She'd die as nothing more than a footnote in history, while the Nazis slowly built their 1,000-Year Reich.

A strange sound like tearing paper filled the clearing as the ground rumbled underneath her feet. The Nazis were confused as to what was going on, and as she took full advantage of that confusion to flee back into the mine.

"What are you doing?" the Nazi leader screamed at his men. "Forward! After her!"

In that moment, a shot rang out. One of Keck's aides was violently hit in the head by a sniper shot, and everyone instinctively took cover.

Far down the mountain, Corporal Mitchell had been left for dead by the Nazi patrols. He'd slowly and painfully been crawling his way up the mountain and happened to find one of the advanced sniper rifles the Germans had been using sticking out from under the body of one of the dead soldiers. It was he who had made that horrific shot. He was trying to hit Keck, but his exhaustion made his aim unsteady. With his last breath he squeezed off the fatal round, and then he fell silent as death finally claimed him.

Jillian closed her eyes, waiting for the bullets that would tear her apart. In that moment of distraction, however, a warm body crashed into her and knocked her to the ground. When she opened her eyes, she found Yanis Miller's face in front of hers. She was lying awkwardly on the ground with him on top of her. His brown eyes smoldered with concern as he instinctively brushed a rough hand across her cheek.

How a near-death experience could pale in comparison to this moment that she was having with a total stranger was beyond her, but that's exactly what had happened.

"It's really 1944? Those are real Nazis?" she asked.

"Yeah, so we'll have to do this quick," he said as he pressed his lips to hers.

* * *

"Where the hell did they come from?" one of the Rangers at Jim's side asked as soldiers started pouring out of the tunnel entrance.

"Who are they?" another ranger asked.

Jim knew who they were. Whoever that woman was, she'd figured out how to use the time travel device that Yanis had been after, and she'd brought an awful lot of help with her. The Nazis were scrambling for cover while the soldiers who had joined the woman grabbed her to pull her back into the tunnel with them. But as soon as Yanis got to his feet, he took off running in the opposite direction.

"Those are our reinforcements," Jim called. "We've got to help 'em break outta there. First and Second Platoons, get those prisoners up here on the double. Everyone else with me. It's time to finish this fight!"

* * *

Keck's rage boiled while his solders fell around him. They'd made no preparations to defend against the tunnel itself, and he alone knew the damage that modern military weaponry could do. This Qualmes woman had come back in time and ruined everything. Yanis Miller had warned her somehow and gotten a message to her. Whatever happened in the next few minutes, however, he swore to himself that he'd have his revenge.

"*Sturmbannführer?*" Reinhold called. "The prisoners!"

The remaining Rangers were charging into the unguarded rear of the troops he'd just ordered to attack the tunnel, while the American prisoners sprinted into the forest. He tried to find Professor Miller, but the situation had become untenable.

"Reinhold, I am ordering you to hold here as long as you can. I'm going to bring the second division up the hill as fast as I possibly can, but you cannot let those soldiers out of the tunnel. Do you understand? Our very lives depend on it."

The adjutant nodded and swallowed nervously. He knew the position was hopeless, but he was a good and loyal Aryan, so he'd fulfill his duty, even if it cost him his life.

Keck left his adjutant to his fate as he sprinted down the road toward the safety of Nazi superiority.

As the devastating rounds of the future soldiers' weapons tore into his men, and as the hillside and road where he'd spent so much time in preparation blurred all around him, he did not see the shape that rose from the forest edge and launched itself into him. All he saw were his dreams crumbling into nothing but ash.

* * *

Jim's Rangers poured the last of their ammunition into the backs of the SS soldiers with a vengeance that was borne *on* the shores of Normandy and realized here at the base of the Zitternberg. As they swept up the final yards of the hillside, the Rangers they'd freed sprinted past.

"Halt!" Jim hollered down the line. "Halt and dig yourselves in!"

Two hundred throats echoed his orders, and he stood to wave the prisoners through. They ran for cover, scarcely believing that they'd managed to survive the ordeal. They picked up any German or American weapons they happened across as they ran, and those that were armed once again dove for cover so they could help to protect the others.

In the end though, there was no need. The strange soldiers who had burst out of the tunnel were incredibly deadly. They fired with a rate of accuracy he could not believe and moved as if each one of them understood where the others were at all times. Even in the clearing with little cover to hide behind, they made steady progress against the outmatched Germans until what few of the SS were left sprinted down the road in full retreat. A group of soldiers took off in pursuit, and Jim was about to join them when he found Captain Dickson climbing up the embankment toward him.

"Sir!" he called.

"At ease, Sergeant," the captain said. Jim gave his commanding officer a weary smile and lowered his rifle.

"Sir, permission to go find out who we owe a favor to?"

"Permission absolutely granted," the captain said.

* * *

"I don't know what the hell just happened, but I think it's over," Captain Leonard said as he re-emerged from the tunnel with Jillian, Yanis, and the other soldiers from the future.

"I owe you an apology," the inspector said. "I shouldn't have just—"

"You were reckless and almost got yourself killed, but you saved lives Inspector. A whole lot of them, and there are some people here who want to thank you," the captain said.

She found a massive man limping toward her in the clearing. His smile reopened a half-dozen cuts on his face, but she found herself shaking his hand without any reservation.

"Ma'am, I'm Sergeant Jim Thompson. I don't know how to thank you," he said gratefully.

"We're with Second Rangers, stationed out of Rome," a man beside the Sergeant said. "I'm Captain Dickson."

"Captain Frederick Dickson?" Captain Leonard asked.

"If you wanna be formal about it, yeah. That's me."

"Don't take this the wrong way sir, but I learned all about you in school."

Jillian left the two captains to their incredulous conversation and drew closer to the sergeant.

"Jim, are you all right?" she asked. The big man wiped tears from his eyes, and then shook his head.

"I thought we were all gonna die up here," he said. "I thought I was gonna get every one of my men killed, but you kept that from happening."

"Well, she wasn't the only one you know," a voice called from behind them.

Jillian turned and saw the man who'd just kissed her a short time ago marching the Nazi leader toward them at gunpoint.

"May I present *Sturmbannführer* Kristock Keck? Mr. Keck is guilty of more crimes than we have time to cover, and he's just been captured by an inferior Jew, which I know just has to be eating him up inside," Yanis said with a cocky grin.

Rage mottled Keck's patrician face, and the man half-turned as if he were going to strike out at Yanis, but Sergeant Thompson rested a big hand on the German's shoulder and offered him a deadly smile. Before Keck knew what was happening, Jim knocked him to the ground with a right cross.

"Damn, that felt good," he said with a grin as he hauled Keck back to his feet and then dragged him off to hand him over to the NATO soldiers, while Yanis and Jillian stayed to talk.

"I'm Inspector Jillian Qualmes," she said and held out her hand, but Yanis didn't take it. He looked at her for a moment as if she were somehow blurry, and he was trying to bring her into focus. Her hair was down, and she'd added highlights to it since he'd last seen her. She was all together beautiful, and he could see in her green eyes that she was glad to see him. He could also see a nervousness there that was likely caused by the kiss they shared earlier.

"Can I ask you just which inspector you are?"

"I don't understand," Jillian said with a confused look.

"Well, I've had a lot of time to think about how this was possible. I mean, what *Der Dom* really is and everything, and the best I can figure it out is that it's not a time travel device at all. I think it takes us to different dimensions, because once you leave your time, everything becomes different."

"Are you asking if we've ever met before?" Jillian asked. His smile was even more disarming in person, and she wondered if he'd made her feel this way in some other timeline.

"Yeah, I guess I am," Yanis said with a laugh. "I'm not very good at small talk, as you can probably tell."

"Neither am I, but let's keep it simple for now. You can call me Jillian."

* * *

From the headquarters where he'd first met his "elder" self, Kristock Keck listened to the progress of the failing battle for *Der Dom*. When the American voices were the only ones he heard, and the last of the rifles fell silent, he switched off the radio and stood there perfectly still.

"*Sturmbannführer,*" Taschner called. "What are your orders?"

Keck didn't answer him right away. He stood there in silence for a moment longer, contemplating the sturdy stone walls, the sky's fading light, and the fact that the only man among the party leadership who tolerated failure less that Heinrich Himmler was Adolf Hitler himself. Perhaps with more experience, he could use their shortcomings to his advantage.

"Come, Taschner," he said finally. "We have much to learn about the new threat that has risen in Bavaria, but we must first make ourselves safe for tomorrow. Do you have all of your papers with you?"

His aide nodded, and then swept open the farmhouse door for his superior. Keck brushed past him stiffly, and then Taschner followed him out into the gathering night, pulling the door closed behind him.

About the Author

J. Channing is a former semiconductor engineer who has retired to Garden City, Idaho. He is a technologist, entrepreneur, and freelance writer. Born in Butte, Montana, he spent most of his childhood roaming around the northwest, living in eighteen different locations before getting through high school. He is an avid fan of all Sci-Fi and loves history and exploring how technology has radically changed possible futures. He loves to read, listen to, and watch space and Sci-Fi programs and loves German Techno, house, and Electronica music. He loves to build custom firearms, specifically AR-15s, and designs and builds new features using 3-D printing to prototype them. He's an avid waterski and snow ski enthusiast (and occasionally does those two activities on the same day) and loves to ride his electronic skateboard on the miles of the Boise area's greenbelt.

Mr. Channing has been interested in military history, time travel, World War II, and weapons technology since he was a small child. The original story concept for *Forever* was outlined on one of his many solo bus rides from the Seattle area to Helena, Montana. It was adjusted and improved over decades and was finally, as a labor of love, completed. The book is a fulfillment of a story that has played out in his head hundreds of times; he hopes the world enjoys it as much as he always has.